PRAISE F ... KAT. ...

Memoirs of a Dragon Hunter
"Bursting with the author's trademark zany humor and spicy romance . . . this quick tale will delight paranormal romance fans."—*Publishers Weekly*

Sparks Fly
"Balanced by a well-organized plot and MacAlister's trademark humor."—*Publishers Weekly*

It's All Greek to Me
"A fun and sexy read."—The Season for Romance
"A wonderful lighthearted romantic romp as a kick-butt American Amazon and a hunky Greek find love. Filled with humor, fans will laugh with the zaniness of Harry meets Yacky."—*Midwest Book Review*

Much Ado About Vampires
"A humorous take on the dark and demonic."—*USA Today*
"Once again this author has done a wonderful job. I was sucked into the world of Dark Ones right from the start and was taken on a fantastic ride. This book is full of witty dialogue and great romance, making it one that should not be missed."—Fresh Fiction

The Unbearable Lightness of Dragons
"Had me laughing out loud. . . . This book is full of humor and romance, keeping the reader entertained all the way through . . . a wondrous story full of magic. . . . I cannot wait to see what happens next in the lives of the dragons."—Fresh Fiction

Also By Katie MacAlister

Dark Ones Series
A Girl's Guide to Vampires
Sex and the Single Vampire
Sex, Lies, and Vampires
Even Vampires Get the Blues
Bring Out Your Dead (Novella)
The Last of the Red-Hot Vampires
Crouching Vampire, Hidden Fang
Unleashed (Novella)
In the Company of Vampires
Confessions of a Vampire's Girlfriend
Much Ado About Vampires
A Tale of Two Vampires
The Undead in My Bed (Novella)
The Vampire Always Rises
Enthralled
Desperately Seeking Vampire

Dragon Sept Series
You Slay Me
Fire Me Up
Light My Fire
Holy Smokes
Death's Excellent Vacation
(short story)
Playing WIth Fire
Up In Smoke
Me and My Shadow
Love in the Time of Dragons
The Unbearable Lightness of Dragons
Sparks Fly
Dragon Fall
Dragon Storm
Dragon Soul
Dragon Unbound
Dragonblight
You Sleigh Me
Axegate Walk

Dragon Hunter Series
Memoirs of a Dragon Huner
Day of the Dragon
A Confederacy of Dragons

Born Prophecy Series
Fireborn
Starborn
Shadowborn

Time Thief Series
Time Thief
Time Crossed (short story)
The Art of Stealing Time

Matchmaker in Wonderland Series
The Importance of Being Alice
A Midsummer Night's Romp
Daring in a Blue Dress
Perils of Paulie

Papaioannou Series
It's All Greek to Me
Ever Fallen in Love
A Tale of Two Cousins
Acropolis Now

Contemporary Single Titles
Improper English
Bird of Paradise (Novella)
Men in Kilts
The Corset Diaries
A Hard Day's Knight
Blow Me Down
You Auto-Complete Me

Noble Historical Series
Noble Intentions
Noble Destiny
The Trouble With Harry
The Truth About Leo

Paranormal Single Titles
Ain't Myth-Behaving

Mysteries
Ghost of a Chance
The Stars That We Steal From the
Night Sky

Steampunk Romance
Steamed
Company of Thieves

AXEGATE WALK

A DARK ONES NOVEL

KATIE MACALISTER

FAT CAT BOOKS

To my darling agent Michelle Grajkowski, who always wanted me to write a small town vampire story.

PROLOGUE

"Blah blah blah."

"Pardon?" Leonid of Corinth blinked at his employer, wondering if the sun hadn't been too much for him. That thought was followed immediately by the question of whether it was possible for Troy to have too much sun.

He frowned, and rubbed his ear. Could Old Gods get sunstroke?

"I said blah blah blah. Is that all mortals do? Talk?" Troy Ilios held out his phone so Leo could see the offending video. "They're all talk and no action. How can this woman have seven hundred thousand followers when all she does is talk in a whisper and tap her fingers on things?"

Leo looked. "She does ASMR. That's what proponents of that lifestyle do."

"Well, it's ridiculous." Troy waved a hand at the massive wall of stone behind him. "Mortals deserve more interesting content to look at that someone tapping her fingernails on a piece of paper. What's the hold up?"

"We're waiting for the drone to be repaired. I told you that earlier. Maybe you should get out of the sun?" Leo asked, studying his employer's face. What did sunstroke look like?

"Why are you squinting at me in that objectionable manner?" Troy asked, leaning back as if Leo were puffing foul breath at him.

"I was wondering what the signs of sunstroke were. You don't feel odd, do you?"

"Odd? Me?" Troy drew himself up, squaring his shoulders and looking down his nose at Leo even though the former was seated. He made a noise remarkably like a snort. "The idea is obscene. Why would you even ask that? Have I ever been odd in all the centuries you have served me?"

Leo knew better than to answer that question truthfully. "I just wondered if spending all day out in the sun mightn't have been too much for you. It is extremely hot."

"Your concern for my well-being is right and proper, but don't allow our time in the mortal plane to taint your memory. I am not a mortal to be so affected by the sun." Troy gave an injured sniff, glanced down the steep slope to a flat bit of road where three off-road vehicles sat, and immediately clicked his tongue in annoyance, asking again, "Why is it taking so long? The light will soon shift and my good side will be in shadow if we wait much longer to stem the void."

"I'm sure they will fix whatever is wrong with the drone so that it can film every second of you climbing the...er... void," Leo said, waving at the tall rock structure behind him that he'd heard someone refer to as a chimney.

"Stemming. I will be stemming the void, not climbing. Really, Leo, how can you not know the terminology by now?" Troy asked, glancing up when Leo's phone pinged. "What is it? Have I hit three hundred thousand followers? How can that whisper woman have more than double the followers I have when I provide so much more interesting content? Anyone can tap their fingers on things. But only a god can climb the most impossible of structures."

"Yes, sir. It does seem unfair. However, I'm afraid it's not a notice regarding your follower count. It's a reminder you had me set last week about appointing a new lord to the Seventh Hour."

"Bah," Troy said, standing to stretch. Leo had to admit that Troy appeared every inch the god who the ancient Greeks had worshipped a few millennia ago, what with his dark curly hair, chiseled jaw, and a physique that had many mortal women doing double takes. But his animal magnetism aside, Leo wished his boss had a bit more going on upstairs. "The Hour is fine. We'd hear something if it wasn't."

"Sir, with all due respect, that isn't necessarily the wisest of attitudes to adopt. If you don't appoint a replacement soon, the members of the Hour are going to notice that you aren't there to contain and police them, and at that point, all hell will likely break out. *Literally.*"

"You exaggerate," Troy said, doing a few deep squats to warm up his legs. "It wouldn't be that bad. Everyone there is, for the most part, well-behaved. Other than a few troublemakers, and they know their place."

"They know their place because up until six months ago when you decided that you were going to take Instagram by storm, they had no other option," Leo pointed out, more than a little exasperated. While he didn't mind being out and about in the mortal world, he missed his dogs, missed his nice little cottage, and most of all, missed the busty ale wenches at the Flogged Bishop inn.

In short, he wanted to go back home.

Troy paused doing his squats, and looked thoughtful, or as thoughtful as a man obsessed with himself could look when it came to subjects that lay beyond his immediate concern. "You think the thanes would really cause problems?"

"Yes. They have sworn to wreak revenge upon those who betrayed them into the underworld," Leo said, a flicker of hope coming to life within him. If Troy ordered him to find a replacement to head up the Hour containing the four thanes who had been cast into its depths, then he could return home and be with his dogs and cottage and ale wenches.

"Their vengeance can mean nothing to us," Troy said after a minute's consideration.

"They want to destroy mortals." As a rule, Leo disliked using abrupt tactics with Troy, since the latter could be as obstinate as an ass when it came to herding him to a desired action, but there were times when it was a necessary risk.

"Meh," Troy said, and started to turn away.

"Mortals who make up your existing and future Instagram audience," Leo said, buffing his fingernails on his shirt as he played his last card.

Troy frowned, his ebony brows pulling together in a manner that had the ancient Greeks who worshipped him falling on their knees in supplication. "Hmm. I suppose you have a point. It wouldn't be at all kind to the mortals to unleash beings who wanted to see them wiped off the earth. Very well. I charge you with picking someone to replace me as lord of the Hour in the next few days."

"But—my lord—I'm not the right person—"

"Of course you're not. Only *I* can appoint a replacement. But you can at least find the individual. So go do that." Troy made shooing gestures.

"Go where?" Leo asked, feeling adrift in a sea of confusion.

"Wherever a suitable replacement can be found. Do not bother me with trivial issues! Go find a replacement, and then inform me so I might make it official, and can focus all my energy on growing my brand. Now, I shall give those idiots a piece of my mind, and tell them to get the blasted drone running so they can get shots of me looking down the belay."

Leo's hope that he might be able to return home fizzled and died even as he sighed, pulled out his phone, and loaded up a search engine to locate any demigods who weren't already attached to a spiritual realm.

ONE

"Go home, Finch. Don't leave your apartment. Don't let anyone in unless it's me. Don't pick up your mail—we'll check it for you. You should hear from me or the OEO about the Witness Security Program in the next twenty-four hours. You might want to pack a bag with the stuff you can't live without. We'll send the rest to you later."

"Pack? Why would I pack anything?" Finch Dante, Dark One, former physician, and would-be author frowned when his friend and next-door neighbor Damon Blackwood exited the sterile police interview room. He bit back the urge to blurt out that he didn't fear any mortal, given how difficult it was to kill a Dark One. Not even the thug he'd inadvertently witnessed committing the execution of a rival. "I don't need protecting. I'm perfectly fine as I am."

Damon stopped to have a hurried conversation with one of the policemen in the hallway, gesturing toward Finch, who felt itchy and irritable. He was an orderly, tidy man, and kept his life equally orderly and tidy. It rankled when mortals' chaotic lives disarranged his.

"Detective Rodriquez here will make sure you get home safely," Damon said before pulling out his phone running down the hallway, not even hearing Finch's words of protest.

Finch sighed to himself, and tapped on his phone.

ME

I won't be able to visit you next month as planned.
Something has come up.

CHRISTIAN

Something pleasant, I hope? Allegra and the children will
be most disappointed not to see you.

ME

I am unable to specify the situation into which I
find myself, but I am taking advantage of it to work, so
that will be productive, if not quite pleasant. I am at a
pivotal point in my book, and the unmentionable situation should provide me with the tranquility I need to
finish it. I will message you when I return to circulation,
so to speak.

CHRISTIAN

It all sounds very mysterious. You would, naturally, tell
me if you are in trouble, and if there was something I
could do to aid you.

ME

I always have.

CHRISTIAN

And I have always appreciated the pragmatic side to
your nature. How long do you anticipate being incom-
municado?

ME

I'm not sure.

CHRISTIAN

Curiouser and curiouser to paraphrase the twin's favorite book. Enjoy your writing time.

Finch tucked away his phone when the detective assigned
to see him home gestured. He was mildly bemused with the
swiftness and ease with which Damon had swooped in when
the police had taken him into protective custody, and set into
motion the improbable idea of a witness program.

It all seemed so helter-skelter, but he couldn't deny the
one shining bright point in the whole situation: he would be
left alone.

This is, naturally, ridiculous, he wrote seven days later in
the digital diary he kept to make notes of interesting points

of discussion for his book. *I can't be killed easily. Not by most mortal means. The idea that I need to be given a new identity and whisked away to safety would be comical if my life was less ordered than it is.*

However, Damon did have a good point when he persuaded me that the small town in which I will be residing should provide ample peace and quiet for finishing my current book. I might even be able to outline the book on the value of emotional control that so many mortals clearly are in need of. Yes, all in all, I think six months in a small, quiet, nondescript town where nothing ever happens will be a good thing.

"I've got the keys to your new car," the marshall accompanying him to Oregon said some hours later when they emerged into a grey, rain-washed sky, of which Finch approved. He adjusted his hat against the daylight, and moved forward when the marshall gestured to an unmarked black sedan. "It should be waiting for you in Ravenfall. You have the information about Marshalll Blackwood's family member who is meeting you? You'll have to get the keys to the shop from them. There wasn't time to send them out to you. Here's the rest."

"Shop?" Finch asked, taking the bulky manila envelope, opening it to spill out onto his lap a new driver's license, an insurance card, a small pamphlet, and two credit cards. He managed to stop from grimacing at the name that he would be living under for the next six months: Jeremy Renfrew. Hrmph. "What shop?"

"Marshalll Blackwood's mother owns a shop in town."

Finch stared at the man in growing horror. "I don't know anything about running a shop. I was told I would be able to work on my book, not hand out groceries to townspeople."

"It's not that kind of a shop," the marshalll said with a half shrug. "Something to do with crystals or runes. I don't know exactly. Blackwood's mother used to rent it to some crazy lady who ran off without paying the last half a year's rent, so he arranged for you to take over. There's an apartment above the shop where you should be safe. We've ordered a security system to be installed in the next few days, just in case."

"That doesn't negate the point that I am not a shopkeeper. And I know nothing about crystals or runes," Finch protested, disliking the fact that Damon hadn't mentioned any of this when he'd persuaded him that the sabbatical—as Finch thought of it—would be best for everyone.

"If you don't want to sell the crystals, that's no skin off my nose. Just don't do anything that the locals would find suspicious. You don't want to do anything that's going to call attention to yourself. Don't let people take your picture—you never know who's going to post something online. One TikTok video of you breakdancing on the sidewalk, and whammo. Two days later they'll be fishing you out of the ocean with a couple of bullet holes in your head."

Finch continued to stare at the man, distraught not over the image of his imminent death, but at being expected to interact with the people of the small town that Damon had promised him would be a balm to his antisocial self. "This is not what I agreed to. I have changed my mind. I will return to my apartment, and take my chances."

"Too late," the marshalll said with far more cheer than Finch thought appropriate. "Just keep your head down, don't draw any attention, and those six months'll go faster than you think."

Famous last words, Finch entered into his phone's note function. He had a horrible presentiment that in this case, he was being remarkably prescient.

TWO

"Are you close to being there? Tat, I'm counting on you! If Damon knows you went off to skulk around an estate sale instead of waiting for his buddy to arrive, he'll have my balls on a platter. And then Mom will light up whatever mangled remains he leaves of me, because she promised him that I would be there to hand over the keys and get his friend settled."

I squinted at the sign reading Forest Road 7N21, shifting the car into low as it bounced its way downward, toward the slate grey-blue water that glistened through the trees. "I'm not quite there, and don't even think of trying to blame me for the fact that you decided to galivant off to San Francisco to be with your latest rather than take care of your brother's request."

"San Francisco?" Rolly's voice was edged with sharp spikes of midnight blue, like mountains viewed against a night sky. "How do you know I'm here?"

"Your voice is dark blue," I answered, swerving to avoid a rut.

"My voice is…oh, your synesthesia. What does blue mean?"

"Usually sexual satisfaction. I assume that means your boyfriend is there?"

"It's like you're a human lie detector," he answered with

a little giggle that came out pale yellow. "Regardless, I hope you get home soon."

"I'm hurrying. I cut short the estate sale as it is, which is a shame, because the late owner had a cracking collection of weird stuff, and I managed to get six porcelain dolls out from under that snobby antique dealer in Raven's Bay. Oh! You'll never guess who I saw there!"

"No clue," Rolly drawled, the blue of his tone starting to turn grey. "Someone exciting?"

"Hardly. Our very own not-so-beloved mayor Jericho Taf's clerk, Mara. She was clearly snooping around looking for those raven dolls that Jerry repeatedly demands I find for her."

"Raven dolls? I know you have some weird stuff, but really, Tat, you're going too far with dolls made out of ravens. Don't they smell?"

"They aren't real ravens, silly. I'll have to show you the ones I have—they're about ten inches tall, and are anthropomorphized ravens. The collection I have is three out of five raven sisters. They're librarians by day, and crime fighters at night."

"Tat," Rolly said, his voice now orange with amusement. "Did you hit the crack pipe especially hard this morning?"

I gave an eye roll at the same time I swerved hard to avoid a pothole. "You know I don't do that sort of thing. The backstory is what the artist gave the dolls. Anyway, what I was going to say before you distracted me—"

"I never!"

"—is that there happened to be one of the raven dolls at the estate, but I hid it behind an armoire so Mara wouldn't see it. She took off after flipping me the usual shit, but I had the last laugh because *I* got the raven doll. Ouch! Man, they need to pave this road." I rubbed the top of my head where it hit the interior car roof.

Rolly made a *tsk*ing sound. "One day Jericho is going to find out you hide things at auctions that you know she'll want, and then there will be hell to pay."

"Meh," I said, peering ahead at the road. "She doesn't scare me. Much. When are you and your boy toy coming back?"

"No clue, and Teddy isn't a boy toy. He's a delicious Nepalese rock climber, and I'm going to be more ripped than you can imagine by the time he gets through teaching me everything he knows. Oh, speaking of that, don't forget to get the keys. And make sure Damon's friend understands that rent is due on the fifteenth of the month. Not the twentieth, or the thirtieth. Mom is still fuming over Ozy stiffing her the last six months, so be firm with Damon's dude, and get the first and last month's pronto."

I grimaced to myself. "About that...did Ozy say anything to you about leaving town? She never once hinted that she might take off suddenly, and it sounds like she left some things behind."

"Not really, just a few odds and ends, some personal stuff in the bathroom, and her collection of rocks. Nothing of value, in any case, which is why Mom is happy for Damon's friend to take over the shop, and have the rent start pouring in again." His voice was definitely grey now, telling me he was bored of the conversation.

I squirmed a little even as I twirled the steering wheel to avoid another deep rut. "I just feel kind of weird demanding that a total stranger hand over cold hard cash to me. Why can't he Venmo your mom?"

"Dear one, if life were that simple, I wouldn't have to run to San Francisco just to get away from my mother's attempts to matchmake me with the perfect gay son-in-law. Just get the money from the guy, and deposit it into my account. I'll zap Mom the money later."

I shifted even lower as the road hair-pinned its way down off the higher elevations, until I made one spectacularly tight turn, and suddenly, the coastline was laid out below me like a three-dimensional map. "All right, but if he gives me even the slightest bit of grief, you're going to be in for a whole lot of bad juju."

"It's not like I'm asking you to castigate him on the doorstep, Tat. Just show him around the shop and apartment, give him the keys, and collect the first and last in cash. Besides, maybe he'll be Mr. Right."

"There is no such thing, at least not for me," I said, trying to keep the bitterness from my voice. I could never see the colors in my own voice, but if I could, I imagined it would be a nasty dark mustard yellow. "Not after the last one."

"The German tourist? How is he? Did they fix his legs?"

"Yes," I said, miserable and guilt-riddled when I thought of the latest of my dating disasters. "He flew home to Munich a few days ago, or so his Facebook says. You'd tell me if you knew that someone in town had cursed my romantic endeavors, wouldn't you?"

"Probably, unless it was coming from someone high up," he admitted. "But I say again that you're not cursed."

"Then how do you explain the fact that most men in town avoid me like the plague, and the ones that don't end up in situations that could be in the next Final Destination movie?"

"The first is due to the fact that everyone thinks you ran off Ozy, and the second is a combination of bad luck and a poor choice in men," he answered, then said in a muffled volume, "Yes, I'll be there in just a sec. I'm just making sure Tat doesn't go off the deep end with the misery that is her sexual self."

I sighed a loud, dramatic sigh that would have won an award if there was such a thing. "You're not far wrong on the miserable love life front, although I didn't do anything to Ozy. You know that."

"I know you wanted her shop."

"She has an excellent location that anyone would covet—" I started to protest.

"You said she drove business away from you."

I slapped the steering wheel. "Three different customers told me she warned them that none of my dolls were haunted! That's tantamount to taking money right out of my till.

And I don't know why everyone ignores the fact that she was so mean to me, saying things like I had it in for her."

"Girl. You named five dolls Pox-Riddle Ozymandra." Rolly's voice was rich with laughter, the grey heading toward a fuchsia color. "Of course she was rude to you."

"I did not drive her from the town, regardless. And it's a moot point since she's gone now, and your mom went and rented that lovely shop to some stranger. You owe me for this, Rolly."

"I know, I know. I promise I'll write up five blood-curdling backstories for your haunted crap."

"Ten." I slowed down to eye the town that stretched along a wide crescent-shaped section of the coast, a small isthmus emerging from the center to sit in the center of a natural bay. The town itself wasn't large—six streets radiated out from the main section, with houses following the curve of the crescent in a single line—but it was a special place, and I loved it almost as much as I loved my shop. "You owe me ten histories for my haunted crap, and at least half of those will be dolls."

"You do not play fair, Tatiana," Rolly said on a breathy giggle. "Fine, ten it is, but I reserve the right to make the histories dank. Seriously dank."

"Doesn't dank mean good?" I asked, confused.

"Does it? I thought it meant moist. Unsavory. Dark and gloomy."

"Well, yes, that's the normal definition, but I believe there's a slang version that is intended to imply something is cool. I can ask Clemmie."

"Lord, I don't keep up with youngspeak," he said with another giggle. "But as far as what I meant, it'll be grim."

"The darker and grimmer the better, so far as my buyers are concerned," I answered.

"You got it. Thanks, Tat! See you next week."

The Bluetooth connection to my phone clicked off as I drove slowly to the center of town, where a bright red and white sign announced Axegate Walk. There were a few parking spots in front of the storefronts, but ever mindful of the comfort of customers, I pulled into one facing the bay, instead, absently glancing toward the café that sat like a beacon on a finger of land pointing into the ocean.

Cthulhu Arms, read a faded, salt-and-wind scrubbed sign with a barely visible arrow pointing out to the isthmus. *Home Cooking. Take Away Available. Catering for Rites—Religious, Sacrificial, and Otherwise.*

My stomach growled as I got out and paused next to my car, wondering if I shouldn't pop in to see what daily special Deacon was running, but a glance at the big clock that sat dead center on the boardwalk had me running in the opposite direction from the café.

A man in what I thought of as an Indiana Jones fedora was standing in the middle of the boardwalk, glancing at his phone before looking up and scanning the storefronts.

"Damn. He would be early. Rolly's mom is going to blame me for this, I just know it—er, excuse me," I said, hurrying up to the man just as he was turning away.

"Yes?" He turned to face me, and immediately my heart started beating wildly, and I couldn't seem to take in a breath.

He had dark chestnut hair, and the faintest hint of stubble, but his eyes were what had me simultaneously sucking in my stomach and straightening my shoulders. They were the color of the water off a Caribbean island I'd been to three years before—perfectly azure, set with a black ring, and the thickest eyelashes I'd ever seen. "Uh…"

"Did you want something?" he asked, a slight crease forming between those two beautiful eyes.

Even his eyebrows were nice, my brain pointed out, my inner Tatiana indulging in a full-fledged squeefest over his straight, dark brown brows, angled jaw, and blunted chin. He looked like he could be on the cover of a men's fashion magazine.

"Yes," my mouth managed to say even while I was processing the slightly curled ends of chestnut hair that ruffled ever so slightly from under his hat.

One eyebrow rose a smidgen. "Would that be something other than staring at me like I was a mouse and you were a hungry python?"

"Maybe," I said before I realized it, then horribly ashamed that I had just stood in front of a stranger and ogled him, blushed furiously. "No, that is...I didn't mean... gah! I'm sorry, I didn't mean to gawk. And I swear to you that I'm really not the idiot you must think I am. Or a...well, I don't know what the female version of a horn dawg is, but I'm not that, either. I just...you have really nice eyes, but I expect you hear that a lot."

"Not really, no," he said, giving me a swift, impersonal once-over. His voice, I noticed, was a forest green. Odd, that. I'd never run into someone who spoke in forest green. The closest I'd ever come to that was my mother's light yellow-green voice. "Is there something you needed from me?"

I bit back any number of risqué comments, and hoped he didn't notice how red my cheeks were. "Actually, it's just the opposite. Are you waiting to meet Roland Blackwood?"

"Yes." He studied me again, this time a little more leisurely, his gaze lingering for a fraction of a second too long on both my breasts and hips before his gaze narrowed on me. "You are Damon's...sister? You don't look...erm..."

"I'm not related to him, if that's what you're wondering. I'm Korean, not Black," I said, giving him my friendliest smile. "Or rather my mother is Korean. My father is Russian, and I don't even know Damon, but I am a friend of his brother Roland. I'm Tat Romanoff."

"Tat?" He took what I assumed was an involuntary step backward, his voice going even darker green. I upped the wattage in my smile, worried I was making a poor first impression.

"It's Tatiana really, but everyone calls me Tat. Or Tatty. Sometimes Titty, but I don't let that by me because you have to have set boundaries, right? You must be Mrs. Blackwood's new tenant. Rolly asked me to help you get settled since he had to go to San Francisco to learn how to climb rocks from his latest."

"His latest what?" the man asked.

I thought for a moment, then gave him another smile filled with the calm reassurance that I was not a man-ogling woman who allowed the name Titty by her without protest. "Whatever he wants. Let's go pick up your keys."

"You don't have them? I was told that Damon's family member would have them," the man said, hesitating a few seconds before falling in next to me as I headed down the boardwalk to the bookstore.

"Nope. I was off picking up some dank haunted dolls from an estate sale. What's your name? Rolly didn't tell me."

"Dank…" He stopped, and from the corner of my eye I caught him doing a little head shake, his jaw flexing a few times as if he was having to stop himself from speaking. "My name is Finch."

"Really? Finch?"

He stopped dead, his jaw flexing again as he blinked incredibly thick eyelashes. "That is, my name is…erm… Renfrew."

"Finch Renfrew? Or Renfrew Finch?" I tipped my head as my libido gave him a fast once-over. The thought that he really was worth the effort passed quickly through my mind before I squelched it. No more romantic escapades for me! "I have to say, you don't look like a Renfrew."

He did something amazing then—he sighed.

Not just a normal annoyed sigh, or even a sad sigh. He heaved a big sigh, a dramatic, soul-deep sigh, the kind that said so much with just an exhalation of air.

He lifted a hand to gesture vaguely. "That's because it's not my name. It's my…" He was silent for a moment before squaring his shoulders and looking me dead in the eye. "It's my pen name. I'm an author. My name is Finch, but I prefer for everyone to call me Renfrew. Jeremy Renfrew."

"OK," I said, biting back the words on the tip of my

tongue. "Do you mind if I call you Finch? It's kind of a cool name."

His jaw worked again, then his shoulders slumped a little. "I suppose that would be allowable."

I gave him another max-wattage smile. "That sorts out the names, then."

"Yes," he said, and we both turned back toward the length of the boardwalk. "I will refrain from calling you Titty, however."

I laughed; I couldn't help it. He had an English accent that I found highly pleasurable, his voice striking some sort of a chord inside me that made me feel like it was part of me.

I wondered about the odd color of his voice, but decided that Inner Tat was close to being smitten on the spot. Such behavior was not to be encouraged, so I dragged my mind from wondering what it would be like to have that delicious voice whispering dark blue sweet nothings in my ear. "But seriously, Finch? Is it your first name or last name?"

"Yes," he answered, marching alongside me without glancing over.

"Finch like the cute little bird? Is it a family name? Is it English? You sound English. I know they have a lot of interesting names like that. My cousin married into an old English family with an interesting name, but it's not as cool as Finch."

He stopped again, this time a martyred expression flitting across his face. "Do you always ask so many questions?"

"Yup. I have a natural curiosity about people. My old therapist—old as in former, not old as in elderly—had me take a personality test, and an interest in people came out as my number one strength. Is Finch a town in England that your family was named for, or did your ancestors raise finches, and the name kind of stuck?"

To my surprise, he gave a chuckle that was fairly rusty in color, like he didn't use it much. Oddly, I was warmed by the idea that I could make him laugh.

"It is a family name, but my ancestors have not, to my knowledge, raised anything but hell, my father in particular."

"Daddy Finch is a bit of a character, eh?" I asked, my steps slowing. I had a strange reluctance to get the keys and get Finch settled. It was far more enjoyable talking to him, listening to his voice, and watching his pretty eyes.

"He was."

There was a sense of finality to his words that warned he wasn't willing to explore that conversational thread, so I just murmured a platitude, then paused to gesture down the boardwalk. "You probably want to know about Axegate Walk. It's been around for over a hundred years, before the red blight came in and wiped out all the shellfish in the 1970s. Ravenfall and Raven's Bay both turned to tourists to keep everyone going, and luckily, we have Axegate Walk. All Raven's Bay has is a weird forest. Morning, Amanda. Morning, Sian."

Two women who had emerged from a shop stopped to clutch each other, whooping in laughter.

"Really, I can't possibly look like that," Sian said, wiping back tears of hilarity. Both women held long strips of photos, the type photo booths spit out. "My teeth! Amanda, *my teeth*!"

"Stop," Amanda said, waving one of the strips at her friend. Both women's voices were shades of yellow, heading to orange for Sian. "I'm going to pee my pants if you don't stop. Besides, I have three eyes in this one. An actual third eye! Did you ever see anything so horrible? I knew the aura photos were going to be revealing, but honestly! A third eye!"

"Got some new pictures?" I asked, craning to see them.

"Oh, hi Tat. Yes, we thought we'd treat ourselves." Amanda wiped her eyes, before turning her gaze on Finch. "Who's your friend?"

"His name is Fi—er—Jeremy," I said, sliding Finch a conspiratorial smile that he did not return. "He's taking over Ozy's shop. Hey, you guys haven't heard from her, have you?"

Sian shook her head. She was taller than Amanda, with long blond hair, heavy eye makeup, and a tattoo of a butterfly on her collarbone. "No. Not since you forced her to leave with all your evil doll juju."

"My dolls aren't evil. They just look a bit dubious," I said, feeling like I was fighting an uphill battle. "Besides, I did not force Ozy to do anything."

"Hrmph," Sian said, turning to eye Finch.

"I heard she went to Seattle to deal with the estate of a relative who left her a fortune after he fell into a volcano," Amanda said. "That's what Deacon said, anyway. Oh, speaking of disasters, how did your date go last week?"

I cleared my throat and slid a quick glance toward Finch, who had pulled out his phone when it pinged at him. "Not great."

"Did you actually kill this one?" Sian said with a sniff. "Or just maim him like you did the others?"

"I haven't killed or maimed any of them," I said, very aware of Finch. Not that I wanted to impress him, but still, I didn't need him getting the wrong idea about me the second we met.

"What about the guy last month?" Sian persisted. "He was taken off in an ambulance."

"It wasn't an ambulance," I said, trying not to look as annoyed as I felt. "Not any longer. And he left quickly because he had a flight to Nepal."

"Right in the middle of your date?" she persisted.

"You know how it is when you have an important appointment with a Nepalese monastery," I said, desperate to get the conversation back on track. "Sometimes, you have a sudden flight out to Nepal, and you end up with a guy driving a decommissioned ambulance to get you to the airport."

Both women stared at me. I refused to look at Finch.

"That bad, was it?" Amanda asked.

"He said something about wanting to join a non-speaking order of monks to quiet the tormented screaming voices of the damned that filled his head, yes, but you can hardly blame that on one date with me," I said with what I hoped was a light, carefree laugh.

"Considering you broke both legs of that German tourist last week, I think it's entirely possible you drove last month's victim to a monastery," Sian replied.

I turned to Finch, unable to keep from telling him, "It's not like it sounds. I met a German tourist, and we decided to go to a putt-putt golf course. He slipped and was trapped in a windmill hazard, and subsequently broke both his legs. I had nothing to do with the unfortunate incident other than being on a date with him at the time."

Finch blinked. "That does sound unfortunate."

"Just how did he slip, that's what I want to know," Sian said, her snark level at maximum.

"Then there was that accountant last year who was doing a walk up the coast for charity," Amanda said with a little frown. "Did they ever find out why his leg dropped off the day after you guys...you know...hooked up?"

"That had nothing to do with me!" I said quickly, shooting a worried look at Finch. He was staring at Amanda with an odd expression that was mingled surprise and something that looked a lot like horror. "It was some rare bacteria or infection that attacked him. The doctors said so."

"Uh huh," Sian said, her lips curling in an obnoxious smile. "And that man who spontaneously combusted when you and he were necking in his car while you sat at the overlook—"

"He didn't combust! Not all of him!" I protested. "Just bits here and there, and he was fine as soon as I rolled him out of the car, down the slope, and into the water. Geesh, Sian. It's like you think I'm doing these things purposely!"

"Everyone knows that a date with you risks potential disaster," she answered with a cocked eyebrow at Finch.

I cleared my throat, feeling a little warmth on my cheeks that I badly wished hadn't manifested. "Yes, well, it doesn't matter since I've sworn off dating for the time being."

Sian gave a short bark of laughter. "It's about time. The men of Ravenfall can breathe easy at long last knowing the Grim Reaper is off the dating market."

"I'm sure none of those accidents were your fault. Although the man who lost his memory and had to be committed later…well, I suppose it's best if we don't speak badly about those with mental issues," Amanda said with a morsel of sympathy, then she glanced at her watch. "Ack. It's after one. I have to run or Deacon'll have my head," she said, taking one last lingering look at Finch before dashing across the street, heading toward the Cthulhu Arms.

"Amanda is a waitress at the local café," I explained to Finch. "They have really good cinnamon rolls, if you like sweets."

"I'm not overly fond of them, no," he replied.

"I just hope you're happy, having driven off Ozy. She was one of the most interesting people Ravenfall has ever attracted," Sian said, tucking away her handful of pictures before heading toward one of the side streets. "Your latest better get some comprehensive life insurance before he ends up like the German tourist…or worse."

"And Sian is a pain in the ass," I told Finch. "Sorry about them deciding we were a couple. And pouring the details of my dating history all over you."

"I found it fascinating, actually," he said, giving me a long look. "The man's leg actually dropped off? There was no injury beforehand?"

"No. One minute he was walking out of my bedroom saying that he knew the supposed curse concerning my romantic partners was nothing but superstition, and the next minute his left leg dropped off, and bounced down the stairs. It landed right at the feet of a customer who was buying one of my haunted tchotchkes." I could still hear the woman's shrieks echoing in my memory. I gave Finch my toothiest smile, and added with a whole lot of false cheer, "Well, I guess we should get going. You're probably anxious to get into your shop."

He looked mildly startled, but turned with me as we proceeded down the boardwalk.

THREE

"Your place is a few doors down, by the way," I told Finch, pointing out the shops as we passed them. "This is Runes, Runes, Runes, which as you might guess, offers rune-stone readings."

The shop was brightly lit, and had little baskets of crystals and such in the window. Inside, three women sat around a table.

"Indeed," he said with what I thought of as frosty disinterest.

Dammit, now he thought I was some sort of dating disaster.

It doesn't matter, I told myself. *There will be no more romantic partners.* I'd decided that right after the last date.

"And this is Tristram's shop," I said, gesturing toward the next shop window, hoping to distract Finch from the sorry mess that was my life.

"Bounties collected," Finch read aloud, eyeing the gold script painted on the door. *"Dog Whisperer. Shaman services available upon request.* What does that mean?"

"It means Tristram is bounty hunter, likes dogs, and is also a shaman. That's a camera obscura studio, but the owner is off back east watching his son get married. And this is the local ice cream shop, but if you don't have a sweet tooth, you probably wouldn't like it much, although they do keep the decor dead accurate to the 1950s. And here you are, number forty-two."

We stopped in front of the glass-fronted shop. I watched Finch, waiting to see what he'd think of it. My lust for better digs aside, I had a fondness for Ozy's shop, and wondered if he'd like it, too.

Mystical symbols painted on the glass didn't obscure the inside of the shop, which I was pleased to see still sported plum-colored velvet curtains pulled back to reveal a plastic skeleton sitting in a chair with a fez on its head, and a book clasped in one of its bony hands. Rolly had been right in that Ozy had left her decor untouched when she'd left…which was odd. Very odd. I couldn't help but wonder…

A rattling sound drew my attention from a nagging speculation.

"The door is locked," Finch said, his brows pulling together as he peered inside. The lights were off, but visible through the dimness was a fanciful silk screen sitting behind a small round table, at which four chairs were arranged. The table was covered with a purple cloth that matched the curtains, and dotted with a variety of miscellaneous objects. A few posters on the wall were of the metaphysical sort, with a listing of chakra locations, a picture of a goat-legged Pan figure, and a note that credit card payments would come with a surcharge. "There is an apartment upstairs?"

"Yup. We'll go get the keys from Mercader. I need to talk to him about the latest crap the Municipal Entity is pulling, anyway." I headed for the used bookstore that resided next to Ozy's shop, admiring as I passed the display of books in the window, everything from Wiccan spells to a guide to trapping fairies, a history of Bigfoot, and the art of understanding the language of plants.

The smell of old books that wrapped around me provided—as it always did—a profound sense of pleasure. A woman with fluffy brown hair stood in front of a bookshelf, her fingers trailing along the spines of the books as she browsed, dressed in layers of gauzy material, with tiny little bells tinkling from various parts of her ensemble. She looked like a fantasy version of Stevie Nicks crossed with Tolkien, as decorated by Martha Stewart.

Opposite her, in an overstuffed red armchair, sat a man with shoulder-length chocolate brown hair, and wearing a sapphire blue velvet smoking jacket. He looked up when a little bell over the door chimed.

"Morning, Mercader," I said.

"And greetings unto you, fair maiden. Have you returned to Ravenfall laden with priceless treasures?" Mercader asked, giving me one of his placid smiles, his voice rose gold as usual.

"A few dolls, but beyond that, no, there was nothing at the estate sale you wanted," I told him, fishing out an envelope and handing it to him. "Here's your money. I wish they had something that you could use, but it was mostly *Reader's Digest* books and a complete set of *National Geographic*s. Nothing even remotely interesting, I'm afraid. This is Jeremy Renfrew, by the way. He's taking over Ozy's shop."

"Reeeally," Mercader drawled, cocking an eyebrow at me before closing the book around one of his fingers, clearly marking his spot. "How very interesting. I had no idea Ozy had left the shop for good."

"Me, either," I said slowly, wondering if something was going on, or if I was making a mountain out of a squashed molehill. "She never said anything about leaving. Not that she spoke to me if she could help it."

"Well, you did name all those horrible dolls after her." Mercader looked puzzled for a few seconds before directing his attention to the woman absorbed by the books in the back of the shop. "Belly, have you heard anything about Ozy taking a vacation?"

"Not a vacation," Belle answered, pulling down a heavy, faded tome and flicking through the pages.

"A shopping trip, then? Or one of her mysterious visits to Portland?"

"No," she answered, putting back the book and absently wiping her hands on her gauze lime and orange skirt. She always wore orange, which meshed well with her vocal color, as did the soft bells sewn onto her clothing. She jingled her way over to the next shelf. "She's left. Do you have the Crawling Eye grimoire? The original Latin, not the one with the crappy translation."

"Annotated or illustrated?"

"Oh, annotated. The illustrated one is pure fiction."

"Back shelf, under the Harry Potter spell books," Mercader said, nodding his head toward the back of the bookstore.

"What do you mean *left*?" I asked, feeling like I had to know what had happened to the woman who had made my life unpleasant during the past year.

"Oh good, you have the spiral-bound version. So much easier when cooking." Belle brought her book up to the desk, giving Finch a side-eye. I was pleased to see he was perusing the nearest bookshelf, feeling for some reason that it was important that he love old books as much as I did. "Left as in left. I did a reading for her three weeks ago, and the cards quite clearly said that trouble was on its way, and then the hanging man turned over for her immediate future, and you know what that means."

"A visit to the state pen?" Mercader guessed, a little twinkle in his eyes indicating he was teasing her.

"No, it means *the man*," the woman answered succinctly. "Big Brother. The police. Or in this case, Sheriff Sharif."

"Sheriff Sharif is the head of our local police," I told Finch, who was flipping through an antique book in what I thought was French.

"So I gathered," he murmured, frowning slightly at one of the pages. "This history of the Boer War is incorrect."

"Ozy said she was going to lay low for a while until the threat passed," Belle continued, pulling out a zippered wallet. She tipped it upside down, causing several cones of incense, a small peacock feather, a handful of live ladybugs, two amethyst stones, and a hammered coin to spill out onto the counter. "She mentioned asking Tristram to watch her shop. Eighteen dollars is a little steep for this version, don't you think? I have fifteen, or I could do ten and a reading whenever you wanted."

"Fifteen will be fine," the man said, plucking the money from her hands, and punching the number in on an old-fashioned cash register. "Not that I don't value your readings, but every little helps. Where did she go?"

"Who?" Belle asked, gathering up her things and tucking the book away in a string bag that was tied to her belt. The ladybugs she scooped up and sprinkled over her head.

"Ozy."

She shrugged. "No clue. Tristram might know. I believe I shall go commune with the sun goddess for a bit before the tea service. I'm going to need her energy to cope with all the tourists. Blessings, Mercader. Oh, Tat, are you here? Blessings to you and your man, too."

"He's not mine—" I started to say, but Belle had tinkled her way out the door before I could continue. I turned back to Finch to see what he thought of the town tarot reader, but he was now studying a book on medieval poison gardens.

"That is Belle Antoine," Mercader told Finch when the door jangled shut. "Priestess of Gaia, and card reader extraordinaire. She runs the tarot card shop at the end of the walk. Are you interested in herbalism?"

"Not really," Finch said, closing the book, his nose wrinkling at the little cloud of old book particles that followed the action, and replaced it on the shelf before turning toward us.

"He's an author," I told Mercader. "Rolly sent me here to meet him, and get Ozy's keys."

"An author," Mercader said, slipping a letter into the book to mark his place. He held out a hand to Finch, who duly shook it. "Always nice to have a man of the literary arts in town. Mercader Davis, bookseller, at your service."

"Keys?" I prompted him, holding out my hand.

"Darling, I would gladly give them to you and our illustrious new resident, but alas, I have them not. Tristram probably has possession of them—you know how tight he was with Ozy."

"That's right, he was," I said, wondering if I dared ask Tristram anything since he always intimidated me. "Thanks, Mercader. See you later."

"On Friday, for sure. The Entity meeting is at six," he called as I headed for the door, Finch following me.

"If they let me in this time," I said with a grim twist of my lips. "After Ozy poisoned them against me."

"Did she?" Mercader asked, retaking his seat.

"She impugned the hauntedness of my creepy dolls to them, and they wouldn't let me attend the last three meetings." I took a deep breath, reminding myself that Finch was waiting, and that he already had a bad image of me. I could rant to Mercader at a later time.

"Well…your creepy dolls *aren't* haunted, though, are they?" Mercader asked.

"Pfft." I waved that away. "My point is that they wouldn't even have thought of me if Ozy hadn't filled their ears with poison. Enough whining. Are you ready…er…Jeremy? Let's go find your keys."

We exited the shop and set off down the boardwalk, my mind twisting and turning like a buttered cat.

Why was I so convinced there was something suspicious about Ozy's disappearance?

How was I going to combat the Municipal Entity's latest move in our battle for superiority?

I slid a glance toward the silent man striding next to me.

More importantly, why did my feeling that there was more to Finch than first appeared make me want to get to know him better?

I gave a mental head shake at that thought, reminding myself it hadn't been that long since my date had ended up running to the airport, swearing the voices of the damned warned him to get away from me.

Under no circumstances should I even think of the intriguing Finch in the light of a romantic interest.

My brain heaved a dramatic sigh, and told me that I had never been one to listen to common sense when it was far more exciting to leap first, and ask questions later.

I hate it when your inner self goes the tough love route.

FOUR

"Why do you sell dolls that are supposedly haunted but aren't?" Finch didn't want to ask the question, but his curiosity was piqued, and he was ever one to gather information.

"Hmm?" Tatiana appeared to be deep in thought, but she glanced at him with eyes made up of a variety of shades of grey, green, and brown, just like shiny rocks in a crystal-clear stream. "Oh, they sell better if people think they're haunted. Like, a whole lot better. Anyone can have a creepy doll, but one bearing the soul of a tormented Victorian child who drowned at sea, or was orphaned and sent to live with a cruel guardian, or locked in an attic until they died a sad and horrific death, sells hundreds of times better. Sometimes even thousands, depending on how good the haunting story is. You're an author—you must know how a good story will sell just about anything."

"I understand the value of intriguing copy, yes, but I was curious why you don't simply sell actual haunted dolls instead."

Her nose wrinkled in an adorable manner. Finch was not a man who admired nose wrinkling in general, but the gesture was more than pleasing on Tatiana. "Because there are no such things?"

"Are you asking a question or making a statement?" he asked, confused.

"Making a statement, of course. I'm a die-hard skeptic when it comes to haunted dolls," she said in a matter-of-fact tone. "But that doesn't mean I'm not going to make a profit off of people who feel differently. What about you?"

"I am told I have a very scientific mind," he answered. "To the point of being almost unintuitive, but that, I believe, is a misunderstanding of a truly analytical nature."

"That's interesting, but I actually meant do you believe in woo stuff?"

"Woo stuff?" Finch gave a little mental sigh at the fact that he was caught up in such a confusing conversation. It was all due to his curiosity about mortals. It was always thus, he told himself. It was just one of the many annoying traits he'd inherited from his heedless father.

"Ghosts, haunted dolls, werewolves…you know, woo stuff." Her bright eyes considered him in a way that left him both feeling overly warm and suddenly aware that he hadn't partaken himself of a woman in two years.

"Ah. I try to keep an open mind," he answered, skating around the subject that he felt was best left undiscussed. He searched for a suitable distraction. "What is an Entity meeting?"

She made a face. "The monthly meeting of the Municipal Entity. If you're going to live here, you should probably attend. We have to keep on top of the Entity. Goddess alone knows what they would do if they thought no one was watching."

"The what, now?" he asked, more confused than he ever remembered being. It wasn't a comfortable feeling.

Tatiana gave him one of her blinding smiles. "Ravenfall isn't the most normal of places."

"Indeed." He wondered if there were members of the Otherworld here. He doubted it—they tended to cluster together in major cities. Certainly no Dark One in his right mind would isolate himself in a small town where his dining habits—or lack of them—might become common knowledge. "It seems pleasant enough, if a bit…eccentric."

"Oh, we have eccentric in spades," she answered with a little laugh that seemed to thrum inside him. He frowned at the sensation. Mortals, even attractive women like Tatiana, were nothing to him other than possible sources of sustenance. Their lives were too disorganized, too chaotic for him. He told the thrum to stop, and instead, focused on what he'd write in the chapter he intended on starting. "For instance, instead of a town council, we have a Municipal Entity. No one really knows who they are, because they never appear."

"I thought you said that a meeting was called—"

"Oh, they *call* meetings," she answered in a scoffing tone, with appropriate gestures that indicated just how ridiculous the situation was. "But then random people show up at the meetings instead of the Entity, bearing a paper with a list of orders, warnings, and punishments from them. The Municipal Entity, that is. I don't know anyone who's actually seen them, though. If it wasn't for the fact that people who challenge them disappear, I wouldn't believe they actually existed, but the proof is in the pudding, as my grandmother used to say, and unfortunately, the Entity's pudding is quick to strike and quite deadly."

Finch had several things to say about the idea of a lethal town government, but kept those thoughts to himself.

"Then there's our police force," Tatiana continued, glancing over her shoulder when a woman going in the opposite direction scowled and muttered something insulting as she passed. "I heard that, Fennimore! I did *not* break his legs, the putt-putt place did that! Where was I? Oh, the Ravenfall police. They're made up of three Wiccan sisters who will smudge the ever-living hell out of you if you cross them."

"That sounds fairly wholesome, in the big picture of life," Finch commented. Despite the still faint sense of resentment and martyrdom at being forced to spend six months in the town, he found himself intrigued.

"It can go either way." Tatiana waggled her hand. "Depends on how annoyed you make them. The biggest eccentricity is the fact people born here bear the Ravenfall boon."

"What sort of a boon? And who grants it?" he asked. He had an almost itchy need to take notes, and wondered if she'd think it rude if he pulled out a small notebook to record what she said.

"It comes from the town, and is dependent on the person born here. I can really only talk about mine—I have a form of synesthesia. I hear colors in voices."

"Fascinating," he said, his fingers twitching for a pen and his notebook, but he resisted, instead committing her comments to memory. He'd make notes on his laptop later. Insight into her personality promised to be quite useful for his book. "And this happens to all people who are born in Ravenfall?"

"No, everyone is different," Tatiana explained. "Clemmie, now—she's my assistant, and also a third cousin or something very distant—Clemmie is ditsy as the day is long, but she's also extremely effective. Whatever she sets her mind to do, she does to a level that I can only envy. For instance, she decided one day that she wanted to get serious about the pictures she takes of my haunted stuff, and within the year she won three international photography awards. Belle has an affinity with insects; you'll usually find bees or beetles or spiders clinging to her. I don't know about anyone else, since most people tend to keep their boon close to their chest, so to speak."

"I can't help but see a dichotomy in your belief system," he commented when she paused at the darkened window of the closed shop he would call his temporary home.

"Oh?" She straightened up from where she shaded her eyes to peer in. "How so?"

"You don't believe in haunted objects, spirits, or werewolves, but you do believe in Wicca, a mysterious group of people who have apparently unlimited power over the town occupants, and a boon granted by a piece of land." He gave her a long look as they resumed their way down the pavement.

"I told you we're eccentric around here." She slid him a glance from the corner of her eyes. "Do you like eccentric?"

"As a rule, yes."

She smiled. It was a smile that warmed him as if he was standing full in the sun without any protective clothing. "Good. That's pretty much it. Oh, there is Deacon."

"Who's that?" Finch asked, temporarily casting aside a mental nested bullet list of points she had covered in the last few minutes. "Your husband?"

Tatiana gave a little half laugh. "Glorious goddess and her nine hairy minions, no. I mean, we dated a few times when he first got here about a year ago and took over the café from the mayor, but Deak is the last person I'd marry."

"What tragedy befell him?" Finch couldn't help but ask. He was more than a little amused by the fact that the lovely, enticing Tatiana was made up of such odd facets to her personality, and even more approving of the fact that she seemed to take the potholes of life with a sense of humor.

"None, actually. He's the only one who didn't have anything bad happen to him," she said with a little laugh, then stopped, frowned, and leaned in close, her breath brushing against his ear in a way that made his penis very aware of her. "He's into old gods. Like, *really* into them."

"Is he?" At the touch of her breath on his cheek, Finch ignored the rush of his libido, reminding himself that he had no need for a mortal lover when there were perfectly fine female Dark Ones with which to disport himself.

The fact that he hadn't done so in two years was something he chose to ignore, telling himself that writing his book claimed all his attention.

Besides, none of his past lovers could hold a candle to the woman next to him. She was almost as tall as he was, with long brown hair that glowed with strands of red, amber, and chocolate in the sunlight. She was what he thought of as substantially built, not one of those women who felt that an emaciated appearance was favorable. Tatiana was just the opposite, a possessor of curves in all the places women excelled in having curves, and for a moment, he was gripped with a hot, red need to touch her, to taste every delicious sweep of flesh.

"Sorry?"

Finch dragged his mind from a vision of Tatiana lying gloriously naked on his bed, her hair spread around her, his hands in full possession of her plentiful breasts. "Pardon?"

"What was that you said?"

He stared at her, the erotic mental image taking its own sweet time fading away. "I'm not sure. Did I say something?"

Her nose scrunched again in the manner he found wholly delightful before he realized he was doing so, then he gave himself another brief lecture about mortals, and the folly of becoming involved with them.

He'd just done so, and look where it had gotten him—cast out from his own home and having to assume the identity of a Jeremy.

He was *so* not a Jeremy.

"Yeah, you made a half-groaning noise in your chest, like you were having a painful gas bubble or something." Her eyes considered him with a mixture of amusement and concern.

Finch clamped down on his body's interest in her, and gave her his sternest look. "I do not now, nor to the best of my memory, have I ever had, a painful gas bubble."

She giggled then. The sound of it fired his blood.

He clamped down on the blood fire, too.

"Sorry, no offense intended. This is Tristram's place." She hesitated as she gestured toward a shop door, casting him a doubtful look. "Er…you might want to let me do the talking. Tristram can be a bit prickly with new people."

It was on the tip of Finch's tongue to tell her that there was no person he had ever feared other than his mother but at that moment, the door was flung open with enough force to bounce off the wall and rebound into the large figure filling the doorway.

"Are you a tourist?" the man demanded to know.

"No. Are you?" Finch asked, meeting the man's steely grey gaze. He was slightly shorter than Finch, but bulkier, with shoulder length dark blond hair, a short beard, and a stance that bespoke a background in the military.

The man's eyebrows pulled together, his fingers flexing.

Aware that his shoulders were tensing in response to a fight trigger, Finch forced himself to relax, but kept his balance on the balls of his feet, just in case this odd man attacked him or Tatiana.

"Of course not. It's just that we have to be nice to tourists," the man said in what was nearly a growl. A muscle in his jaw twitched. "The Entity made us all take an oath. A blood oath. And you know what happens if you decry a blood oath."

"Something abhorrent, no doubt," Finch answered. He had a feeling this man was itching for a fight, and for a moment, he considered giving it to him.

"It's not nice," Tatiana said, moving a step closer to him, a fact that had his body warming up again. "Your testicles shrivel up to little raisins, hair grows out of your ears, and you grow a small tail." She made a quick introduction, ending with, "Mercader says you have Ozy's keys."

"I don't call a tail sixteen inches *small*." Tristram the shaman gave Finch one last long, antagonist stare before jerking his head toward the interior of the shop. "Keys are inside."

Tatiana quirked her lips at Finch in what appeared to be an apologetic half smile, following the man into his office.

Finch entered, noting absently that the office furniture consisted of a couple of desks and a long green overstuffed Victorian couch that looked remarkably comfortable, which was currently inhabited by a large, snoring bulldog. A flat-screen TV was mounted on a wall, next to an assortment of video game machines and controllers. Tristram rummaged in a desk before pulling out a key with a hot pink rabbit's foot hanging from the keychain. "Here's the key. It opens both the front and back door. There's no separate one to the apartment upstairs. Don't go in the basement. It's cursed."

He turned his heel, and marched out of the room after handing Tatiana the keys, leaving Finch standing there wondering just what sort of place he'd stumbled across.

"Who has a cursed basement?" he said aloud before he realized he was doing so.

"You, evidently," Tatiana said, giving him another of her blood-warming smiles before urging him back onto the sidewalk. "Some people have all the luck, huh? Wow. Still no tourists, and it's almost three. Oh well, the few days we have before tourist season really gets going gives you time to get settled in."

Seagulls wheeled overhead, but even they were strangely silent. Their footsteps echoed while they walked toward Finch's temporary home, making him feel twitchy. He cast a glance back toward the water, noting absently that the tide was out, although the smell of salt and seaweed seemed to hang thick in the breeze that blew off the water.

At the parking area where his rental car sat, three other vehicles had joined it, one a low-slung red sports car of some Italian origin, a sensible silver four-door sedan, and a blue and purple VW Bug, decorated with runes.

Out on the quay that ran to the isthmus, a woman walked, a long scarlet scarf fluttering behind her. When she approached the building, a shadow broke away from the wall and swept forward, pausing before her for a moment before the two figures suddenly began to move together. Finch shook his head at the odd behavior of the mortals waltzing around a restaurant, saying, "How long has your family lived here?"

"About a hundred years, going back to when the town was founded. My mom moved away when she was young, but came back when she was pregnant with me, after my dad ran off to shack up with one of his students. He was a geology professor, and not a very good one, according to Mom. Here we are, home sweet home." She flashed him an oddly unreadable look, and unlocked the door.

"Abandon hooooope," a sepulchral voice intoned. Finch glanced up as they entered the shop, and saw a small white plastic box above the doorframe, clearly a movement-sensitive device that acted in place of the usual shop bell.

"I hope you don't get the willies from Ozy's stuff. She wasn't here long enough to really build up a steady clientele. Dammit, I should have asked Tristram about her leaving town so suddenly, but he always intimidates me. He used to do something with black ops, and is scary as hell when he wants to be," Tatiana said, glancing around.

The previous occupant had obviously set up the room to resemble that of a stage fortune-teller, complete with a wall of framed vintage crystal ball reader posters, below which a row of four faded red velvet cushioned chairs sat. The shop front was a massive window that ran almost floor to ceiling, with three stylized eyes in a vertical line above the words *Ozymandra's Emporium of Other* in fancy gold script. Below all that, in a much simpler block print, read *Crystal Readings*.

"The apartment is in the back?" Finch asked as he moved past a desk and two faded wingback chairs to a narrow hallway. A door to the left led to a small bathroom, clearly for clients since it contained a toilet and sink, and a sign reminding visitors that those who didn't wash their hands would not be served.

"Upstairs. I haven't been in the back of her shop, but if it's like Mercader's, there should be a kitchen and breakfast nook." Tatiana followed him as the hallway opened into a dimly lit space bearing a small Formica table with two chairs that had probably been first put in use some sixty years ago, a staircase leading upwards, and a two doors situated at right angles to each other. The window next to the door opposite indicated it opened to an alley behind Axegate Walk. "Ooooh! It's so much nicer than my shop. You have an actual kitchen. And a downstairs bathroom. All I have is my shop, and two minuscule bedrooms, and an equally tiny bathroom upstairs."

Finch opened the second door, which led to a narrow wooden staircase that plunged into darkness.

"Ugh. Cursed basement," Tatiana said, backing up when he flipped on the light and descended a few steps to examine it. "I wouldn't go down there if I were you!"

"I thought you didn't believe in woo?" he asked, using her own term.

"Yeah, well, there's saying you don't believe in were-wolves, and then there's not wanting to go into creepy, dark, obviously curse-laden basements," she called down to him.

"I am very hard to curse," was all he answered. The light didn't illuminate much of the small, closed space, but Finch identified the familiar shapes of a water heater, and small furnace that looked many years of out date. There was also a collection of discarded and dirty furniture against the wall, stacked with a neatness that appealed to Finch's orderly nature.

He didn't sense any sort of a curse whatsoever, nor did he see any wards or signs of occupation by any denizens of the Otherworld.

"It's just a basement," he said, returning to the kitchen, locking the door behind him nonetheless. "Musty and ill-lit, but there's nothing frightening there, unless that furnace is as inefficient as it looks."

Tatiana shuddered, and handed him the shop keys. "I wouldn't know, and honestly, I'd like to keep it that way. Shall we go see your apartment?"

Finch had just started up the stairs when he heard from the front room, "...all ye who enter," in the same tinny mechanical voice that had sounded when he'd entered the shop.

"Tat? You in here? Mercader says there's a dishy Englishman in town, and you've been showing him around—oh, hi." The words ended in a giggle, and Finch found himself facing a young woman of about eighteen or nineteen.

"This is Clemmie," Tatiana told Finch. "My assistant who is supposed to be watching the shop. I hope you didn't leave people in it like last time."

"I locked the door so they couldn't steal anything," the young woman said, then giggled again. "No one is there, but that buyer from Portland who scooped up the jointed kid-body dolls is downright rude with his demands for you to call him back."

"I'd better go," Tatiana said, giving Finch a conspiratorial wink before gesturing her assistant toward the door. "Gotta keep the customers happy, right?"

Finch fought the need to make up an excuse to keep talking to Tatiana, desperately searching his mind. What happened next was the last thing he expected. "If you are not busy tonight, perhaps we could dine at the café I saw on the spit."

Tatiana's face lit up for a second before the pleasure in it dimmed. "Oh. That's sweet, but I really did promise myself that I wouldn't do the dating thing for a while. It seems fate has me in its crosshairs, and I wouldn't want to put you at risk."

"If I told you that I am notoriously difficult to harm, would that make a difference?" he asked, warring with the smart side of his mind, who pointed out that not only was he *not* looking for involvement with a mortal, but even if he was, he couldn't. It would be far too dangerous for her if the murderous gang found him. According to what Damon had told him, the miscreants would have no qualms harming her in order to get to him.

"Well…I shouldn't," she said, glancing toward the young woman. "The whole date thing is…discouraging."

"You can have dinner together without it being a date," Clemmie pointed out with a big smile at him.

"That's true," Tatiana said, the light returning to her face. "So long as it's not actually a date, dinner would be nice, but it'll be my treat since you are the newcomer here. The Cthulhu Arms has a really kicking spaghetti Bolognese."

"I'm free tonight," Clemmie said, her expression hopeful.

"No, you aren't," Tatiana told her firmly, which just made Clemmie giggle more.

Finch disliked giggling women. He thought for a second, then amended that statement to exclude women who weren't Tatiana. She had a pleasant giggle, more like the laughter of a burbling stream.

He decided that the dinner would offer a good opportunity to learn more about the eccentric Tatiana. Perhaps he could use her in his book. That thought cheered him up, and quelled the little voice that pointed out he was only interested in her because she appealed to his libido. "The spaghetti sounds delightful."

"Awesome!" Tatiana's smile seemed to brighten the dark kitchen. "I'll meet you here at seven, OK? I'd better go eat a couple of apples so I don't starve until then. I missed lunch, but Deacon's Bolognese is worth a few hunger pangs."

"I'm hungry, too. And I love Bolognese," Clemmie said with a plaintive note that Tatiana obviously ignored as she pushed her out the door, the chime speaking its words of doom as she did so.

Finch stood there for a moment, his brow drawn, rubbing his chin and wondering at his reaction to the intriguing Tatiana.

He disliked discordant influences on his life, and Tatiana looked just such a thing. Then again, it would have been the purest folly to ignore her when she might offer insight into the chaotic workings of the mortal mind. He owed it to his book to get to know her better. And once he was done learning everything there was to know about her, he'd tuck her away in an emotional compartment as he did all chaotic mortals who touched his life. One where she couldn't distract and discompose him, and all would be well.

The ironic side of his mind laughed and laughed and laughed at such optimism.

FIVE

"Why do I suspect there's something you're not telling me?"

I arranged an innocent expression on my face, and peered through the darkness at the source of the voice. "What do you mean, Finch?"

A dark shape moved in the murky light. "For one, there have been several references by citizens of the town to you having driven off the woman whose shop I am now inhabiting. For another, the server seated us here, in the back depths of the restaurant, with lighting so poor a single tallow candle could probably do a better job than the illumination present. Also, there was the fact that you had to threaten the server before she actually allowed us to sit down."

I pursed my lips, squinting a bit to try to get a look at the expression on Finch's face, but it was too dim to see more than a vague oval shape.

His voice was its normal forest green, though, so I assumed that meant he was not unhappy or upset. "If I told you that I was innocent of all wrongdoing, would you believe me?"

"Yes," he answered to my complete surprise, then amended the statement. "Probably. You seem like a truthful person, but perhaps you are under a misapprehension. I assume it is in reference to Ozymandra?"

"It is," I said with a sigh, and after seeing a familiar shape appear at the far end of the restaurant, where actual lights allowed the patrons to see, I leaned out of the back booth that was never used, put two fingers in my mouth, and gave a piercing whistle. Finch gave a little jerk at the noise. "Sorry, didn't mean to startle you. It's just that I see Deacon, and I'm going to demand he bring us some light."

The figure I had spotted turned at my whistle, and after staring down the row of booths to our inky spot, started toward us. The café was shaped like a horseshoe, with the kitchen in the center, and tables at the top and running perpendicular on either side. We were placed on the left side wing, at the distant back.

"I would have been happy to request a better location," Finch said.

I sensed censure in his tone.

"I'm not making a good impression on you, am I?" I asked, which was not what I had queued up in my head to say.

"Do you want to make a good impression?" he countered without answering my question, which was pretty much an answer in itself.

"Of course. I like people. I like you. I don't want you thinking I'm the sort of uncouth person who whistles at café owners instead of getting up and politely requesting help, but trust me, if I had done so, we wouldn't be getting the same result we're about to have. Hello, Deacon."

"Hullo. Who—" Deacon Owain stopped at our booth, clearly not able to see us very well. "Er..."

"This is Jeremy Renfrew," I said, introducing Finch. "He's a writer, and he's going to be staying at Ozy's place for a bit. I was wondering if you couldn't find such a distinguished visitor a better table than the Black Pit of Calcutta?"

"Who—" he started to say again while squinting at me, then straightened up with a sigh. "Oh, it's you, Tat."

"Yup. Deacon, can we please have another table? I can't even see the water glass, let alone read a menu."

"We're full," he answered in an obstinate tone that unfortunately I was very familiar with. "There are no other tables."

"Perhaps you could bring some light, then?" Finch asked in a silky tone of British politeness, beneath which there was an interesting thread of steel.

Deacon sighed again. "Fine, but you know that this table is reserved for those who wish to indulge in romantic escapades, and you shouldn't have chosen it for your date if you didn't intend on enjoying the privacy offered by it."

"This isn't a date. I swore off those. It's just dinner," I said in a tone that sounded false to my ears.

"Whatever. Just don't do anything to this poor man that ends up harming the café." He moved off before I could respond.

"You know what I dislike?" I asked the Finch-shaped shadow. "People who drop sentences like that and then leave before you can dispute the fact that you are on a date. Or damage places due to dates. Or don't want to have romantic shenanigans. But that's Deacon for you."

Finch was silent for a few seconds before he asked, "Have you always been so unfortunate with your romantic partners? I apologize if that seems like an intrusive question—there's no getting around the fact that it is—but I find myself curious as to why a woman like you apparently has such a difficult time with the partners in whom you are interested, romantically-speaking."

"No, it's only been the last six or seven years," I said with all honesty. "I was married for fifteen years, but then he left to find himself, and Clemmie needed a home, so I took her on as an assistant. After my ex, I didn't date for a few years, because...well, just because. Then I decided enough was enough, and I started looking around. Wow. I really opened up a stream of consciousness on you, didn't I? I'm sorry. Clemmie says I could talk the back leg off a zebra if I set my mind to it."

"There's no need to apologize. For one, I asked, and for another, I'm interested in why everyone perceives you to be cursed in the romance area of your life," he said. "And the shenanigans?"

"I really wish I could see your face," I complained. "It makes it hard to decide if you are seriously interested in the question because you want to shenanigan with me, if you're teasing me, or if you're bent out of shape because we've been banished to the darkest depths of the café due to Sonia the server being annoyed with me simply because I went on a date with her brother six years ago, and he left town the next day to join the merchant marines, and hasn't been heard of since."

"Seeing my face wouldn't help you," he answered. "I have an extremely good poker face. My emotions seldom—if ever—touch my expression."

"Uh huh. That's why right now you're secretly laughing?" I asked, acknowledging the rich thread of amusement in his voice that lightened the green to golden-emerald.

"I never secretly laugh," he said with a placidity that again was laced with amusement. "Although I will admit to being entertained by this situation despite the inconvenience. What did Sonia's brother do that made him run?"

I stared at the dark shape that was Finch for a few seconds, my admiration of him growing a few levels. "What makes you think that Brendan did something and not me?"

"You are an interesting woman who is quite straightforward in conversation and manner despite your reputation for doom. Surely any person who consented to go out with you must realize that. Thus, if there was a problem, it seems reasonable to chalk it up to the other party not understanding your somewhat eccentric nature before you went out together."

"Do you understand my eccentric nature?" I couldn't help but ask, a warm glow of pleasure starting in my belly and spreading outward. The second I realized it was doing it, I tried to shut it down.

This is not a date, I reminded myself. *Just dinner. Stop thinking nice things about him.*

"I believe I have a good grasp on it, yes," he answered in that same measured, calm tone, one that you would use to a fractious cat, or a child throwing a tantrum. "I am writing a book on the ordered mind, and how structure and organization can bring satisfaction to a chaotic life."

"I can't tell if that means you think I have a chaotic life that needs structure and organization, or if I'm an example of an ordered mind."

He said nothing, but I could have sworn I felt how uncomfortable he was.

"I'm sorry, that was unfair of me to put you on the spot like that," I said quickly. "I'm not a particularly structured person, so please don't feel bad about that."

"I have never met a woman like you," he said slowly, his voice tinged butterscotch with wonder. "Although my uncle's wife speaks her mind like you do. Still, she doesn't say things that I don't expect."

"Butterscotch," I said, startled.

"Pardon."

"Your voice. It's butterscotch. Wonder is teal, but your wonder voice is butterscotch. Odd."

Finch was silent for another few seconds. "And here we have another example of you speaking in an unexpected manner."

"It's my boon, the synesthesia. Are you familiar with what that is?"

"Moderately so, although other than you, I have not met with someone who has that ability," he answered before saying with obvious hesitance, "Would it be rude of me to ask how you hear colors?"

"It's not rude at all. Honestly, I think it's a pretty neat boon. I think I told you that I only hear the colors for voices. Not any other sounds. And because everyone always wants to know, your voice is a nice dark forest green normally. But it went fully butterscotch, which I've never seen. Or heard, rather." I frowned at that thought. Usually, the people I met all fell into tidy color containers.

"How interesting. I'm sorry—would you mind if I took notes? It's for my book," he explained, obviously feeling I would be offended.

"Feel free to note away, although how you can see any-thing—oh."

His face lit up as he tapped on his phone, clearly making a note on it.

"I've never known anyone with synesthesia," he said, his fingers moving quickly on the screen. "But I would like to talk to you further about what it is you hear, and if you have any way to influence the colors."

"Er…" I stifled a giggle. "Yeah, I can, sometimes, but it's not something I can show you."

"Oh?" He tucked away his phone, the darkness consuming us again as his voice went back to green. "Why is that?"

"It would require me touching you in a way that gave you sexual pleasure. Oh good, here comes Deacon."

"Here," the man himself said as he slapped down a tall black object, flipping a switch so that the camping lantern filled our inky corner with blue-white light. "This is the best you're going to get." His glare was prodigious, but just as I was about to comment that he could put some lights in the booth for those customers who didn't need the privacy, he cast a glance toward Finch, and froze for a few seconds, his eyebrows high on his forehead.

"Is there a problem?" I asked, a bit disconcerted by Deacon's stare at Finch. "I told you Jeremy Renfrew is—"

"A Dark One," Deacon interrupted.

It was my turn to stare at him. His voice, normally russet, went a pale, watery pink. I'd only ever heard that color once, and it was when Clemmie's birth father had locked her into her room, and threatened to burn the house down around them both.

Why on earth was Deacon scared?

"What's a Dark One when it's at home?" I asked him.

Finch, who had scooted the light to the back edge of the table, also seemed to freeze at Deacon's statement.

"Vampire." I could have sworn Deacon spoke without moving his lips. The word seemed to hang in the air in front of us before dissolving into nothing.

Finch's eyes, which I could once again see, studied Deacon for three seconds before he asked, "Do I know you?"

"No," Deacon said, and seemed to snap out of whatever possessed him. He backed up two steps, shaking his head. "No, you don't know me. I…I need to go."

I watched him hurry out to the main part of the café before disappearing into the kitchen area. "He's scared," I said, my gaze shifting to Finch. "No, not scared, terrified. What did you do to frighten him? Why did he call you a vampire?"

Finch narrowed his gorgeous eyes at me, his fingers tapping on the table. I had a feeling he was looking inward, and not really seeing me.

"You're not answering me," I said, my confused thoughts settling into one word. "You're afraid to answer me because I'll know you're lying, aren't you? Oh my goddess—you *are* a vampire! Is that why your voice is green? Is that why you wear a hat and a long coat on a day that doesn't really need either? Holy shitsnacks—would the sun fry you if you weren't wearing them? Oh my goddess! It's true! You're a vampire, a real vampire. I know a vampire. I am sitting across from a vampire. I have had sexy thoughts about a vampire."

Finch, who had started out looking stunned, quickly donned an expression of martyrdom that made me want to giggle. "If I offered you ten dollars to stop saying the word 'vampire,' would you take it? Or would you, instead, stand up and point at me while screaming, 'He's a bloodsucking master of the night?' No. Don't answer that. I suspect I wouldn't like it."

I couldn't help myself. I let the giggle that I had been holding back loose. "I wouldn't do any such thing, actually. Mostly because I like you, and you don't look like a bloodsucking master, although you sure put the fear of the twelve gods into Deacon, but also because your voice is still foresty, and not at all deceptive."

"Out of idle curiosity—" he started to ask, pulling out his phone again.

"Deacon? Brown." I made a face. "And not a pretty brown. Just kind of…well, brown. Basically the same color as his hair. Wait, you *were* asking what color Deacon's voice is, weren't you?"

"Yes." He made a note then put away his phone and considered me with a solemnity that had me sitting up a bit straighter. "Your synesthesia aside, it would appear that you have stumbled across a fact about myself that I prefer few people to know."

"Holy cats in pajamas," I said, lowering my voice when Sonia started toward us, a sour look on her face. "That's pretty amazing."

"Has it shaken your woo-sense?" he asked, glancing up when Sonia pulled to a stop next to him.

"Well?" she asked, her voice brittle, the color of damp slate.

"Bolognese for me," I said, and glanced at Finch. "Er…"

"I'll have the same," he said, his expression giving nothing away, and yet I could tell he was going butterscotchy again.

"Fine," she almost snapped, then whirled around on her heel and stomped off.

"She really took it hard when I told her brother he was deceptive and a liar," I said by way of explanation.

"Ah, you saw that in his voice colors?"

I nodded.

He paused a moment, then added, "And was he?"

"Yup. Stole from Mercader—he was working there part time—and left town rather than facing the Municipal Entity. But that's old news, and not even remotely as interesting as the fact that you're a—" I glanced around, although it was a silly thing to worry we'd be overheard, since there was no one at this end of the horseshoe. "And just how did Deacon know? Why was he so scared? I mean, other than the fact that you're a bloodsucking not-master of the night. You do suck blood, don't you?"

"I try to make it a rule not to suck anything," he said in his plummy accent, his color now richer, as if someone had splattered gold ink across his forest green. "If you mean do I drink blood to survive, then yes. I am what is referred to as a redeemed Dark One. My parents had bonded before I was born, and thus I have a soul."

"You mean you guys don't normally have one?" I asked, my flesh crawling at the idea of anything so horrible.

"Not unredeemed Dark Ones, no."

"I'm making you uncomfortable. We'll change the subject. Um. Let's see…wow. All of a sudden, I can't think of anything that isn't vampire-related." I poked desperately through the dark recesses of my mind, avoiding the several dozen questions I had about Finch.

"Why don't you tell me what you know about the owner of this establishment?" Finch asked, sitting back, steepling his fingertips.

"OK, but you look very Bond villain right now." I thought for a moment. "Although I don't remember there ever being a vampire villain in those stories. Do you…are your fangs hollow? Wait, you do have fangs, don't you? Or do you have normal teeth and you gnaw someone's neck for blood? Or is it something else entirely, like a hypodermic needle, or something surgical? Is there such a thing as a medical vampire? I mean, wouldn't working as a phlebotomist be an ideal career for vampires? Dammit, I'm doing it again. Sorry. Don't mean to pepper you with questions you'd rather not answer. It's just…and you're…OK. Moving past all the thoughts tumbling around in my brain. Er…what was it you asked?"

Finch gave a little sigh and stopped the finger steeple. "Deacon?"

"That's right. I don't know a ton about him, despite going on a few dates." I became aware of the disbelieving air that wrapped around Finch, although he was careful not to allow that to leech into his expression. "No, I have not dated every man in the area."

He jerked back like he'd been stung. "I don't believe I said that you did."

"Didn't you?" I raised one shoulder in what I hoped looked like nonchalance. "Maybe I anticipated that since pretty much everyone else implies it. I haven't even dated much since I got divorced. Just the normal amount, really. And you know, it's unfair for everyone to blame me for those weird accidents. Just because I was present doesn't mean that I caused them. It's more likely that they were due to the men themselves. People in Ravenfall, as I've mentioned, are a bit different."

He said nothing to that.

"Odd that you, a vampire, came here," I couldn't help but point out.

He gave a tiny flinch, almost so faint I missed it. "My reasons for coming here have nothing to do with the town itself, or the residents therein. And I have cast no aspersions on your romantic history, nor do I intend to do so."

I shot him a wary look, but decided that his voice couldn't lie to me. "That aside, Deacon and I did go out a couple of times, and I thought that at last things were returning to normal since nothing horrible happened to him, but then I realized he was giving off weird vibes."

"What sort of weird?" Finch asked, his voice going dark.

I thought for a few seconds, trying to put my feelings into words. "Disconcerting. Worrisome. Uncomfortable. He started talking about an old god he wanted to bring into our world. Like something out of a weird speculative TV show." I chuckled until it struck me that Finch didn't look at all amused by the idea. "Oh no. You're not going to tell me that Deacon wasn't being delusional, are you? Holy cats, I can see it in your face. There *are* old gods? It's not just a thing that he made up because he's read too much Lovecraft?"

"I have not met one personally, but yes, they exist, although I assume they reside outside of the mortal plane." Finch looked thoughtful. "It's interesting that he should seek to bring one forth."

"Interesting or terrifying?" A little shiver rippled down my back. I rubbed my arms against the goose bumps that followed. "Thank the goddesses I decided he was a bit too strange, and stopped seeing him. He's been a bit snippy with me ever since because he—" I stopped, not wanting to reveal anything else weird about me.

I felt Finch had seen enough of my quirky nature to last him a long time.

"Because he what?" he asked, cocking an eyebrow at me. It just drew my attention to his beautiful eyes again, now somewhat washed out in the flat light of the camping lantern.

"I didn't fall in with some plans he had," I said carefully, pushing down the guilt that immediately swamped me before continuing. "He hasn't been here that long, relatively speaking. He moved to the town about a year or so ago, and bought the café from the mayor, Jericho Taf."

"You don't know where he came from?" Finch asked, a little frown puckering his forehead. I had a mad desire to run my finger across the frown to smooth it out.

No! I told my fingers. *No touching his brow. No sweeping fingertips down his slightly stubbly cheeks. No focusing on his mouth, and how his eyes made me feel as if I'm rushing from a sauna to a plunge pool.*

Finch, who had been wearing a tie and sports coat, loosened his tie, and asked, "Tatiana?"

I stopped imagining him in a sauna, covered with nothing but steam. "No, sorry I don't know where Deacon is from. He wasn't overly forthcoming with his life before he moved here, although I do have a vague memory of him saying his family always raved about his cooking. Is his past important?"

"I'm not sure," he said with obvious hesitance. He ran a finger around the inside of his shirt collar. "I admit to being curious about him since he could tell at a glance what I am. Is it overly warm here? It seems a bit humid."

I set down my glass of water that I'd been guzzling to combat my brain's attempt to drive me insane with Finch-in-sauna thoughts, and instead, focused on him. "I was wondering about that. I don't see anything about you that screams vampire, so it is really curious that the second Deacon clapped eyes on you he knew who you were. Is there… do you guys have an overt trait that makes you obvious to people in the know? I don't see a tattoo, and you don't have weird eyes, or even a bad aura."

"There are no overtly visible traits, no," he said, his voice going a bit grey with annoyance. "Although some beings in the Otherworld can recognize Dark Ones, it's not a common situation."

"Other—?"

"It is the name for the society comprised of beings of a non-mortal nature, Dark Ones amongst them." His gaze slipped to his hands, which were stroking the condensation on the outside of his water glass. I watched his fingers with an avidity that had my nether regions interested.

What would those fingers feel like touching me? Teasing me? Entering me?

His hand jerked, tipping over the glass.

"Woops. Here, I have some napkins." We mopped up the water, and I sat back, giving my rampant libido the lecture of its lifetime. I refused to damn another man to whatever horrible blight had settled on my life, and I certainly wouldn't want to see someone as interesting as Finch harmed simply because I couldn't keep from thinking smutty thoughts about him.

"You said he moved to Ravenfall a year ago?" Finch asked.

"Hmm? Oh, Deacon? Yeah, about then."

He shook his head quickly. "There's an aura about him, a sense of something that I am unable to pinpoint. It's almost as if he is familiar, and yet, I have never met him."

I had a feeling he was speaking more to himself than me, so I simply sat quiet, fascinated with the idea that I was sitting across from a vampire, a real, honest-to-goddess vampire. One who snacked on other people in order to survive.

Snacking? More like feasting, he said.

"Really?" I asked, somewhat startled by the rush of heat and tingle of sexual awareness that accompanied his unexpected words.

"I admit it's unlikely, but the sense remains nonetheless."

"Huh?" I stopped picturing him *feasting* on me. "I think I'm lost, conversationally speaking."

"I was referencing the odd feeling that I've met Deacon," he explained, his eyes glittering in the light despite its harsh illumination.

"Yeah, but I mentioned—never mind." I shook my head, about to ask him why he had chosen to come to Ravenfall if not for the town or people, but at that moment Sonia reappeared with two plates of salad, one of which she slammed down in front of me.

"Thanks," I said, scooping up the bits of lettuce, parmesan, and croutons that had scattered with her gesture.

She snarled something wordless at me, flicked a fast glance at Finch, sniffed, and spun around, marching off with a twitch of her shoulders.

"I'd apologize, but I don't feel particularly responsible for her bad behavior. I am sorry she's taking out the vendetta against me on you, however. Oh well. I have half a salad left, and I love Deacon's homemade Caesar dressing."

I looked down to rearrange the salad that Sonia's delivery had left me, and after savoring a mouthful, looked up about to say something when I noticed that Finch's plate was empty.

"Holy cats, man. I thought I was a fast eater—my mother always said I ate like the house was on fire—but you got that down in seven seconds flat. You're going to get heartburn if you keep that up."

"That's highly unlikely," he answered, setting down his fork. His voice was tinged with a touch of grey again.

"Sorry. Didn't mean to annoy you with talk about your digestive system," I said, applying myself to my salad.

"I'm not annoyed in the least," he answered.

"Your voice says you are," I said around a mouthful of romaine. "You've got spiky grey bits around the edges. It's OK, Finch. I have a habit of getting personal before people are comfortable with it. I'll keep any such further comments to myself. I hope you enjoyed the salad."

He gave a long, soft sigh that was just on the edge of my hearing. "I assure you that I am not annoyed by your personal comments, despite never having had a dinner with a woman where she expressed interest in my internal workings. In fact, I appreciate the concern."

"And?" I asked, pausing my forkful of salad en route to my mouth.

"And what?"

"You didn't finish your thought," I said, pointing the loaded fork at him.

"How do you know that?" he asked, an incredulous expression visible for a second.

"It's all in the voice," I said, eating another bite. "Teal means you are holding back what you'd really like to say. You were very teal."

This is almost as invasive as a mark, he said.

"What kind of mark?" I asked, chasing a cherry tomato around my plate. I hated the little buggers, and wanted to put it onto the bread plate where I'd placed all the salad Sonia spilled.

Silence, thick, heavy, and filled with disbelief wrapped around us. I glanced up at him, his gaze meeting and holding mine as he leaned forward. "What did you say?"

"I asked you what kind of a mark. You said that my synesthesia was almost as invasive as a mark, but I'm not sure what you mean by that."

"No," he said, leaning back against the booth cushion. *This can't be. I am redeemed.*

"What does your soul have to do with anything?" I asked, crunching a bit of crouton.

How can this be happening? It makes no sense. I know it is possible, but why me?

"Why you what?" I stopped in mid-chew, swallowing with an effort so I could speak clearly. I shook my empty fork at him. "Wait a second. Wait one freakin' second. Your mouth didn't move when you said that."

A mark is a connection made between a Dark One and his Beloved.

"Dude!" I said, a flush warming my cheeks as I set down my fork. "I'm not saying that the urge to get to know you better isn't there, because I think you're interesting, and I love your eyes, and how you talk and think, but I'm not in the market for a man. Even a casual hookup is out at this point, and I wouldn't want that with you. I'd want more. I want to talk to you about things. And be with you doing non-sex things. And sex things, but those are a given, right? Regardless, that can't happen because if it did, then you'd end up losing your ears, or finding yourself suddenly in the Bermuda Triangle, or whatever other inventive horrific event fate worked up for you just to make me feel like I'm a pariah. So no, even though—all things considered—I think that I would like to hook up with you, for your own good I'm not going to."

He gave me an odd look. "Did I have some sort of a time slip where I asked you to bed?"

"Didn't you?" My cheeks burned even hotter now. "Oh goddess, you didn't. But when you said beloved, I assumed that meant you liked me, and wanted to do highly erotic things to me, like nibbling all over me, rubbing your whiskery cheeks on all sorts of sensitive places, your fingers touching and teasing and tormenting right before you bite, savoring each exquisite sip of blood—" I stopped, sitting up straight. "What—what the hell was that? It was like I was feeling what you feel when you…when you…"

"Feed," he said, looking a bit stunned about the eyes.

I knew just how he felt.

SIX

I dipped the edge of my napkin into the little bit of water left in my glass, and patted my heated face. "Sorry. I don't know what came over me to say such inappropriate sexual comments to you."

They weren't inappropriate, or unwanted, as you are thinking.

I stared at him, my mind trying to understand. "OK. That time you definitely did not speak. Your mouth didn't move at all, and yet I heard your voice in my head."

He sighed into my mind. That's the best way I can describe what happened—he sighed into my head, and then said, *Dark Ones have Beloveds. They are life partners, the one person who is perfectly matched with them. Usually the Beloved serves the role of redeeming the Dark One, but for men like me, who already have their soul, they are simply...companions.*

"Companions as in a buddy? Acquaintance? Someone you walk with a couple of times a week in order to get your cardio in? Because I already do the last one with Clemmie, although getting her out of bed in the morning for exercise is an epic feat in itself."

"That's not quite the sort of companion I meant." A few lush images danced around my mind, and I realized they originated with him.

"Holy shit." I reached across the table and wrapped my

fingers around where his hand rested. "Are you saying I'm a vampire's girlfriend? One who can read your mind?"

He did that mind sigh thing again, then lifted my hand and kissed my knuckles before releasing my hand. "No. Yes. Some of each. You are not a Beloved for several reasons, the biggest of which is because we are not—we have not—consummated a relationship. You can, however, converse with me mentally. It is an interesting situation, and one in which I never expected to find myself. It does pique my curiosity, and I would be interested in exploring it further...so long as you understand that nothing can come of it."

"Nothing like...sex, you mean?"

"Yes. Sex would further us along the path to the point where you would become a Beloved, and I can't have that."

Hurt chased embarrassment, followed by shame. I busied myself stacking up the sodden napkins used to wipe up the water he spilled. "Of course not. I already said I wasn't interested in dating, and it's clear you're of the same mind."

"It's not that I wouldn't like to—" He stopped, regret flashing across his face. "The simple fact is that I can't have a Beloved."

The hurt dug into my chest, forcing me to struggle for a few seconds to get a breath. "Gotcha. As I said, none of my past dating history was really my fault. Although I did feel guilty about the one date whose car exploded, and set a small forest on fire."

Finch, who had been avoiding my gaze by continuing to toy with his now-empty glass, suddenly shot me a look. "Your history with men who are clearly deficient has nothing to do with my decision. The situation is complicated, I'm afraid, and not one I feel up to explaining now. You'll have to take my word that I have a valid reason for taking such a stand."

"Sure. No problem." I was hurt again, but I reminded myself that not everyone was as forthcoming as I was with every thought that came to mind. "Just...er...out of curiosity, if things were different, if I could have a lover without damning him to goddess-knows-what calamity, and you could have this Beloved person, would you want to—"

"Yes," he said quickly, his eyes going a little liquid. Erotic images came to my mind again, causing me to fan myself with my soggy napkin.

"That's good to know. Well, not good, because nothing is going to happen."

"Nothing can happen," he agreed.

The images shifted into a higher level of intensity. I poured the last few drops of my water on the napkin, and patted my cheeks again. "Is that coming from you, or me?"

"What?"

I revisited the mental image of him rubbing his stubble on my inner thighs, and gave a little sensual shiver. "There's this scene that keeps replaying in my head of you rubbing your cheeks on sensitive parts."

Ah. That, I believe, is one of my thoughts. I apologize. I had no idea you could pick up on the ideas my libido gives me, although I will admit to being appreciative you are receptive to the idea.

The sexual tension rolling off him and swirling around me was epic. My stomach felt like it was filled with champagne bubbles, and the material in my bra rubbed across my nipples in a way that was highly distracting. I was more than a little heated over the idea that Finch wanted to bite me on my hips.

I like your hips. They are highly attractive.

You can hear me? I asked, stunned.

Of course.

I was silent for a moment, my mind a whirl of erotic thoughts, desires, needs, and most of all, amazement. A bona fide, mind talking, sexy-eyed vampire was sitting right across from me, and he wanted to bite my hips, and rub his stubble all over me. "This…wow, this is pretty wild. But we should stop, shouldn't we? Since nothing is going to happen?"

"We should stop, yes." His pupils were huge dots of black in a sea of pale blue. "Why do you feel like you are not worth my attention?"

"The women in my family are prone to being what Clemmie euphemistically refers to as abundant. I am more so because I'm over forty, and abundance hits the over-forties with a vengeance."

"I do not understand why you are not comfortable with your appearance, since you are attractive and enticing. But I know many mortal women have body dysmorphia, and thus will simply tell you that what you see as an unwanted abundance, I think of as a lush, tempting goddess meant to enjoy the pleasures of the flesh. If anyone has told you otherwise, they were a fool."

I leaned forward. "Can we clone you and give you out to every plus-size woman around? Hell, I'll be generous—every woman who has a doubt about her body, which I think is pretty much everyone alive, because you, sir, are extremely good for the ego."

He smiled, filling me with warmth and need. "Thank you for that compliment."

"No, thank you. And in case you were wondering, I reciprocate your interest and nice thoughts about your handsome self."

"I gathered that from the way you dwelled on thoughts of licking my nipple while simultaneously dragging your nails across my scrotum," he said with a deadpan expression, but his voice gave him away.

"You liked that, did you? I put in the bit with the balls just for you," I said, giving another shiver at the look in his eyes.

His jaw worked. "If I asked you to stop, would you?"

"Yes. But I thought men liked—"

"We do, but you're going to make it difficult to walk if you continue on with such thoughts. Not to mention the fact that although I enjoy thinking of things that make you tremble as you just did, it serves no real purpose. We are of one mind that we cannot be together in a physical or emotional manner."

"You're right," I said, regretfully setting aside a thought I had about his inner thighs. "It's like a weird mental sex fencing game, and it's going to do nothing but leave us both frustrated and wondering how much an online porn subscription costs."

Perhaps you could have one more, he said, his breath hitching in my mind as I imagined nibbling up his thighs. *Christos, yes. That was good. I like that.*

"OK, that's it, though—" I suddenly sat up straight, my breath caught in my throat, my breasts now heavy and needy and badly wanting out of the confines of my clothing. "Oh, you do not play fair, Mr. Scraping Your Teeth Gently Over My Nipples."

He was silent for a few seconds, then to my utter delight, smiled again. "I would apologize for that, but it was particularly good, wasn't it?"

"It would be much better in person, but yes." I fanned myself with my hand. "Although no more, please. It's kind of a mean game, considering we can't do anything about it."

"You're right, of course," Finch said, and reluctantly pushed aside thoughts of my nipples. "It's not wise in the least, despite the mark. You are not a Beloved, and I am in no need of salvation."

The sexual interest buzz I'd been riding for the last few minutes fizzled out to nothing at his words. "Right. Here comes dinner, and just in time. I was going to see how you feel about your own nipples and my teeth."

You really are going to make it impossible to walk.

Nipple man, are you? I asked, hoping he didn't feel the dismay that filled me.

Dismay and something very akin to rejection wrapped around me. I'd been enjoying our mental flirting, not just for the sake of attention from a man who was attractive and interesting, but the pleasure faded when he made it clear that although we had some sort of a connection, he didn't want to pursue it.

Not to my knowledge, but somehow, I feel like you might swing me that way.

I stifled a laugh as Sonia slammed down our plates of spaghetti Bolognese before shooting me a glare, and storming off without even offering extra parmesan or garlic bread.

"Again, I feel like I should apologize because normally, service here is much better," I said, pushing down my emotions, determined to enjoy the dinner with Finch despite my disappointment. I twirled a bit of spaghetti on my fork, glancing up to see Finch with an open napkin next to his plate. He froze. "What…eh…what are you doing? If you want to take it back with you for later, you can ask for a to-go carton."

"I'm a Dark One," he said after an obvious moment's mental struggle.

"And?"

I can't eat food.

"Oh!" I glanced at the napkin. "Is that how you got rid of the salad so fast?"

"Yes."

I eyed his plate, then leaned out of the booth and made sure Sonia wasn't returning. "This is probably going to give you a horrendous idea about how much I normally eat in a day, but I never did get lunch, and I'm ravenous, so if you don't mind…"

He slid his plate my way. "Help yourself."

I did. And while I worked my way through a plate and a half of the Bolognese, we both kept to strictly non-sexual topics. I told Finch about my shop, and how I'd found a raven doll earlier in the day, along with some less-odd dolls that I planned to sell as highly haunted.

"I'm not sure that I've ever seen a raven doll," he commented when I divided up the remains of the Bolognese so that it looked like we'd both eaten most of our respective servings.

"No? They're pretty uncommon, but given the name of the town, I've always had a fondness for them. I have three. This one is named Natasha." I pulled up the big blue and white striped canvas bag into which I threw everything, and rustled around until I found the raven doll, setting it on the table in front of me. She was about seven inches tall, made of black velvet and cotton cloth, had the head of a raven, and was dressed in what I thought of as old-time Eastern European clothing, with a black lace veil, maroon and gold overskirt, and a gold silk underskirt decorated with a couple of matching tassels. "She even comes with a couple of spells, see?"

He looked at the artist label folded into an envelope and pinned to the back of her skirt. Although it carried no artist name—just a stamped image of a raven with the name Natasha—the words "Open for spells" were written in handwriting that looked like a spider had dipped its feet in ink and danced across the paper.

"What sort of spells?" Finch asked, looking askance at the doll.

She stared back at him with eyes made of tiny hematite beads.

"I don't know. The envelope is glued shut, and I didn't want to tear it trying to see. Not that I plan on selling the dolls, since I like them, but there's no sense in ruining their value just for idle curiosity. And to be honest, it's probably luck or happiness or something positive like that. A lot of artisans do that sort of thing with their goods." I tucked Natasha away in my bag, and with a pointed look at Sonia as she served a customer the next booth over all the while ignoring me, signaled to her that I'd like the bill, sighed to myself and gathered up my things. "Are you done pretending to eat?"

"Yes, thank you," he said, glancing down at his notebook before tucking it away again.

We emerged from the depths of the abyss that was that end of the café, pausing long enough for me to pay for our dinner—Finch politely offered to do so, but I refused. I'd told him I really did want to treat him, especially since he hadn't eaten a thing.

"But what about you?" I asked, following the line of my thoughts as I pushed open the door, and emerged into the night.

The air was salty, and just chilly enough to make me thankful I'd worn a long knit tunic along with my heaviest leggings. The breeze caught a few tendrils of hair, whipping them around my face until, annoyingly, they glued onto the corners of my mouth.

"What about me?" he asked, pulling on his long duster coat.

"You didn't eat." I looked at him, biting my lower lip for a second while I thought. "Do you want to…er…should I offer…is it polite to stick out my wrist? Neck? Some other easily accessible body part?"

"Are you offering to feed me?" he asked after a moment's silence.

"I guess so. I mean, if the world was different, we'd be together, right? Wait, will it hurt? Not that I want you to starve, but I have a low tolerance for pain, and if it's going to be along the lines of a slasher movie, sort of gory with blood gushing everywhere, then I may need a couple of shots of vodka." I bit my lip again. "Although I also have a low tolerance for alcohol, so I'd probably be knocked off my feet if I drank more than a tablespoon of vodka, and also, wouldn't the booze get into my bloodstream? Would it make you drunk, too? I can't imagine a drunk vampire is a good thing. What if you were ripped off your tits and started telling everyone who you are, or flashing fang, or even turn into a bat right on the middle of Axegate Walk? The next thing you know, gangs of people with garlic and wooden stakes will be banging on your door."

His eyebrows rose. *That was quite the stream of consciousness.*

"I know. I'm just a bit nervous. I've never fed a vampire before, and I'm not sure what is the protocol for feeding one."

"I appreciate you being concerned for my well-being both with regards to feeding me, and ensuring my safety from the stake-bearing crowds, but there is no need. I'm fine."

"Oh." I felt a bit let down, because I was already picturing myself as Tatiana, Priestess of the Night.

"I have no ability to name you a priestess of anything," he said as we strolled toward our shops.

I gave a start at his comment. "This mind thing is going to take a bit of getting used to. I keep forgetting you can eavesdrop."

"I wouldn't dream of being so intrusive. You are projecting thoughts at me."

Really?

"Yes." We passed his shop. I paused, looking at it. He took a few more steps before turning back. "Is something amiss?"

"What are you going to do with Ozy's shop?" I asked, gesturing toward it. He retraced his steps and stood next to me, looking in through the glass. He'd left one light on in the small hallway which spilled out into Ozy's front room, casting a ghostly glow over everything.

"I suppose my first order of business will be to pack up her items and place them in the basement, assuming she left no forwarding address. After that, I will do what I've intended to do—continue work on my book."

"Now, that's just a waste," I said, putting a hand on the glass and almost pressing my nose on it to peer inside. My heart sang a sad little song of unrequited desire as I assessed the size of the shop.

"My book may not be to everyone's taste—"

I nudged his arm, trying hard to ignore both the fact that he was standing close to me, and the lemony scent that clung to him, which I swore drove my body insane with lustful thoughts. "No, I meant the loss of the shop. For one, it's a desirable size, and is in prime tourist location. For another, we're just a few days away from the start of tourist season, and the Municipal Entity likes shops on the Walk to be open. All the other shops are going to open up, and it'll really stand out if yours doesn't."

He looked thoughtful for a few seconds, then shook his head. "I don't know anything about crystal readings. Who does the reading, the crystal or the person holding it? What sorts of things can it tell? How do you do a reading—do you touch the person with the crystal or simply hold it in your hand and divine the future?"

"I don't know, but it's easy enough to get the info." I glanced up and down the walk, but although there were a few early tourists strolling down the walk, most of whom ended up at the ice cream shop, no one was near enough to hear us. "I'll tell you something I've only mentioned to Clemmie—Ozy was a fraud."

"Oh?" Finch's eyebrows rose, and his voice went rose-colored. I had no idea what that meant since other than Mercader—who had a reddish-gold voice—I'd never heard anyone speaking in that same colored tone. "How do you know that?"

"She used the same online hokey certificate place I used to acquire a paranormal research expert certification." I took a step closer to him, reveling in the slightly spicy citrus smell that seemed present around him. I wondered if it was his aftershave, and if I could get some for myself since I loved spicy perfumes. "I got a coupon for a class on this website that offers all sorts of out-there certifications—angel translations, animal past life regressions, chakra relocation, that sort of thing. And then there was the crystal reading course. After I got my certification—which was a joke, let me tell you, since all they had me do was read a bunch of stuff on the history of spiritualism and ghosts and stuff—I decided to take the crystal reading class since Ozy was going on and on about how she loved to help people using it. And what did I find but some comments from her on the class message forum. Clearly, she'd taken the same course, and judging by her comments, she was utterly new to the subject."

"Perhaps she was trying to educate herself on an interest," Finch replied in a manner that irritated me because it made total sense, and didn't in the least justify my theory about her being up to something. "I'm sorry if I didn't contribute to that theory, but I don't see what is so outrageous about her taking an online class about a hobby."

I ignored the fact that he peeked at my thoughts again, and tried to put into words what bothered me.

I didn't peek. You are sharing.

"It's the fact that she presented herself as an old-timer with the crystals," I said, reluctantly taking a step back from the shop window. "That's deceptive."

He pursed his lips. "More so than selling dolls you claim are haunted?"

"Ouch." I gave him a look that I hoped would part his hair, and turned to continue down the walk toward the end, where my little hole-in-the-wall was located.

I stopped when he put a hand on my arm. "That was unkind of me, and I apologize," he said, his eyes shaded since we were in the dark pool in between the yellow streetlights, but I heard the sincerity in his voice (a rich bluish-green).

"It stung a bit, but you didn't say anything that isn't exactly true," I said, pausing while once again, I tried to make some sense out of my jumbled thoughts. "The thing is, all the residents of Ravenfall know the truth about my shop. They know my dolls are just a bit weird, and not actually filled with the residue of malcontent spirits. Yes, I sell the dolls with descriptions of their haunted histories, but I do put a disclaimer on each and every doll saying that their history was just an interpretation by me, and intended for entertainment purposes only. If people chose to ignore that, and believe what are clearly outrageously ridiculous stories about the dolls, well…"

He said nothing as I let the sentence dribble to a stop.

Dammit. I continued down the walkway toward my shop. *You could have at least interrupted me when I couldn't continue with that bullshit.*

It didn't seem to be bullshit to me. You are simply justifying your business.

"Yeah, but you're right—it really is no better than what Ozy did, even if I don't claim that I, personally, have abilities like she did. Dammit." I shot him a glance that was mingled amusement and irritation. "Now I'm not sure I want you to make me Tatiana, Dark Mistress of the Obsidian Hours if you're going to be so pedantic."

He laughed again, a sound that filled me with joy. "If I told you that I do not have the powers to make you any such thing, would you continue to offer to feed me?"

"Yes," I answered without thinking, stopping at the door to my shop. "For one, we all but had mind sex in the café, and despite you not wanting a fancy, soul-saving girlfriend, there might come a time when things worked out between us. If I can figure out who cursed me, that is. For another, I like you. If you're hungry and I can feed you without being gacked out at the blood and gore, then I will happily do so."

"I don't think—" He stopped himself, and my spirits drooped. I was really batting a thousand tonight. "I don't think I've received such a generous compliment in quite a long time."

I smiled, a warm glow of pleasure forming in my belly, unwilling to ruin the moment with an offer to indulge in intimate activities. Instead, I dug through my bag to find the key, and gestured at the periwinkle blue door. "This is mine. As you can see, my shop is a whole lot smaller than yours. Which brings me to a point that I've been wondering about all afternoon. What would you think of having me take over your lease for Ozy's shop? I know there are a couple of mother-in-law apartments around town you could rent for less, and you'd have a lot more privacy, all without the Entity breathing down your neck for having a non-functioning shop. I could really use a bigger storefront for my haunted stuff, and Clemmie would be thrilled for us to have an actual kitchen, and not just a microwave and hot plate that were located in my bedroom."

"You are kindness personified to be so concerned about my happiness," he said in that polite British tone that made me want to giggle when he spoke which so much Downton Abbey elegance. "But I am not comfortable with the idea of giving up my place since the arrangement was for me to stay there."

My shoulders slumped. "I heard that."

He looked confused for a moment.

What you said in the back of your head. The bit about me wanting the shop for my own purposes. I mean, it's true, I have wanted Ozy's shop for a long time, but that wasn't the only reason I offered to take it off your hands. You seem genuinely unhappy about the idea of running a business.

"I am. I am a writer, thus I write, not read crystals," he pointed out.

I stared into the darkness of my shop, the light from the streetlamp picking out a few shelves bearing some of the creepier of the dolls. I made a mental note to design a new layout for the scenes Clemmie set up in the front window. "Is there any reason you couldn't do something that you know about? Like…could you do something vampish that tourists would pay to see or experience?"

"I can think of no surer way to draw attention from those people who would prefer to see Dark Ones destroyed," he said in a tone so dry, his voice was the color of straw.

"Oh. Good point." My shoulders slumped even more.

"I'll say goodnight. Thank you for dinner, Tatiana."

"That you couldn't even eat," I said, suddenly possessed by a glumness, as if an Eeyore cloud of depression had settled over me. I was about to go in, but to my surprise, Finch was right behind me, his eyes like shallow water over white sand.

"You permit?" he asked.

Huh?

May I kiss you?

"Oh, hell yes," I said, and gave in to the urge that I'd fought ever since I first laid eyes on him, lunging forward just as he moved toward me, resulting in me smashing my nose into his cheek, and him poking me in the boob as he reached for me.

"Ow!" I rubbed my abused breast, my nose wrinkling with the need to sneeze.

"I'm terribly sorry," he almost stammered, a horrified expression crawling across his face. "I would never—but you moved, and I wasn't expecting—did I hurt you? I am a physician, so if you'd like me to look at your injury, I will be happy to do so."

"Dude!" I said, now rubbing my nose and laughing at the same time. "You did not just ask to look at my boobs!"

"Of course not." He squared his shoulders. "I simply offered to look at the injury I inadvertently caused. As I said, I have been trained as a physician—a number of times, given that I do not age as mortals do, and I wish to keep that fact from the licensing organizations—so if I've bruised your breast, I feel obligated to tend it."

"Tempting as that offer is, I'm fine, really. It was just a little poke." I leaned in to kiss him, but at that moment, I caught a risqué mental whisper concerning the word poke, and I burst into laughter.

He reeled back a step, looking highly offended.

"Stop," I said, laughing even harder at his expression, tears leaking from the corners of my eyes.

He continued to look outraged, his nostrils flaring dramatically. "I apologize if I have suddenly become distasteful to you. I interpreted your lunge at my head as a willingness to kiss me—"

"No! That is, yes! Hang on, I can't brain. Laughing too hard." I pulled a wad of tissues out of my bag and mopped up my eyes before dabbing at my nose. "Stop thinking that you've done something to offend me. Far from it. It was your not-so-modest thought about how if you were to poke me the way you wanted, I wouldn't be using the word 'little.'"

You didn't hear that!

I did.

"It's not possible. I deliberately shielded that thought from you," he insisted.

Carefully, so as not to repeat the incident with my nose and boob, I leaned forward, and allowed my lips to brush his. *I think you need to check your brain shield. Kiss me, Finch. Kiss me like I can feel you wanting to kiss me.*

That was all it took. One second I was teasing his mouth

while I threw caution and common sense to the wind, and the next, I found myself pressed up against the glass door of my shop, the coolness that seeped into my back countered by the heat of Finch on my front. His body was made up of hard, solid planes, his scent filling my head. His mouth was like fire on mine, nipping at my lower lip in a way that had me moaning. He took the opportunity to explore my mouth, his body hard moving against mine as he pinned me against the door, his hands starting at my waist, but sliding down to my behind, pulling me up even closer.

By the goddess, I panted into his mind, even as I wriggled against him, my tongue twining around his. *You really know how to do this.*

Kiss? Woo? Seduce?

All three. Can I touch—

Anything. You can touch anything you want.

I slid my fingers into his hair, the sensual feeling of its silky lengths making me shiver. His tongue got even bossier with mine, my body now tense and tight with a need that was part me, part Finch.

"Why don't you…I can feel how much you want to bite me…maybe we should do this in private. My bedroom is upstairs—" I tore my mouth away from his in order to catch a few fast breaths.

I very much want to drink from you…and more, he said into my head, making me shiver with the desire that swamped me. My body was as taut as a bowstring, wanting desperately to be rid of the constriction of clothing.

And then he stepped back, his head down, his hands fisted.

I felt the loss of his body as if a part of me had dropped off, rolled down the stairs, and come gently to rest next to a tourist.

"I cannot, Tatiana. I'm sorry," he said, his voice maroon.

I'd only heard maroon once before. It was the day I told Clemmie that try as I might, I couldn't afford a bigger shop, and she'd answered that we'd be fine where we were.

Regret. His voice was filled with regret. *He* was filled with regret…but not enough to drive him back into my arms.

"I understand," I said, lying.

He lifted a hand, brushing back one of my long curls that had clung to my cheek. "You don't, but I can't explain it to you. There are…reasons I—"

"No, it's OK," I interrupted, getting hold of the emotions that were tangled together in an impossible knot. "We just got done telling each other that nothing could happen. Nothing sexual. Although I am serious about my offer to feed you—"

"Tat? Is that you out there? You're not being sick on the doorstep again, are you? You know shellfish doesn't agree with you, and I have a hair-trigger gag reflex, so there's no way I can clean up all your ralph spew." A skin-twitching squeaking noise sounded above our heads as Clemmie turned the crank that opened the antique window in her bedroom. "How did your date go? Did it end in disaster, like the others, or did Jeremy survive intact? You will notice I didn't text you since you made it clear you'd fire me if I interrupted your fun time, but that buyer in LA who wants the dozen dolls for a TV show called three times and he says if he doesn't speak to you tonight, he's going to buy his haunted dolls from someone who answers his calls in what he referred to as a timely manner, so you'd better call him back pronto if you want to be able to pay next month's rent."

"Shit," I said under my breath, then took two steps out and looked up at where Clemmie was hanging out of the window. "I am not vomiting in the doorway or anywhere else. Seriously, Clemmie, I have an allergic reaction to shellfish *once* years ago, and you still hold it against me that you had to hose off the sidewalk? Until this moment, the dinner with Fin—Jeremy was going pretty good. Not that it was a date."

Finch moved out of the shadow to stand next to me.

Clemmie's eyes widened, and her mouth made an Oh! before she retreated silently back into her tiny bedroom, the squeak of the window as she cranked it close making me wince.

"Remind me to bring you some oil for that fixture," Finch said.

"It wouldn't help. I've WD-40ed the ever-living hell out of, and it insists on sounding like a herd of Kardashians scraping their nails on a blackboard. I suppose that ruined the moment, huh?" I studied his face. He really was the handsomest man I'd ever laid eyes on, and I badly wanted to lay a whole lot more than just my eyeballs on him.

Like to be on top, do you?

A blush washed up from my chest as I mentally damned my inability to remember to keep smutty thoughts to myself.

"You didn't ruin anything. It was a delightful evening, but I should be going home. I had planned on writing tonight after I cleared up the belongings of the previous tenant," he said, his voice still maroon.

I knew just how he felt, but I reminded myself that we'd met just that day, and despite finding out about his unique nature—and the fact that I had some sort of a tie to that nature—life was simply not going to allow me to fling myself on him and beg him to make me his Dark Queen.

My inner parts grew sad at that thought, and glumly returned to their pre-Finch state of general disinterest in the world.

I tried to pull together lemonade out of the lemons that fate had handed me. "Tell you what—I'll come over tomorrow once I've packed off what I hope is going to be a lucrative sale to the set director in LA, and help you with Ozy's stuff. And then maybe we can talk about anything other than how you can kiss the breath right out of my lungs, and leave my legs feeling like jellyfish. And not the big, aggressive kind, but the little blobs that wash up on the beach."

"Why?" he asked.

"I don't know for sure, but I think it's like a whale beaching itself. Or maybe they simply die and the tide brings them up. I'd have to Google—oh, why do I want to help you clean house?" I tried to keep my thoughts tucked away in the back of my awareness. He'd already seen farther into my psyche than I was comfortable with. "Mostly just curiosity. I want to see if Ozy left behind anything that explained why she ran off without a word to anyone."

"Ah. I, myself, like to know the answers to things that strike me as odd," he said, nodding with what was obvious understanding.

I was more than happy to let him think it was pure curiosity that had me interested, and not a fear that something had been going on that might end up biting me in the butt.

His eyebrows rose in question when I watched him for a few seconds, half expecting him to make a mental thought about biting my butt, but evidently, I had mastered the art of hiding my thoughts. I gave myself a moment of smug satisfaction over that fact, but was distracted when Finch's lips twitched.

"Thank you for your offer of assistance, but I didn't see enough there to require a second person," he said in a voice that was dark green streaked with brown, like dirt seen through a field of pine needles.

"Oh. OK," I said, somewhat hurt. "I wasn't trying to intrude on your privacy. I just thought you might like someone else to help you."

"A fact I appreciate, but there's no need to take time away from your business for something so trivial."

I blinked at him a couple of times. I'd never been much of a "can't process; must blink to reboot brain" sort of person, but there I was doing just that. *Why do I have the feeling you're trying to…I don't know…break up with me?*

"We are not together, so there is no us to separate," he said gently, his gaze skittering away from mine. "Although there is a sympathetic link between us, as I've said a few times, I'm not in a position to claim a Beloved. And since you seem quite happy in your life here, I think it's better for us both if we continue to maintain a friendly, yet platonic, relationship."

Now that really did hurt. *And yet just a few minutes ago, you were ready to go upstairs with me, and do the bitey thing.*

I lost control of myself. I regret that. I regret that I lead you on.

"You didn't lead me on," I said, feeling particularly martyred, heading straight for a pity party. Why did a rejection of a relationship yet to be hurt so much? "I was just as willing as you."

"I believe I did. Or at the least, I gave you expectations that I can't meet. Tatiana—there are things I can't tell you, but I assure you I'm just as unhappy as you are that they prohibit further exploration of what we could be together."

"Then I guess it's good we did nothing other than having a little mental teasing session, and one steaming hot kiss," I told him, my gaze on his mouth. His upper lip was a normal sort of lip, there, but not overly intrusive into the whole mouth situation. But his lower lip had a sweet, sweet curve that had me feeling alternately hot and cold.

"Yes," he said, his voice now green-grey. "Thank you again for an enjoyable evening."

"Thank you for that humdinger of a kiss," I said, and spun around, hustling my now-depressed psyche into the shop lest I fling myself on him right there on the sidewalk.

"How'd the evening with Jeremy go?" Clemmie asked when I went upstairs a half hour later, after having soothed the irate set director, and promised him a shipment first thing in the morning.

"Dinner was fine. Deacon's cooks always are good. The company was…" Wonderful. Fascinating. Sexy as sin. "Less so. The man in question seems determined to keep me out of his shop, and most likely, his life."

"Oh?" She stood in the doorway to our tiny bathroom, toothbrush in hand as her normally sunny demeanor faded. "I was willing to bet he wouldn't let a little thing like the Curse of Tat's Hoohaw scare him off."

"My hoohaw and all my other parts are not cursed," I answered. I thought about explaining further, but realized I couldn't without revealing that Finch was a vampire, and I wouldn't do that without his permission. I knew that Clemmie would not pose any threat to him, but it wasn't my secret to tell. "I think I'll have to chalk it up to a Deacon-level date: not lethal or dangerous, but not ending well, either."

"Aww," she said, watching when I slumped my sad self into my bedroom. "Hang in there, Tatty. I'll do a reading for you tomorrow, and see what the cards have to say about finding a man who doesn't let you buy him dinner, then won't so much as scratch your itches."

"There's more to it than a need for some rompy time between the sheets. Good night."

"Night," I heard her say as I closed my door, and considered my cold, lonely bed.

I looked out of the window, unable to see the window above Ozy's shop, but knowing that just down the road, Finch was probably getting ready to do his writing. Or muck out Ozy's belongings. Or, hell, maybe mind-talking with some other woman.

"It doesn't matter," I told myself firmly, closing the blinds, and turning away from the window while fighting the urge to reach out to him with my mind. "He doesn't want you, so let it go. Besides, he's right. You have a good life here. There's Clemmie, and everyone in the town who doesn't think you drove out Ozy, or pose a threat to every single man. That's enough."

Was it, though? an inner voice asked. It might have been before I met Finch, but now…

I shut down that line of thinking before it got started.

I had a horrible feeling that since meeting Finch, my life had changed, and not for the better.

SEVEN

Finch chastised himself all the way back to his digs.

"It's not as if you are a young, untried Dark One who has had his first sexual encounter," he lectured as he let himself into the dark shop through the front door, ignoring the comment from the plastic motion sensor. He made sure the door was locked, then went upstairs, all the while damning his inability to keep Tatiana from his mind. "She's just a mortal. All right, perhaps she's more than that if she's actually a Beloved, but I don't need a Beloved. I am perfectly happy as I am, not to mention, I can't have her in my life. Not while I'm here incognito."

Coward, a voice in his head said.

He hated that inner voice. It was prone to pointing out things that he never appreciated having brought to his attention. But because he was nothing if not an honest man, he amended his statement.

"I can't have a Beloved because I don't want to kill her." There. That satisfied his need for honesty, and quelled the annoying inner narrator. "It is for her own good that I reject her Belovedness. She will remain a fascinating, tempting woman who has an oddly troubled history with men, and I will live my life knowing I have saved her from a hellish nightmare."

That felt good. That felt noble. He couldn't follow up the

kiss that had damn near brought him to his knees because he was an honorable man. He was only thinking of Tatiana.

"It's just a matter of keeping her at arm's length. That can't be difficult." He glanced around the front room of the shop. Perhaps he'd been overly hasty in spurning Tatiana's offer to help him pack up the previous tenant's belongings. "She was just trying to be helpful," he told the skeleton wearing a fez. "There's keeping someone at arm's length to avoid killing them, and then there's being rude. I was the latter. I should apologize."

His voice echoed slightly in the room, giving him an uneasy feeling that he couldn't explain.

"I'm a Dark One," he said aloud before clicking off the light and heading toward the stairs that led to his bedroom. "There's little on this earth that I fear, and certainly nothing that can be found in an odd town on the coast of Oregon."

That thought held him over for a half hour as he opened up his laptop and perused the notes he'd made on the plane ride to the West Coast. Then he sat starting at a blank, empty screen for a good forty minutes before he closed the laptop lid with an annoyed click of his tongue.

"I'm overly tired. And hungry." He opened the window in his bedroom, breathing deeply for a half minute, enjoying the sting of salt air with its slight overtones of rotting seaweed. He leaned out to look down Axegate Walk toward Tatiana's shop, wondering what she was doing. He could reach out with his mind and ask...no. That way lay madness. He was right to set boundaries with her, boundaries that he would keep even if it killed him.

He couldn't see her storefront, but just the knowledge that she was there, tantalizingly close, kept his hunger foremost, and his penis ready to spring into a full-fledged erection should he require it to do so.

He thought of finding someone to feed from, remembered the kiss with Tatiana, and instead, got into bed. He'd made it up with the new linens, and was pleased to discover the mattress was comfortable.

"I don't need you," he told his penis after he got settled, then made a face at it. "I'm not the sort of man who talks to his genitalia. The fact that I'm explaining this to you proves that I am overtired, and although I am hungry, I have been hungry in the past, and survived. I will now go to sleep, so that I don't have to be the sort of Dark One who is a worry to his family because he holds full-fledged discussions with his penis."

He wondered what Tatiana tasted like...all of her.

His penis donned a distinctly hopeful air.

"No!" he told it. It now bobbed about merrily.

"I'm ignoring you," he said, propping his hands behind his head. "I'm going to think of the chapter I wish to write on how mortals use social media to encourage their biases. Doom scrolling, it's called. I will think about doom scrolling, and not about how Tatiana's mouth tasted like a deep, rich red wine, full of subtle notes that went immediately to my head. Or that her body was the personification of the word lush, and how she fit so perfectly against me. And her hips. Her hips deserve odes written to them. The way she walks could make a eunuch hard."

His penis agreed with everything he said.

"That just shows you have good taste," he acknowledged.

Had that been hurt he'd seen flash in her eyes when he'd refused her offer of help with his shop?

She had glanced away when he'd told her that he had reasons he couldn't be with her, but he'd seen the pain nonetheless. He'd hurt her feelings. No doubt she'd taken his statement as a rejection of herself, rather than the fact that he was in a situation that didn't allow him to dally with a potential Beloved. She had probably already chalked him up as yet another of her disastrous dates who treated her poorly.

His penis drooped at the idea that he would do anything so callous.

"You were there," he said, trying to shift the guilt that clutched at him with barbed fingers. "Why didn't you stop me?"

Silence filled the room. It was the sort of silence made all the more poignant by a sad, deflated penis, and a Dark One who knew he earned the scorn of a lovely, enticing woman who deserved better.

"I'll apologize in the morning," he said aloud, clicking off the light. Shadows flickered across the ceiling from the streetlights outside. He watched them dance for a few seconds before adding, "I'll make her understand that it's nothing to do with her, and everything to do with the fact that I can't be who I want to be. I won't damn her and her seductive hips. She'll thank me one day."

Idiot, his inner voice said.

Finch couldn't even enjoy feeling nobly martyred. He just felt hopeless.

It took every ounce of his self-will not to reach out to mentally to Tatiana the following day, or stop by her shop to explain how unreasonable it was for her to feel hurt by the fact that he couldn't submit to her hips' demands that he seduce her as she deserved to be seduced, but he had a suspicion that if he gave in to his mind, body, and soul's desire to contact her, he wouldn't stop with a simple apology and explanation.

Instead, he left his apartment in the early morning, his hat and coat protecting him from the pale sun, the salt air lashing him in a way that was both invigorating, and tear-inducing. Although he saw several people out and about, he hesitated each time he picked out a likely source of sustenance.

None of them appealed to him. None of them had the same heady wine sense about them that wound around Tatiana.

None of them made his penis feel martyred. Only Tatiana did that.

"Fine!" he told himself, and went home, coming perilously close to slamming the door to the shop before reaching up for the door chime. It barely had time to pronounce,

"Beware all—" before he ripped it off and flung it across the room. He was annoyed enough with himself that he slid into another lecture. "You can just be hungry, then. Or find some blood sources elsewhere. Christian probably knows a supplier in Oregon."

He sent off a quick text to his uncle.

ME

I hope all is well in London. I find myself in a situation where I might need to purchase a supply of blood indefinitely. Do you know of anyone in the Oregon area who could supply me?

That done, he marched his annoyed self upstairs, and sat in front of the laptop until dusk fell.

Tatiana didn't once visit him.

"She could have at least stopped by to see how I was doing," he complained to the skeleton as he stood in front of the big bay window, his hands clasped behind his back while he watched the shop lights flicker as the visitors to the town strolled up and down Axegate Walk. There were definitely more people today than there had been the day before, and several had approached his shop until they'd noticed the closed sign. "Maybe there is something I could do…"

He stopped, realizing just how asinine that thought was.

"No. I am not a shopkeeper. I have no skills from which mortals would benefit other than those based on medical needs. I am here to write my book."

Muffled laughter drifted into the room from a gaggle of young women who were strolling down the pavement.

"Perhaps I'll stop by Tatiana's shop this evening. I wouldn't want her to think I was harboring ill will against her. I will explain as best I can the situation, and then she will be easier in her mind."

His penis stirred.

He ignored both it, and the pleasant sense of drawing in his inner thighs that followed when he relived—for the fortieth time that day—the kiss he'd shared with her the night before.

CHRISTIAN

You're in Oregon? Can you tell me what this mysterious situation is that prohibits you to feed from mortals? Are you in danger? Two of the Four Horsemen are on the West Coast, and if you are in need of assistance, I have no doubt they would be eager to provide what help they can.

ME

There is no need to send anyone to my aid. I'm perfectly well. However, I might need to find an alternate source of food, and I thought you would know of a provider. I will conduct a search online, since there must be something on the West Coast.

CHRISTIAN

I do know of a provider, and I will attach a screenshot of the information. I assume the situation is not dire if you are not in any distress. Allegra sends her love. Do you have any news on when you will return to New York? We were hoping to visit you at the end of the summer, since we've promised the children they could see one of those interminably long Broadway shows based on comic books.

ME

I'm not sure. The situation is somewhat fluid. Regardless, I will update you when I know the date of my return.

CHRISTIAN

I feel obligated to repeat my offer of aid if you need it. You are, after all, my favorite nephew.

Finch smiled at that text. Christian was as unlike his father as two brothers could be, but Finch was much more like Christian than his wild, adventurous father.

ME

I am your only nephew, and the affection is returned. My love to Allie and the children.

By the time darkness claimed the town, Finch was restless, wandering around first the upstairs rooms, then the lower level. He even went and stood in the basement for a few minutes before the smell of earth, cobwebs, and mustiness drove him back upstairs. He spent a little time packing up Ozy's things that were spread amongst the three rooms upstairs, telling himself he'd feel better once he got everything removed, but he did nothing with the shopfront other than pick up a bowl of crystals and examine them before setting them down, and moving over to study a poster.

"Enough," he told himself when he contemplated his reflection in the small downstairs lavatory. "Go make your apology and explanation. Then, perhaps, you can get on with your doom scrolling chapter."

He mentally rehearsed his explanation as he strode down the pavement to where Tatiana's shop was located. He paused for a second, staring in surprise at the vignette she'd arranged in the big window. There were several dolls of an antique variety that lay in a gruesome scene of carnage, with a viscous, red substance splattered against the backdrop, dripping off the dolls' respective torsos, and even small pools of it visible on what appeared to be fake grass. But what gave him pause was the approximately three-foot-long doll dressed in Edwardian wear, with a China head and uncannily realistic eyes. The doll had been plastered against the window, staring straight out at the passers-by, its visible pearly teeth stained red, while its bloodied hand bore a wickedly sharp letter opener.

"Heya." Tatiana's cousin Clemmie looked up from where she sat behind a long wood and glass case when he entered the shop. To his surprise, the interior didn't smell at all like the musty antique shops of his experience—instead, small enamel bowls of potpourri filled the air with scents of spices and flowers. "You like the window scene? Tat thought it up. She wanted to go full CSI, but I thought a murder scene would be better. Eye-catching, right?"

"It's definitely that. Erm…is Tatiana in?"

"Nope. She went off to see if she could find the Entity." Clemmie gave a little shake of her head. "I told her that she was just asking for trouble, but she got some sort of nasty-gram this morning, and went off to see them about it. So. You and her didn't hit it off last night, eh?"

"On the contrary, I thought we did quite well together, however, my situation is such that I can't entertain further such interludes," he said, aware that he sounded priggish, but unable to do anything to stop himself.

"Dude. Please tell me you didn't use that line on her," Clemmie said, shaking her head again.

"If you would tell her that I called, and will stop by later, I would be grateful," he said, once again in that same damned stilted voice. Idly, he wondered what color Tatiana would call it. It felt like all colors had been thrown into a blender and ground up until they made a muddy soup.

Lovely. His lack of control led him to having mud soup vocal tones.

"OK, but you have no one to blame but yourself if you end up without any nookie tonight." Clemmie looked point-edly at him, but he decided there was nothing more to say.

He left the shop and glanced down the walk, wondering if he shouldn't return to his doom scrolling chapter.

His penis twitched.

"Very well," he said grimly, turning and striding down the walk to the seafront. He would ask someone where the town hall was located, and see if he could find Tatiana there. "But you have no one but yourself to blame if she says cutting things about me."

Well aware that not only did that *not* make sense, but he had evidently reached a point where having casual conversation with his genitals wasn't at all disturbing, he decided there was no further use in debating the odd bent his mind had taken since he'd met Tatiana, and went off to see if the bookstore owner could provide the information he sought.

Ten minutes later, he held a scrap of paper upon which a crescent had been drawn, with six lines radiating from its curved side. The main line was Axegate Walk, while two streets away Mercader had placed an X, marking the location of the city hall.

As he strolled through the streets, Finch kept an eye out for a likely mortal from whom he could feed, since the blood he'd ordered from his uncle's supplier wouldn't be there for twenty-four hours, but just like earlier in the day, none of the people tempted him.

"I'll get over this fascination," he told himself as he rounded a corner, and spied a two-story red brick building with cream stone molding around the roof and windows. "It's simply a matter of not having had a woman in some time, and a potential Beloved disrupting my peace of mind. Clarity. I just need to keep hold of clarity, and all will be— what the hell?"

The building was surrounded by several trees, more or less shrouding the windows, and no doubt making it very dark inside. But it was the large cream stone gargoyles that clung to the roofline, leaning out to peer down at the pavement below, that had Finch pausing. Floodlights lit up the front of the building, and combined with the movement of the trees' leaves in the breeze that came off the water, Finch had an impression that the gargoyles moved.

Keeping a wary eye on them, he approached the main door, but it was locked.

He pursed his lips for a moment, then spun around when he heard a rustling in a large deciduous bush that sat between two of the trees. He approached the shrub, saying aloud, "I know you're in there. Come out."

"Shhh! They'll hear you!"

To Finch's immense surprise, a hand shot out of the shrub, grasped his wrist, and jerked him forward into its leafy confines.

"Tatiana? What—"

"Shh!"

Branches poked at him, stabbing into his hair, dislodging his hat, and dribbling leaves down his back as he squinted in the darkness at the Tatiana-shaped shadow. To his surprise, once he knelt down, there appeared to be a hollow space inside the shrub, as if it was an umbrella. *What are you doing here?*

Waiting to see the Municipal Entity. There's a meeting tomorrow, and I'm determined to see if they leave the building tonight.

"If there's a meeting," he said softly, shifting to a spot where he wasn't kneeling on a rock, "wouldn't they be arriving rather than leaving?"

"You don't know the Entity. They inhabit the building, but are never there when meetings are called. Thus, they have to leave. This spot lets me watch both the front and back exits. See?"

Tatiana parted some leaves, allowing Finch to see that she had chosen a good—if uncomfortable—location.

"What makes you think they will vacate the premises tonight?" he asked, making himself comfortable by sitting on the ground, his ankles crossed as he leaned back and eyed the Tatiana shadow.

Just being near her drove the hunger to a point where it almost consumed him, her nearness causing the fine hairs on his arms to stand on end. The scent of earth and green, growing things mingled with a slightly salty tang that had nothing to do with the ocean air, and everything to do with the woman next to him.

"Just a hunch." She moved next to him, peering through the branches, her arm brushing his shoulder.

His penis, already pleased to see Tatiana, now struggled to achieve a full erection despite the close confines of his jeans. He tried his best to ignore the sensation of the drawing in his groin, ordering his mind to focus on what was important. "Do you intend on spending all night here?" he inquired, his mind now divided between trying to quell the hunger that gripped him, and the need to keep to his plan of distancing himself from the tempting, tantalizing woman next to him.

Damn. She must have hosed herself down with pheromones, because her salty scent seemed to wrap around his head, filling his senses.

"No. I figured a few hours ought to do it. Why? You don't have to—" She had released the branch and sat back on her heels, turning to face him as she spoke, but her breast brushed against his arm, making him feel as if he'd been struck by a lit torch. "Oh," she said on a breathy exhalation.

His fingers curled into fists as he struggled to control the hunger, hunching over against the pain as it crawled across his mind.

"Finch? Are you OK? What am I saying; it's obvious you're not. You said you were a doctor—is there something I can do?" She moved again, her hand soft on his arm as she leaned over him.

He drew in a ragged breath, knowing he shouldn't give in to his body's demand, knowing it would just intensify the agony, but unable to keep from doing so. Her scent sank into his mind, driving the hunger before it.

Yes. Don't touch me.

The pain that he felt when she withdrew her hand stabbed deep into his soul.

It's not you, he reassured her. *I like you touching me. Too much. I can't—*

You need to eat, she said, her thoughts touching his awareness more than he could bear.

Yes.

Her hesitation swamped him. He felt instantly guilty, and hurt.

"If I…I know we talked about this, but if I was to feed you…er…"

"It's not gory, no." It was an effort to force the words out, and although he desperately wanted her, he couldn't lie to her just to scare her away.

"And if I was to feed you now…Finch, you hurt. The pain is all but leeching out of you. I don't like you hurting, but I…goddess, I never thought I'd have to say this…I don't want to become a vampire. I may not be any great shakes as a human being, but I don't want to be undead, and go around sparkling and shit like that."

He chuckled despite the hold the hunger had on him, wracking him with wave after wave of pain at her nearness. He struggled against the voice that told him to claim his Beloved, and said instead, "Dark Ones don't do that. We aren't undead, we don't sparkle, and I'm not going to prey on you."

Dammit! I thought I hid that thought from you, she said, embarrassment filling her mind.

You never need be embarrassed with me, he answered before he realized the wisdom of making such a claim. He tried to remember why he had decided to keep her at arm's length, but at that moment—with her so close to him that he could feel the beat of her heart—all he could think of was possessing her. Tasting her. Giving her pleasure.

You're sure? she asked, and for a moment, he was confused.

"About not being undead or sparkling? Yes. Popular media has a different idea of what Dark Ones are. My uncle is partly to blame for that, since he wrote a series of books—but that is neither here nor there."

"OK, then." She took a deep breath, and held up her wrist, the feel of her skin on his lips pushing him to the very limits of his control. "Go ahead."

He hesitated, the voice in his mind telling him this was a step he couldn't reverse. There was blood on the way to appease the hunger, the voice pointed out, but the agony of having Tatiana next to him, with her skin touching his, and the scent of her blinding him to everything else was simply too much.

Still, he fought it. He tried to reason with the voice. Feeding just once from her wouldn't bind her to him. It wouldn't mean she couldn't live on if he died. It wouldn't damn her to a lifetime of misery and despair.

Would it?

"Please, Finch. I can feel how much it hurts. I want you to eat."

She was too close, too warm, and too enticing. He pulled her onto his lap, ignoring the pain of her sitting on what was now a full erection, and nuzzled her neck.

He struggled against the primal nature that possessed all Dark Ones, knowing that to go further was to risk it all.

She moaned softly as he nibbled on the spot behind her ear that she had thought of the night before, during the dinner that had ended up being unexpectedly erotic. *Oh, goddess yes, right there.*

Her pleasure was his undoing. He gave in to the need, allowed the hunger to swell up until it consumed him, his teeth sinking into her warm, inviting flesh. She jerked, tensing for a second before the endorphins that followed the bite filled her, making her moan again.

Goddess above and below, Finch. That's...I can feel the pleasure it gives you. It's all tied up with the sensation you are giving me. It's so...so...I think I'm... She moved restlessly against him, and for a second, he thought about taking her right there.

Feeding can be a sensual experience, he reminded her, aware that his control was just a hair's breadth away from snapping.

Are you—do you— She gripped his arms when he swirled his tongue over the bite, ensuring the bleeding would stop.

Yes. But not here. I draw the line at making love in the shrubbery.

Your place?

If I can walk, yes.

Looking back on it, Finch wasn't entirely sure how they made it from the town hall to his domicile, but as he approached the door leading out into the alley, he was well-aware that he was about to take a step that might have re-percussions that lasted his entire life.

Worse, it could doom Tatiana. And he'd be damned if he repeated the mistakes of his father.

"I had no idea that eating could do that to you," Tatiana said, rubbing her arms as she gazed at him with eyes that were smoky with passion. "Would you think I'm the bra-zenest of hussies if I told you that you can dine at Café Tat any time you like?"

He was about to answer her when he reached for the door, his keys in hand.

The door swung open.

"That was pushy, wasn't it? I'm so sorry, but I've never had a necking session like that where I was suddenly go for launch," she said, moving into the small kitchen area, setting her large striped bag down on the table. "Necking! Ha. Kind of a pun."

Finch entered slowly, glancing around the room, his senses heightened. He didn't feel the presence of another person, but that could mean nothing.

"Finch?" Tatiana gave him a doubtful look. "Are you OK? Oh lord. You're having second thoughts, aren't you?"

"The door was unlocked." He moved to the entrance of the short hallway and checked the front room. Everything there appeared to be normal.

"Was it?" She paused, evidently realizing the gravity of the statement.

He took the stairs three at a time, but the upstairs was empty of anything but furniture and his possessions.

"Everything OK?" Tatiana asked when he slowly came down the stairs. To his surprise, she held a large gold statue topped by a bird.

"Yes, although if there had been someone lurking above stairs, I'm not sure your weapon would have done much to dissuade him."

She glanced at the object, and tightened her grip on it. "Don't you believe it. This thing weighs a ton, and would handily brain anyone who threatened us. It's a racing bird trophy I picked up at the antique sale I went to yesterday. I've named the bird Herbert Pigeon. Did you forget to lock the door, do you think?"

"No. I'm very careful about that."

"Oh."

They looked at each other for a few seconds, then simultaneously turned to look at the door leading to the basement.

"I knew it was cursed," Tatiana said, giving the door a dark look.

"It's not. I was there earlier today, and felt nothing but the dust of almost a hundred years." Regardless, he opened the door and flipped on the switch, starting down the stairs. To his surprise, Tatiana was close on his heels, the large trophy clutched to her chest.

The room was empty of any intruders. He'd stacked the eight boxes of Ozy's belongings tidily against the wall, and they appeared to be untouched.

"Is that your stuff?" Tatiana asked, gesturing with the bird trophy toward the stack of boxes.

"No. I cleared out Ozy's things this morning. She had a lot of things tucked into cupboards and drawers."

"Hmm," Tatiana said, narrowing her eyes on the boxes before turning to retreat to the kitchen. "No one would break in just for the fun of it. You must have forgotten, and left the door unlocked. That or—" She stopped abruptly.

He closed the door to the basement. "Or what?"

"Nothing. My mind is a bit numb around the edges because of the effects of feeding you. That sure was something." Tatiana stood at the base of the stairs, looking deliciously tempting.

He watched her, wanting badly to take her into his arms again, but knowing that the madness that had come upon him was partially sated by feeding.

His penis lodged an objection to that statement, but he ignored it. "About that. I realize that things got a bit out of hand in the shrub."

"Yes, they sure did," she answered immediately, moving toward him, then halting, her gaze flickering to the door to the basement. "Would you…I hate to feed and dash, but I should really go back to watching for the Entity. They sent me a letter today saying they were reviewing my lease after complaints were lodged against me. I just know it has something to do with Ozy."

"I wouldn't want to hold you up from your stalking time," he said politely, his mind warring with his body. Christ, he wanted her, but he had to rise above that. His body was all for having his cake and eating it, too—literally—but his desires did not rule him. He was, if nothing, a man of order and structure.

"OK, then," Tatiana said, lifting her hand in an awkward gesture. "See you later."

He made a slight bow, and held the door open for her. She paused as she passed him, swore under her breath, and standing on her tiptoes, pressed a kiss to the corner of his mouth before dashing out into the alley.

He watched her disappear into the darkness before closing the door, locking it, and after double checking it, turned to consider his empty domain.

"She didn't want to stay. And yet, I could feel her desire. She wanted me as much as I wanted her." His body sang a silent song of loss while his mind tried to puzzle out her inconsistent actions. He started up the stairs, warning his penis, "Don't even start with me tonight. I'm going to take a cold shower, then work on my book, and we are going to forget the interlude in the shrubbery."

The mocking voice in his head told him it would be a very long time indeed before he forgot anything to do with Tatiana.

EIGHT

"Your boyfriend came by a little bit ago." Clemmie was in the process of closing up the shop, printing out invoices for items purchased on our online storefront when I returned home. She stapled a couple of sheets together, smiling broadly. "He liked the display."

"Did he?" I asked, guilt riding me hard. How on earth could I even be thinking about doing what I wanted to do when a few minutes before, I'd been ready to frolic all over his naked body. "That's good."

"Yup." She stuffed the invoices into the drawer in which we kept our cash lockbox, and pulled out her phone. "I'm going to join Becca and Tamsin at the café. It's Ouija board night, and we're hoping to get in contact with Tamsin's grandpa again, since the last time we summoned him he told her that before he died he buried a couple of grand in her backyard, but wouldn't tell her exactly where."

"Have fun. I hope grandpa's ghost comes through," I said without thinking, my mind still focused on Finch, Finch's mouth, and the boxes in his basement.

"Really?" She paused at the door, slanting an odd look my way. "Since when do you believe in ghosts? You always tell me that the Ouija board nights are rigged by Deacon so that people spend more time there buying expensive drinks."

"I was wrong," I said simply, not wanting to go into reason why I now believed in things like ghosts and old gods and sexy-as-sin vampires who made my body feel like it was one giant erogenous zone.

"Nice to know you don't mind admitting that. What are you going to do tonight? I thought you might be seeing Jeremy again."

I froze in the act of locking the cash drawer. "What do you mean? Why would you think that?"

"Because he came looking for you. Didn't he find you?"

"Ah. That." I cleared my throat. "Yes, he did. I'm not going to do anything in particular tonight. Certainly nothing illegal."

She blinked. "Huh?"

I damned my inability to keep from blurting out every thought. "It's nothing, silly. I'm just a bit tired. Have fun with your friends, and don't be out too late. I'd like to have the shop open early tomorrow to catch the first of the tourist busses."

"Aye aye," she said, saluting before exiting the shop.

I went upstairs to my small room, contemplated the contents of the refrigerator that sat in the hall, and with no better option, tossed a frozen meal into the microwave that sat on my dresser while I changed into black leggings, tee, and hoodie.

Waiting the two hours that I judged would ensure Finch was upstairs in his bedroom stretched my patience almost to its limit. "I can't believe you're doing this. This is not just illegal, it's immoral, and what's worse, if Finch knew, he'd never want to think sexy thoughts about you again," I told myself as I skulked down the alley on Finch's side of Axegate Walk. Although there were light fixtures at each shop's back door, many of them contained bulbs that were burned out, or nonexistent, leaving only a couple of pools of light down the length of the dark alley.

I pulled up my hood, and with a cautious glance around, slid into the shadows, hurrying down the length until I came to one of the doors that fortunately, didn't have a light. Evidently Ozy hadn't seen fit to make sure the back door was illuminated.

"All the better for me," I said softly, pulling out the lanyard upon which hung my keys, and with another furtive glance up and down the alley, slid the key to my shop into the lock.

It turned easily, and slowly, ever so slowly, I opened the door, peeking in to make sure that Finch wasn't downstairs. I'd seen the light from his window when I approached the alley, and since the lower floor was filled with darkness, I breathed a sigh of relief.

The door hinges gave a few squeaks that I prayed weren't audible above. I opened the door only as wide as I needed to slip inside, closing it just as carefully.

"Let's hope Finch was correct in that the basement isn't cursed," I told myself in a whisper as I eased open the door to the basement.

The odor of old dirt wafted around me when I silently made my way down the stairs, the lone bulb overhead as dusty as the rest of the basement. I paused midway down the stairs to make sure there was nothing else in the room, but it was reassuringly empty of monsters, boogeymen, or the undead, all of which I was absolutely prepared to believe lurked in its depths.

"You're just discombobulated because you found out vampires are real," I said softly, and with a glance to reassure myself that I had pushed the door almost closed, but hadn't latched it, I moved over to the stack of eight boxes. "OK, Ozy. Let's see what you were really up to, and why you have it in for me."

I pulled the lid off the nearest box, quickly sorting through various items of a bathroom nature. "She sure liked her bath bombs," I murmured as I set the box aside, and turned to the next one.

That's when I noticed something so out of place, my brain staggered to a halt.

I stood with the lid of the second box in my hand, just staring at the object on the floor behind the row of boxes. It was a black tennis shoe.

I looked at the shoe, then my gaze slid upward. An ankle was visible above the shoe, disappearing into the inky blackness cast by the boxes.

"No," I said aloud, trying to reboot my brain. "It can't be. This is a joke. It's Ozy's skeleton. For some bizarre reason, Finch has dressed it and hidden it here so it would scare the ever-living shit out of me."

I blinked a couple of times, then realized the cardboard of the lid to the nearest box was cutting into my hands. I loosened my grip on it, and carefully setting it down, moved around to the end of the boxes.

A body lay prone, squished between the stone wall and the boxes. All I could make out were the shoes and ankles.

"Holy cats," I swore, my brain suddenly filled with thoughts that chased each other like deranged hamsters on a wheel. "It's a body. A real body. Finch has a body in the basement."

And with those words, a horrible image rose in my mind—a man who was so sexy, so fascinating that it drove all common sense from my brain. One who drank blood in order to exist.

Everyone knew vampires killed people. That was a common theme in all the vampire movies I'd seen.

"Holy cats," I repeated, the skin on my back crawling. "I kissed a murderer. I fed a murderer my blood. I was ready to bonk a murderer. What the hell am I going to do?"

I thought of pounding up the stairs and confronting Finch to demand to know why he'd let me make a fool of myself with him when he was a murdering bastard bloodsucker all along, but almost immediately, the tiny shred that was my self-preservation warned me that wasn't the best idea I'd ever had.

"Maybe the person isn't dead," I said softly, moving around toward the head end of the boxes. "Maybe he's keeping dinner on the hoof, so to speak, and they are just snoozing?"

I knew even before I got the words out that it wasn't true, but I wouldn't be able to live with myself if I didn't at least check that the person was still alive.

It took a minute to drag away the four boxes at the other end, since they were extremely heavy, but at last I wrestled them away, and stood with my phone in hand, shining its light down on the person.

"Shit," I said, blinking in disbelief.

"Is there? I didn't see any earlier. I admit there may have been a rodent living here some time ago, but I didn't even see droppings, so I assume they are long gone."

I whirled around at the voice and stared with horror at Finch, who stood at the bottom of the stairs, leaning against the wall with his arms crossed. *Fuck!*

Really? I'm happy to oblige, of course, but I thought you would be bush-bound to continue your stalking of the city forces.

"I can't believe I fell for you," I said, suddenly furious. How dare he speak so casually into my mind? How dare he be so amused, his voice was positively orange with it? Without thinking of the wisdom of my actions, I flung myself at him, punching him on the center of his chest. "You murdering bastard! I was thinking about falling in love with you!"

He rubbed the spot on his chest, his delicious chocolate brown eyebrows pulling together as he considered me with eyes that darkened to sapphire. "You were thinking about it? It's not something that happens?"

"Oh, it happens," I said, my anger rising. How could I have been so stupid as to allow him to work his way into my mind and affections? How could my body, even now, want him in a way I've never wanted any other man? "It happens a lot. I'm forever falling in love at first sight. Ask Clemmie. Ask Mercader. Ask anyone. It doesn't mean anything. Not one. Damned. Thing."

He studied me for a few seconds, then to my surprise, slid his arms around my waist and gently pulled me against him, his mouth curving in a smile as he feathered kisses along my lips. "Is that so? That's not what your body is saying."

"My body lies," I said, melting against him despite myself.

"Sweetheart, your body is many things—delightful, delectable to the point of making me drool with desire, and sensuous as the day is long—but a liar is not one of those things."

He kissed me then, and for a moment, I let him, reveling in the feel of him, of the slightly spicy taste of his mouth, and the way his body fit so well with mine.

And then I remembered I was kissing a murderer, and managed to pull away from the lure of his seductive self.

"Why did you kill Ozy?" I asked.

He stared at me as if I had grown a second set of arms. "I what?"

I pointed to the boxes. "That's Ozy. Why did you kill her, Finch? Did you want her shop that badly? I mean, I get it. It's a great shop, and goddess knows I've tried like crazy to get Rolly's mom to let me have it, but I never once thought of killing Ozy to get it!"

Finch continued to stare at me for a few seconds, then released my arms and strode past me to stand next to the remaining boxes. Then he knelt at Ozy's head, but didn't touch her.

I took a few hesitant steps toward him, guilt overwhelming me. "Is she alive?"

"No." He stood up and looked at me, his face a study in confusion and dismay.

"Are you sure?" I peered around him. "You didn't check for a pulse."

"I didn't have to. She was beheaded."

"What?" My voice came out as a squawk. "No! I saw her head. It's right there at the top of her body."

"It's placed there, but it's not connected. I can show you—"

"No!" I screeched, backing away while holding up both hands. "I'll take your word for it. I told you how squeamish I am about blood and guts."

"Oddly, there are neither." He studied the body. "In fact, judging by the black marks at the point of severing, I assume some sort of sword spelled with dark power did the job, but the only beings I know who have those are wrath demons. And they do not frequently leave Abaddon."

"What's—" I started to ask.

Finch turned to the boxes, and started rustling around in them. "Abaddon is what mortals think of as hell. There are seven princes who rule it. Each prince has legions of demons, including wrath demons, their elite guards." He pulled out two neatly folded blankets, and spread them on Ozy's remains.

"Are you—" I had to stop to try to find a nice way to ask my question. "Are you part of that? Of Abaddon?"

"Me?" His brows pinched together. "Far from it. Dark Ones originated from the wealden, thanes who tried to destroy Abaddon."

I took a step toward him, unable to resist the lure of those eyes. And his chin. And goddess help me, the rest of him. "Your ancestors tried to close down hell?"

"More or less. They didn't succeed. The mortal race betrayed them, and the four thanes were imprisoned." His eyes fairly glowed with intensity when he pinned me back with a long look. "What did you hope to achieve by placing the body here?"

"Me?" My voice came out a squeak. "I didn't put her here. Besides, I couldn't have if I wanted to. You're the one who killed her."

"I did no such thing."

"She's in *your* basement," I pointed out.

"One that evidently others have access to," he said, glancing at the lanyard, which I'd slung over my head. "How do I know you don't have a blade imbued with dark power, and decided to rid yourself of a rival?"

"Because I didn't!" I straightened up and squared my shoulders, outraged he could even think such a thing. "I couldn't! For one, I am not a murderer, and for another, I get squicked out at blood, which I've told you twice now. I doubt if there's a way to lop off someone's head without having blood gushing everywhere. Not to mention the fact that I don't have an evil hell wrath sword."

You broke into my house. I found you in the basement with a body. It was a natural conclusion.

Oh! I like that! I didn't break in, I just used my key.

"You have a key to my home?" he asked, moving over to where I stood.

"No, I have a key to mine. It just so happens that some of the locks on the Walk haven't been replaced, and Mercader and I have keys that work on them. I wondered earlier this evening if Ozy's lock was one of them when you said the door was open."

His lips tightened. "Evidently it is. If you didn't let yourself in to leave a body, then what were you doing in the basement?"

My face grew hot. "I had a feeling you weren't going to forget about that."

"It is a point of curiosity," he admitted.

"I couldn't resist searching Ozy's things," I said, my shoulders slumping at the confession. "Obviously, I couldn't do that when her stuff was upstairs, where you live, but down here in boxes? It just seemed like too good an opportunity to miss."

His expression changed from skepticism to speculation. "What, exactly, did you hope to find in the boxes?"

"There's no exactly about it, because I don't know. Proof that Ozy had it in for me? That she was making a targeted attack against me? Information about why she was doing it?" I shrugged. "I don't know because I don't understand her motive."

"I packed her things earlier. I saw nothing that mentioned you," he said. He glanced back at the body.

I took another step toward him, unable to keep from putting my hand on his arm. He wore a tank top and flannel sleeping pants, his chest and arms drawing my gaze like he was a magnet and I was a particularly befuddled bit of metal. His skin was warm and soft, but the muscles that lay beneath it bespoke a man who lived an active life. It was an effort, but I managed to drag my mind off the need to touch and taste and nibble, and ask, "You really didn't kill her, did you?"

Do you think I'm capable of such a thing? he asked, and I could sense pain behind the words.

I put my other hand on him, searching his eyes, but there was no guile there, no sense of betrayal, just confusion and hurt.

No. I did, but as soon as I said the words, I realized how stupid it was. You're not a killer.

He closed his eyes for a moment, then his arms went around me again, this time in a much looser grip. "I served in several wars in the medical corps as a doctor. I did not take arms against mortals, but there were a few occasions when I had to defend the injured from attackers. My soul is not as stainless as you believe."

I wrapped my arms around him, holding him against the sorrow that leached blackness into his voice. "You are a protector, Finch, not a murderer. I'm sorry I accused you of being one. I should have known that I couldn't fall for a man who could harm others."

He was silent for a moment, accepting the comfort that I offered, then gently set me from him. "You are a Beloved."

"So?" I watched him, unsure of why he was wrapped in a sense of regret.

"Dark Ones and Beloveds are, for lack of a better expression, programmed to be captivated by each other. What you're feeling isn't actual love. It's your body chemistry reacting to my body chemistry."

"Oh, really?" I didn't know whether I should be angry that he was so clueless he didn't understand falling in love if not on sight, then damned close to it, or amused that he was clearly in denial. Annoyance gained the upper hand. "So you're an expert in my feelings, now, are you?"

"No, I am an expert in Dark Ones, and I know how they work," he said in a maddening tone of reason.

"You know," I said after a moment's thought, deciding the present wasn't the best moment for the argument I wanted to have with him. "As much as I would love to talk about how wrong you are, not to mention wanting quite badly to go upstairs so I can frolic all over you, there's a dead body just a few feet away, and I'm perilously close to freaking out."

"Point taken," he said. "Although I don't understand why you turned me down earlier when I invited you to go upstairs. Has something happened to change your mind?"

I gave a little cough, and studied my hands for a second. "Yeah, well, before…I just couldn't, Finch. Not when I knew I was going to try my key to get in here after you went to bed. If you and I hooked up before that, it would have felt… icky. Like I was using you. I couldn't do that."

He looked thoughtful, and I realized that I couldn't hear his thoughts.

Did our mental radios go out, or are you simply not transmitting?

The latter.

A pang of regret stabbed into my heart. I wanted to go into full pity-party mode over the fact that even though I had deliberately avoided putting him in a position where he might have felt used for my own purposes, I had still ruined whatever it was we had between us.

I pushed that pain and guilt aside. This wasn't the moment for selfish introspection.

Finch must have felt something even though I was careful to keep my thoughts hidden in the shadows of my mind, because he examined my face before saying, "I agree that knowing you intended on breaking into my home would have made any intimate activity viewable in an unfortunate light, but it does make me wonder why you decided to loot my basement in the first place."

I gave in to a tiny bit of self-pity. *I told you. I didn't want her to win.*

Ozy?

Yes.

I don't understand.

"This whole thing between us," I said, gesturing at where Ozy lay. "You don't understand because you weren't here being the focus of her attention, but I can assure you that I'm not being paranoid when I say she had it in for me. She bad-mouthed me to the Entity and several people in the town. Powerful people, like the mayor and the sheriff, and several other shopkeepers. And before you say it's just a perception on my part, it's not. There were tangible results to Ozy coming to Ravenfall and taking an instant dislike to me. For one, the people in the bank wouldn't give me a loan when I wanted to buy my shop from the city. And then there was the way the Entity started taking an interest in me after she visited them."

His brows pulled together in a flat line. "I thought you said that nobody has seen this mysterious group?"

"No one has…no one but Ozy, and now she's dead." I pointed with a suitably dramatic manner to the boxes. "And if you expect me to believe that's it's a coincidence she's seen them and now is lying here with her head lopped off, you're crazy."

"I can't address that situation, but I agree that you appear to have been the target of malicious attacks by her. You're sure you did nothing to harm her?"

"Quite sure. I'm not a Wiccan, but I hold with the idea that what you put out in the universe returns to you, multiplied by a factor dependent on how harmful your actions are. It's kind of embarrassing to admit, but karmic backlash is more or less what keeps me on the straight and narrow."

"And yet you named dolls after her," he said, his voice going a bit mauve.

My cheeks warmed. "That wasn't nice of me, but didn't really do any harm. It just irritated her more than anything. I told you that I put disclaimers on all my haunted stuff, the dolls included."

"Mmm," he said with a noncommittal tone, and returned to view Ozy's remains.

"What are you doing?" I asked, biting my lower lip. I didn't want to see the body again; although it wasn't particularly gory, I didn't have any desire to look at it.

"Checking for any other injuries. I don't see anything other than the obvious, which means she either knew her attacker and didn't try to protect herself, or she was taken by surprise and didn't have time to react. I'll check if there's anything in her pockets."

He made a quick search of Ozy, but stood up with his hands empty, staring down at her in silence until I asked, "What's wrong? Other than the fact that Ozy's remains were stashed behind a bunch of boxes in your basement, that is."

"She's cold," he said, his voice spiked with butterscotch tendrils.

"She's dead. Doesn't that make sense?" I moved a few steps to eye the top of Ozy's head, which was all that was visible around the boxes.

"It would if she were outside. But it's fairly warm in here, and she should be at room temperature. She's not."

"Someone brought her in from outside?" I asked.

"I don't know." He shook his head and sighed, looking at his phone. "It's not that cold out. If I didn't know better, I'd say she had been held in a refrigerated facility like a morgue."

"Which makes it weird that someone brought her here and hid her behind your boxes." I sat down on the box the most distant from Ozy, my body wanting to curl up on itself. "What are we going to do?"

His lips thinned. "Call the authorities."

"I had a horrible feeling you were going to say that. Don't you think we could…you know…take her somewhere else?"

Finch made a face, his eyes a pure, rich blue. "Tempting as that is, it would be disturbing the scene, and I'm sure the mortal police will have something to say about that."

I glanced around, bracing myself, but the basement was oddly free of blood, gore, or other carnage that indicated it was a crime scene. "Is it, though? A crime scene, that is."

He looked thoughtful, then returned to the body for a moment before straightening up to make a quick visual survey of the basement. "I believe you are correct in that supposition. There is no sign that she was killed here. Regardless, I'm sure the police wouldn't like us interfering."

"You don't know the local cops like I do. They don't follow normal police procedures in Ravenfall. But...do we really have to call them? Maybe there's something else we could do." I pinched my lower lip, creating and discarding a number of unreasonable options.

"Such as?"

"I'm afraid I don't have any bright ideas on how to make Ozy disappear," I admitted. "My brain has failed me. I blame kissing you. My mind simply doesn't want to function when it can keep reliving the kiss, and feeling sort of giddy over the fact that I snogged a vampire. I don't suppose you have any suggestions?"

"Other than calling the police?" Finch looked like he wanted to sigh, but stopped himself in time. "No. I make it a policy to live by mortal rules whenever possible. Oh, Christ."

"What?" I asked, a little spike of fear piercing my belly. "Is this going to out you? Do you think people are going to say you killed her just because you're a vampire?"

"No to both. However, I'm going to have to call a friend and tell him what happened." He ran a hand over his face, and for the first time, I noted lines around his mouth. "He will be less than pleased."

Something inside me shifted at the unhappiness in his voice, and with that, a need followed.

I wanted to help Finch. No, not just help—I wanted him happy. His happiness had somehow pushed its way to the top of my primary interests. What was going on with that? I liked Finch, and if I wasn't the queen of cursed relationships, wouldn't at all mind having a physical relationship while we explored the connection we had, but other than taking Clemmie under my wing a few years ago when she needed a home and job, I had never put someone else's welfare and wishes ahead of my own.

What was that?

What was what? I asked, panicked that my inner narrative had once again been broadcast to him.

You were thinking something that flittered around the edges of my awareness. Did you wish to say something, or are you practicing your control?

"Neither. Both. Oh, hell, how do I know? I just committed my first outright crime by breaking in to your basement, discovered a body, and the handsomest man I've ever seen is not only a vampire, he thinks I have a couple of screws loose."

Finch smiled, warming me from within. "I don't. I think you are delightfully unexpected, but that is not a bad trait. I also think you are caring, a peacemaker, and most likely a middle child."

"How did you know that? My mom had my sister with a guy when she was really young, before she met my dad, and then when I was in my teens she married my stepdad and had two boys."

"I made a study of mortal birth order personality traits. You exhibit several traits such as rebellion, peacemaker, impulsiveness, and wanting to please people, all appropriate to middle children."

"I don't know about caring all that much about pleasing most people—other than my friends and customers—but yeah, the other parts are mostly true. Are you a middle kid, too?"

"No. My parents had only me." He put a hand on my back, and gently urged me toward the stairs, which I started up, after a last glance toward Ozy and the boxes.

"And what are only kid personalities?" I asked, interested despite the horrible situation into which we found ourselves. Finch was fascinating, and not just because he was a vampire.

"In general, they are achievers. Structured. Conscientious. And can be controlling, although I don't see any but the structured trait in myself."

I shot a glance at him over my shoulder to see if he was joking.

He wasn't.

"Do you have the number for the local police?" he asked when we reached the kitchen. He closed the door, but I noticed he didn't lock it.

And it was at that point that I decided I couldn't just stand by and let Finch and me be railroaded.

"Sure," I said, and pulled it up on my phone.

He noted it, then glancing at his phone, made a face that perfectly matched the frustration (grey) that tipped his voice. "I need to make a phone call first. Er...it may take some time."

"I'll stay here and guard the door," I said, taking a seat at the table. "How long do you think you'll be? Should I make coffee, assuming Ozy left some?"

"I'm not sure how long the call will take. My friend will no doubt have many things to say to me once I inform him about the body. By all means help yourself to whatever beverage you can find. I haven't stocked anything, I'm afraid." He headed up the stairs and disappeared into the room at the top, quietly closing the door after him.

My phone was out a second later.

"Yo, Tatty-pants." Clemmie sounded somewhat out of breath, but also very giggly. "Wazzup?"

"I need help moving a body. Are you at the café? Can you leave your friends for a couple of minutes to help me?"

"Sec." She evidently placed her hand over her phone, but not enough for me to not hear her say in a stage whisper, "My cousin has gone batshit crazy, and I may have to talk her down off whatever ledge she's on. No, I don't think so. Let me ask. Tats?"

I stood and paced to the basement door and back to the table. "I am not batshit crazy, Clementine!"

She giggled again. "Sorry. Are you on a ledge?"

"No, I'm in Ozy's kitchen. Will you please come to the back door pronto?" I glanced up the stairs, but the door to Finch's bedroom was still closed. "I need help before Finch gets off the phone."

"Huh?" She sounded slightly less giggly. "What are you doing in Ozy's place? And who's Finch?"

"Look, I don't have time to answer your questions, OK? There's a body in the basement, and you and I both know what Sheriff Sharif is going to do if she has even the faintest whiff of me being involved with it. Finch doesn't see it, but he's very only child, evidently. So tell your friends you'll be back in ten, and come help me. I'll leave the door unlocked."

I hung up before she could do more than start to sputter a protest, and with another glance up the stairs toward Finch's closed bedroom door, took a deep breath, told my inner Tat she could do this, and went into the basement.

Nothing had changed, which was oddly reassuring, although I sidled around the blanket-covered form of Ozy, half expecting it to sit up in the best horror movie style.

"You kissed a vampire," I told myself, moving around to the head end. I decided that although Finch swore there was no gore, it would be best to keep everything as covered as possible, and drew out a large bath towel from the box into which Finch had packed Ozy's linens. "You fed a vampire. You can do this."

"You fed a what?"

The sudden voice, accompanied by a slight creak of the stairs, had me stifling a squeal as I whirled around clutching the towels to my chest, my heart beating so loudly that for a few seconds, it drowned out everything else.

Clemmie stood at the bottom of the stairs, weaving slightly, a couple of paper drink umbrellas stuck into her hair. "What are you doing with those towels? And who's this Finch person? Does the dishy Jeremy know you are here?"

"Thank the goddess," I said, telling my pulse it could return to a more reasonable rate. "You can take the head. I'll drag the rest of her."

"The head of what? What's going on, Tat? Hey. Is that—"

I averted my gaze and peeled back one of the blankets to expose Ozy's head.

"Holy shiznits!" she gasped. "That's Ozy!"

"Yes, and keep it down. I don't want Finch to hear you. Here. Take this, and wrap the head in it. Then help hoist the rest of Ozy onto my shoulder."

"By the god and goddess, you've finally snapped," she said, and gave me a look that I won't soon forget. "You killed Ozy? You decapitated Ozy?"

"Don't be ridiculous," I said, tossing the towel at her, and moving around to consider how best to lift up Ozy and still keep her covered. "You've known me your whole life. I'm no more a murderer than you are. Now take her head and park it somewhere so we can lift the body."

"Tat—"

"For the love of the twelve goddesses!" I slapped my hands on my thighs in utter exasperation. "I didn't murder her! Neither did Finch. But if the sheriff finds her here, there will be all sorts of hell to pay, and frankly, I don't think Finch understands that."

"Who—"

"Jeremy Renfrew. Finch is his real name," I said, giving her a little shove toward the body.

She looked first at the towel, then over to the body, then back to me. "Is he the vampire you fed?"

I thought quickly. "That was...I was remembering a line from my favorite book."

"What book?" she asked, her expression neutral.

"Does that matter?" I asked, fighting back the need to break into hysterics. Why was everything and everyone crossing my simple attempt to get rid of Ozy's body?

"Sure. I might want to read it. Is it one of those vampire books that my mom loved?"

"No, it was…something different."

"How different?" she asked, leaning against a box, evidently prepared to have an in-depth discussion about a non-existent book.

I gently banged my forehead against the nearest box. "For the love of all the gods!"

"I mean, a good book is worth the time to find out the title," Clemmie pointed out, hoisting herself onto the box. "Do you remember the author name? Or what the cover looked like? I can ask the local library if they know—"

"It's not a book!" I said, pushed beyond the point of sanity. "I lied, OK?"

She blinked at me. "Then what were you quoting from?"

I did the head on box move a couple of more times. "Nothing. It was just me speaking aloud my inner narrative."

"Really," she drawled, her eyes narrowed. "You met a vampire?"

I slumped against the box.

"Vampires are real? You met a real vampire? Man." She looked thoughtful. "Clarita swore that they were, but I thought she'd hit the crack pipe or something. But you're saying they exist? Wait…are they the big bun-hair guys from the 90s, or the skinny sparkle pony dudes?"

"We are not having this conversation," I told her, straightening up and squaring my shoulders before I pointed at the body. "Later, perhaps, I will explain. But not now. Not while there is a body poised to bring nothing but a hellish nightmare smack dab on top of Finch and me."

"Finch! He's the vampire? You hooked up with him?" She slid off the box, her expression going from scandalized to fascinated. "But you never do that with guys you just met. Wow. Did he use his vampire super powers on you? Do you have an urge to eat bugs? To wear slinky outfits and seduce unwary young men to your lair?"

"I am so changing the password to the Wi-Fi," I told her with a meaningful look. "You're watching far too much TV. Now, can we move past the subject of vampires and onto something more mundane?"

"I dunno," she said, glancing over at the body. "A decapitated body in a vampire's basement seems pretty wild to me. I'm going to want the full story, you know."

"I know, but I don't have time to explain now. Get the head."

"I'm a little unclear on what your game plan is," she said, moving over to the far end of Ozy's body. "Also, I need to verify that this is what you say it is. You might have hallucinated it."

"I am not the one who was clearly indulging in alcohol and herb," I told her, having caught the faint whiff of smoke about her. "I didn't hallucinate Ozy's body."

"I didn't smoke anything," she said, lifting the cover off Ozy's head. "Clarita did, though."

"I'm glad to hear that. I need you to have your wits together," I said, spinning around so my back was to the body. "Cover up Ozy when you're done. You know how I am about bloody things."

"I know, but honestly, Tat, what are you doing with— wow. That really is Ozy." There was a little rustle as I assumed Clemmie knelt down. "Yup. She's dead all right. It's kind of neat how her head fits right there, but you give it a little push, and boom. It's not connected."

"How bloody is it?" I asked. "Finch said there was no gore, but he's a doctor and a vampire, and both of those means he has a higher tolerance to such things than I do."

"There's no blood." Another rustle followed. "So that's a spinal cord? Huh. It's kind of interesting, really. Tat, you should see this. It's like one of those anatomical books."

"I can do without seeing it, thank you," I told her. "Please re-wrap the head and put it on a box, so you can help me with the body."

"I'm not sure we should move it. The sheriff is going to be pissed if you move her."

"Ozy wasn't killed here," I pointed out, turning around when Clemmie moved in front of me. I was dismayed to see her hands were empty.

"How do you know?"

"You really need to listen to some of those true crime podcasts I recommended. For one, there's no blood anywhere. And for another, Finch and I were down here earlier, and she wasn't here. Plus he said she might have been refrigerated."

"All very interesting points," she agreed. "But even so, the sheriff—"

"Will have me in jail so fast your head will spin if she finds Ozy here," I interrupted, moving over to the body. "You know how much she hates me."

"Well, you *were* responsible for her husband leaving her," Clemmie said, looking down on the body.

"I was no such thing. I simply told him that her voice was so brown it could have been dirt. It wasn't my fault that he realized she was lying about her visits to the gym, and her relationship with the well-oiled Ricardo."

"Ricardo," she said on a long breath. "I really need to get him to be my personal trainer, too."

I buoyed up my sagging spirits. "You'll have to fight just about every other woman in town. I heard the waiting list for him is at least a dozen deep. Right. Help hoist Ozy onto my shoulder. She was pretty tiny, so I should be able to carry her."

"Carry her where?" Clemmie asked, but bent when I did, and managed to keep the blanket wrapped around the body as we lifted together.

I staggered a little under the awkward burden, but was able to get a rough approximation of a fireman's carry on the body. "Man, she is a lot heavier than she looked. Don't forget the head."

"Tat!"

I staggered toward the stairs, stumbling twice, my breath coming short and fast. "It's fine, just fine. No need to worry—gah!"

Clemmie caught me when I did a seriocomic trip over a shoebox, fortunately catching Ozy's body before it slid completely off my shoulder. "Here, let me take her."

"No, she's my problem—"

"I'm bigger than you, stronger, and younger," she said, hoisting Ozy's form with apparent ease. "You can get the head."

I made a face to her back as she carefully started up the stairs, snatching up the head in a towel, immediately dropping it when it seemed to deflate upon my touch.

"Shit!"

"Don't tell me you dropped the head," Clemmie said, only her legs visible as she was almost to the top of the stairs.

"Of course not," I said, grimacing when I used the edge of the towel to carry the head. I whispered an apology to Ozy for mistreating her body in that way, praying she understood that I really had to get her out of there.

"You still haven't told me your plan," Clemmie whispered when I entered the kitchen, and closed the door to the basement behind me.

"Oh, that's easy. I'm going to take her to the town hall. She was working with the Entity, so they can just have her back and deal with the ramifications of her death."

"You know how I'm always telling you that you act first, and think later?" Clemmie followed me when I went to the door and opened it for her. "This is a prime example of just what I'm talking about."

"What you call impulsive is really nothing more than quick thinking," I said with a fast glimpse up the stairs, but Finch's door remained closed. Good. With luck, I'd have Ozy parked at the town hall and would be back before he was done making his phone calls. "I'll be damned if I do anything else to have the Entity and the sheriff on my ass. Or Finch's."

"A prime example," Clemmie repeated, and I marched resolutely out of the shop, and into the alley.

Straight into Clemmie's back.

When I moved to the side, I froze, noting with horror the group of three people facing us.

"Hello, Titty," the foremost woman said, a smirk curving her mouth in a way that reminded me of a fox eating a chicken. It wasn't very well-lit outside of Ozy's shop, but it there was enough light spilling down the alley to glint on the metal handcuffs held in her hand. "What's that your cousin is holding? Looks very much like a body to me."

I looked from the sheriff to the two women behind her, both of whom held thick, smoking smudge sticks, and sighed.

NINE

"I'll get hold of the local police, but for the love of god, Finch, will you please keep your head down, and your door locked? I can't promise to keep you safe if you insist on harboring headless bodies in your basement."

"It's not like I invited people to park their dead in the basement," Finch protested, but it was a moot point. They both knew that the situation was problematic, but where Damon was worried about Finch being harmed, he was more concerned about Tatiana.

The following ten minutes were painful, at best, but at last he managed to end the conversation.

"If I had stood out in the midday sun, I would feel less burned," Finch said to himself as he hung up on Damon. He had thought briefly of telling Tatiana just why he was in Ravenfall, but the tongue blistering he'd received from his old friend made it clear that such a thing was not advised. "Someone somewhere is having a very big laugh at the fact that I found my Beloved at the exact time when I was least prepared to welcome her to my life."

Um. The touch of Tatiana's mind against him was a welcome distraction, although it drove home the bad timing of their meeting.

Regardless, he couldn't resist her. *Hello.*

Hi. Er.

Finch consulted his contact list, prepared to call the local police per Damon's instructions. *Got lonely down there, did you?*

Not really. He felt an odd sense of reluctance from her. *Don't leave your shop.*

His eyes narrowed on his phone. *What?*

Emotion swirled around her, but he couldn't pick out just what it was she was feeling. Damn. She had taken his words to heart, and was now doing an exceptionally good job of keeping her thoughts to herself. He found he didn't like that one little bit.

Don't leave your shop. Just sit tight, OK?

Why? he asked, his fingers tightening on the phone until his knuckles turned white.

Silence filled his head, but he could feel Tatiana thinking. Finally, she said, *Just…uh…because?*

He sighed into her mind. *Did you go down to the basement and look at the body? Are you upset because you saw the head separated from the body?*

Oh, it's much worse than that.

He was on his feet before he realized it, heading out of his bedroom. *What is wrong?*

It's kind of a long story. Just sit tight. Clemmie should be able to tell you what's up later, but I don't want you involved.

Involved in what? He raced down the stairs and after hearing voices from the alley, yanked open the door, skidding to a halt as soon as his feet hit the pavement. *What are you doing?*

Outrage filled his mind. *I was trying to save us, but as usual, fate has shit upon my life. Honestly, Finch, other than a few specific cases—such as rescuing Clemmie from her abusive father, and having my shop, and of course, meeting you—other than those instances, I swear that everything that could go wrong does. It's like I'm some sort of voodoo doll that people keep sticking pins in.*

Ahead of him, a small cluster of women were moving toward the main street. One of the women had a firm grip on Tatiana, who appeared to have her hands cuffed behind her back. Faint sounds of sputtering and coughing reached back to him. *What happened? Who are these women? Where is the body?*

Tatiana spun around. "Dammit! I said *don't* leave the shop." She stopped for a paroxysm of coughing before glaring at one of the women. "Will you stop smudging me! It's setting off my asthma."

"Who—oh." The woman holding onto Tatiana's arm studied him. He returned the gesture, noting she had dark eyes and hair, was clad in a black uniform, and bore an expression that he felt boded ill for everyone. She released Tatiana and strode forward to him. "I'm Sheriff Nadia Sharif. You are Mr. Renfrew?"

"I am," he said, wondering how he could have left Tatiana sitting in the kitchen, and now all hell had apparently broken loose.

A figure appeared at the end of the alley, backlit by the street lights that dotted the crescent making up the main street. "Hey! What's the hold up? I'm not going to haul Ozy around all night waiting for you slowpokes. Let's shake a leg, people! I have a whole lot of drinking to do before Deacon closes the café."

It was at that moment that Finch realized that Tatiana's cousin Clemmie was evidently carrying the body from his basement, and the large object wrapped in a towel, and held by one of the women bearing smudge sticks, must be the head.

He couldn't help but give Tatiana a pointed look.

She gave it right back to him.

You kidnapped the body? he asked.

I was trying to save us! she responded, obviously disgruntled. *I told you what would happen if the Sheriff found Ozy in your basement. And look! I was right.*

"Just what is your role here, sir?" the sheriff asked him, her eyes narrowing further until they were to glittering obsidian slits. "I assume you know Titty, here?"

"Don't answer her," Tatiana said loudly, her glare a razor's edge of fury. "You have the right to a lawyer. You don't have to talk to her without one."

The sheriff cast her glance skyward for a moment, then spun around and hands on hips, said, "I'm not arresting him, you idiot. I'm simply asking if he's involved in this with you. Now settle down before I have my sisters smudge you again."

"You do and I'm suing for asthma-related trauma," Tatiana snapped, twitching when one of the two women waved her smudge stick at her. "You're loving this, aren't you?" she added to the woman, who smiled.

"How about it?" the sheriff asked Finch, her gaze filled with speculation. "You in this caper with Titters?"

"Her name is Tatiana," he said, giving her a level look that he hoped made it clear he was not amused by the obvious attempt to shame her prisoner. "And I don't know what caper you are referring to, so I am unable to answer that question. I am, however, acquainted with her. She's—"

"This is ridiculous! You're harassing this poor, innocent man of whom I have barely any knowledge," Tatiana interrupted, ducking when the non-head bearing smudge sticker grabbed at her.

What are you doing? Finch couldn't help but ask her as the sheriff turned back to Tatiana.

Protecting you! she answered. *This isn't your problem. Go back to your shop, and I'll make sure she doesn't bother you.*

Finch felt out of his depth for the first time in several decades. No one had ever tried to protect him other than his uncle, and that had been when he was a very young man.

I don't know what to say to that, he admitted, not sure he liked the emotions that Tatiana had stirred in him. Protection towards mortals—that he understood. It had been bred into him, both his parents being adamant about his duty to help those who needed aid. Even considering Tatiana as a potential Beloved made sense with regards to the need he had to keep her safe. That was also his duty, but never, in any of his experiences with mortals, had any of them offered him the same consideration. *Do you seriously think I'm the sort of Dark One who would allow his Beloved to put herself at risk just for his convenience?*

He tried hard to keep his mental tone stern, but he had a horrible feeling that she could feel the warmth in his mind that came with the knowledge that this woman, this mortal, was putting him first in her thoughts.

He had a sudden urge to dance and sing and shout to everyone that he had a Beloved, and she was thinking about falling in love with him. He wanted to revel in the fact that someone worried about him. Someone put herself at risk on his behalf.

And then reality blotted out every last shred of joy, reminding him of just what happened to Beloveds. He wouldn't put Tatiana through that. Not so long as there was a breath left in his body.

"Sheriff, I'm sure the situation looks suspicious at best, but I can assure you that in this case, appearances are quite deceptive. Ms. Romanoff may be guilty of what is perhaps an inadvisable method of trying to bring your attention to the fact that the deceased was found in my basement, but she is in no way at fault for any more serious charge than that of moving a body."

"Oh goddess. You're talking to her." Tatiana's shoulders drooped. "Now you're doomed."

You have a very poor idea of me if you think that, he told her with a tenderness that was both new, and yet seemed to have been a part of him for eons. Just because he couldn't protect her as he ought to do, didn't mean he had to treat her poorly.

"I think we'll do our talking back at the office. Shall we?" The sheriff took Tatiana by the arm and hustled her down the alley.

Not of you—of the sheriff, Tatiana replied. *She works for the Municipal Entity, Finch. They are beyond dangerous for you.*

I assure you, Dark Ones are very resilient.

Not if the Entity outs you, Tatiana answered, her emotions once again out of his mental reach. It was as if she'd slammed shut a door, leaving him feeling bereft.

He thought of reassuring her there was little a small-town organization could do to him, but decided to hold that conversation for a later time, instead following the group while pulling out his phone and sending a text to the lawyer that Damon had recommended if one was needed.

A half hour later he sat down at a big ebony desk, one that almost entirely filled the sheriff's office. The room itself was stuffy, the air smelling of stale popcorn, a slight case of dry rot, and a popular wood soap. Outside the window, the building housing the city hall loomed, its shadow casting inky fingers across the floor of the sheriff's office.

For one fanciful moment, Finch felt as if the building was a living entity…one that was extremely aware of him.

"Now," the sheriff said, tapping on her laptop. "I've heard what Tit—er—Tatiana has said for herself. Perhaps you'd like to give your side of the story. Let's start with who you are."

Finch recited the facts of his assumed persona, and presented the sheriff with the documents that had been given him.

"Jeremy Renfrew," the sheriff said slowly, pursing her lips as she tapped on the laptop keyboard. "I thought I saw… ah. Yes. Here it is. It would appear that the governor has had some things to say about you. Must be nice to have such powerful friends."

"I am not acquainted with the governor," Finch answered truthfully. "Although I appreciate his interest in the matter. I assume that Tatiana and I are cleared of all charges?"

"I haven't laid any charges against you…yet," she said, slamming shut the lid.

Finch winced at such callous treatment of the laptop. He had a fondness for electronics.

"Tatiana Romanoff is another matter."

"She did not kill Ozymandra," he said primly, wishing he knew the woman's last name.

"No?" To his immense surprise, the sheriff gave a little shrug. "As to that, I'm in agreement. Tat doesn't have the wherewithal to lop off someone's head. She prefers to annoy them to death. That doesn't, however, explain how Ozy ended up in your basement."

"She was the former tenant," he pointed out. "Perhaps whoever killed her simply returned her to her home."

"Yees," the sheriff drawled, tapping her fingernails on the desk in a manner that made Finch feel like ants were crawling on his skin. "But I'm more interested in just what you and Tat were up to. Don't deny it was something—one of the deputies told me you are dating her. Not only that, but you didn't run screaming into the night after your dinner date, which puts you in a completely different camp than the other men she's blighted."

"My relationship has nothing to do with the situation concerning Ozymandra's death," he said calmly, his protective instincts firing up. For a moment, the quirky side of his mind, the one that always enjoyed the oddities that were mortals, admitted that he had a better understanding of his parents' relationship. He'd always assumed his father was the overly emotional partner, storming around making dark threats and outrageous declarations whenever he'd perceived a threat to his Beloved, but now…now Finch was starting to understand the emotions his father had felt.

What's going on in there? Tatiana asked. *Is she tying you to a stake and threatening you with heinous tortures that I can't name because if I do, I'll start to retch?*

No. She told me she knows you didn't kill Ozy, he answered.

She what?

"And yet…" The sheriff leaned forward, her eyes like hematite in sunlight. "And yet there's something about you. Something about you and Tat together. Who are you, Mr. Jeremy Renfrew?"

"I have provided you with as much documentation as I have," he said, trying to get a sense of whether the woman was something other than mortal. Unfortunately, the prickly awareness of city hall continued to fill his mind, leaving him unsure. "I am a writer who seeks peace and quiet."

Finch?

"And Ozy's shop? You're going to take over her business? Or are you handing it over to Tat? Deus knows she's wanted it long enough. Maybe you two arranged for it to become available to her, hmm?" There was a threat in her voice, but Finch wasn't sure if it was directed at him, or Tatiana.

OK, now you're freaking me out. Did she knock you unconscious?

No. He tried to keep the edge of annoyance to himself. *She's trying to pry into my past, and I keep being distracted by the way the city hall building is breathing at me.*

The silence that followed that statement was almost loud in its absence of thought.

"If there are no other questions that aren't pure speculation—false speculation, it need not be said—then I will collect Tatiana and return home," he said, getting to his feet. He cast another glance out the window at the dark shape of the city hall, the hairs on the back of his neck standing on end when he could have sworn that one of the gargoyles on the roofline swung its head around to look at him.

Tatiana's touch on his mind was evocative of an antelope approaching a watering hole. *Did you say the building is breathing at you?*

Yes. Don't you feel it?

"I don't believe I've released Tat," the sheriff said, her lips pursed in a petulant expression.

He pulled out his phone. "Then I will engage a lawyer on her behalf—"

"Fine." The sheriff got to her feet, and with a dark look at him, crab-walked sideways in the small space between the edge of the desk and the wall, shooing him before her. "I'll let her go, but I'm keeping the charge of tampering with a dead body. You're lucky that the deputy's familiar didn't find any evidence in your basement of either Ozy's death, or the method of her delivery to the premises, else there'd be charges regarding disturbing a crime scene, as well."

"The deputy's *familiar*?" he asked, searching his memories for those Wiccans he had met over his lifetime. He hadn't known one to have a familiar, but admittedly, he wasn't terribly well versed in their beliefs.

"Yes." The sheriff gave him a challenging look, obviously daring him to make an objection, before suddenly relaxing, and adding in a much less defensive tone, "It's her son Ray, actually. But she has always said the lord and lady blessed him at his birth with foresight, cunning, and empathy…and also, he's a semester shy of graduating with a forensic science degree, so if there was anything there, he'd find it."

Finch, are you sure that the sheriff hasn't done something hinky to you? Did you drink anything she gave you? Eat some mushrooms? Maybe had a little smoke of a fun herb?

I only drink blood, don't eat, and have found that the plant you are thinking of does not affect Dark Ones.

*Wow. That's kind of sad. But…*breathing *at you?*

I'm on my way. The sheriff is releasing you.

She cheered into his mind, and he waited a few minutes in the large central room into which two desks were arranged in front of a bank of antique filing cabinets; three heavy wooden benches lined the opposite wall. An elderly man was stretched out asleep on the first bench, while the second was occupied by a middle-aged woman who eyed him sourly.

He sat down on the third one, glancing at the clock, hoping it wouldn't take long for them to release Tatiana.

A swirl of salty air had him turning to watch as a man with short, curly cropped black hair entered the room, a large messenger bag slung across his body. His clothing was nondescript but rumpled, as if he'd slept in them. There were lines around the man's eyes and mouth that hinted he was close to exhaustion.

The man scanned the room, his gaze passing quickly over the others on the bench, pausing on Finch for a few seconds.

Finch cocked an eyebrow, but the man merely looked away, shuffling over to the reception desk where one of the Wiccans sat typing diligently on a keyboard.

"Hello. I was told that you would be able to direct me to one—"

"You must wait until called," the woman interrupted, and nodded toward the benches without lifting her gaze from the monitor.

The man appeared to ignore her, instead patting down the pockets of his beige jacket before starting on his navy-blue trousers. He clicked his tongue as he pulled out a handful of paper, quickly sorting through it. "Er…Jericho Taf is the name. If you could tell me—"

"You must wait until called," the Wiccan repeated.

The man glanced back at the others before appealing to the woman. "I don't need to see a police officer. I just need information about the mayor."

"Look," the Wiccan said, her head snapping up as she pinned the man back with a gaze that Finch mentally applauded. "I've told you twice. You. Must. Wait. Now go do that before I call my familiar to take care of you."

Finch wondered what a student in forensic science would do to the newcomer, but decided he didn't want to know. It was bad enough he studied mortals—he didn't need to be involved in their minor scuffles.

The man seemed to deflate for a few seconds, before squaring his shoulders, and with slow steps, took a seat next to Finch.

"I don't suppose you've seen a demi-god in the area?"

Finch, who was making a few mental notes for his chapter on doom scrolling, turned to look at the man next to him. The voice was pitched at an intimate volume.

"Pardon?" he asked, not sure that he heard him correctly.

"Demi-god," the man said, his lips barely moving as he slumped against the back of the bench, his eyes on the Wiccan at the desk.

"Why would you think I know a demi-god?" he asked.

"Well…you *are* a vampire," the man said.

Finch glanced beyond him to where the others sat, but the man's voice hadn't carried. Part of his mind was annoyed that evidently everyone recognized him for what he was, when he, himself, had no sense of other about the town.

Except the building next door.

"So have you seen one?" the man asked, wriggling his shoulders to make himself more comfortable, his head against the wall, and his eyes now closed.

"No, I haven't had the pleasure of meeting a demi-god. Er…would you mind me asking who you are?"

"Leonid of Corinth. But call me Leo. Most everyone does. I'm looking for the mayor. She's supposed to know about this demi-god. If you find her, would you let me know?" With a little grunt, the man named Leo rustled around in his breast coat pocket for a few seconds before he pulled out a battered card, and set it on the bench next to Finch. "It's important."

He took the card. "Are you with the Watch?"

"Not really. I'm the steward, personal assistant, and general dogsbody for Troy Ilios."

Finch's brows pulled together. That name seemed familiar. He poked through the distant, dusty memories of his past, when he was a child, and his father and uncle were teaching him about the history of Dark Ones.

"Troy Ilios…"

"Troy Ilios," Leo agreed. "Son of Simeois, and grandson of Oceanus and Tethys."

With a flash, memory of his youth returned, and Finch turned to stare at the man, who despite having his eyes closed, smiled at his reaction. "The lord of the Seventh Hour?"

"Thought you would know who he was."

Finch studied him, but even knowing that the man wasn't mortal, he couldn't pick up a sense of other about him. "Every Dark One knows the story of the four wealden, the thanes who started our race. Why are you here and not in the Hour if you work for the lord?"

"It's a long story, and not very interesting, frankly." He opened his eyes, turning his head enough to pierce Finch with a look filled with warning. "But if you see the mayor, it's vital you call me."

He was about to ask why, but at that moment, one of the smudgers emerged from a back room with Tatiana.

"—and see that you stay out of trouble, or I swear to the god and goddess that I'll sage you up one side and down the other, see if I don't," the woman said, giving Tatiana a quelling look.

"You do, and I'll start a new line of haunted dolls," Tatiana answered, biting off each word. "Ones all bearing your name and famed for misanthropic spirits who caught all sorts of venereal diseases in Victorian times."

"Oh!" the deputy said on a gasp, her eyes round. She held a hand to her chest as if protecting herself. "That's low, Titty! Very low."

"If the sage fits…er…" Tatiana paused for a few seconds before finishing, "Smudge it!"

"That makes no sense," the deputy snapped.

"I know, but I'm annoyed and tired from wrestling with a dead body, and Fin—Jeremy is waiting for me, so that's the best you're getting." Tatiana sailed past the sputtering deputy with her head held high, all the while saying, *Fly, you fool!*

Are we doing movie quotes now? he asked, getting to his feet while casting a hesitating glance toward Leo, who appeared to be asleep.

No. Maybe. Also, I really want to get you out of here.

Because you think I'm insane, or because you fear the sheriff?

"I don't fear her," she said, taking his arm and more or less pulling him from the building. Finch couldn't help but keep his gaze narrowed on the city hall building as they passed it, but it had evidently stopped breathing at him, and was now back to being just a building. "But as I said, she reports to the Municipal Entity, and they…well, they are a whole different kettle of fish. Thank you for getting me out, by the way. Do I owe you any bail money?"

"I would like to take credit for your release, but I didn't do much but threaten to hire a lawyer for you. I suspect the sheriff knew she had little to hold you on, and would have released you regardless. And no, there was no bail. Do you wish to go home?" he asked politely.

"What I wish is to have a bottle of wine, a comfy chair, and about a hundred questions answered."

"I can provide you with a chair, and what answers I know, but I don't have any wine."

She hesitated a moment, sliding him a glance out of the corner of her eyes. "Is that an invitation to go back to your place?"

His lips curved in a small smile, the sort he kept for those close to him. "Yes. I, too, have some questions I'd like answered."

She thought for a moment, then with a heavy sigh, slid her hand into his. "I'll go without the wine. My apartment is bound to be full of Clemmie making all sorts of statements. I take it she left earlier?"

"Right after we were fingerprinted," he said as they turned onto Axegate Walk. There were a few people out, mostly drifting down the pavement from the café, which evidently did a booming business at night.

He felt an odd tugging at something inside of him, a sensation he couldn't put a name to until he realized it was contentment. Right there, at that exact moment walking hand in hand with Tatiana, while anticipation buzzed around them filling the air with sexual tension, he was happy.

"Good."

"Yes. It is good," he agreed, making a decision that he felt he had moved toward since the moment he'd met her. He wouldn't bind Tatiana to him as a Beloved, but he owed it to her to protect her. Now that he saw for himself that someone clearly had ill intentions toward her, he could do no less than to offer his help when it was needed. He ignored the mental comment that such protection would, naturally, require him to maintain close contact with her, and she would be hurt if he didn't give in to their shared need. He'd just have to keep them from fulfilling all seven steps of Joining. "This may be a bit premature, but since we have a block to go, perhaps we can address the subject now—do you have a form of birth control that you are using, or would you prefer that I equip myself?"

She stopped dead, causing him to swing back toward her when he realized she'd done so. "Wow. You just came right out there with it."

"Yes." A moment of disquiet caused him to add, "Was that rude? Do you not feel the sexual attraction between us? It is common with Dark Ones and their Beloveds, as I have mentioned."

"Oh, I feel it." She slid a glance toward the fly of his jeans, which instantly made his penis aware of the situation, and started putting its full effort into not disappointing either of them. "I've felt it ever since I fed you. That was…hoo! And the answer is yes, I have an implant."

Once again, he felt over his head, this time confused as well, but in addition, contrite. It was not an enjoyable cocktail of emotions. "I apologize for being so forthright with sexual discussions."

"You know, you have the most intriguing ability to sound like you are something out of a Merchant Ivory film, all stuffy British upper-class Victorian, but tempered with a sexy, sexy vampire." Tatiana's smile warmed all the dark recesses of his soul, but just made his confusion more profound. Did she want him to speak his mind, or was she seeking a more traditional approach to a sexual relationship?

"What do you want me to do?" he asked, hoping she didn't hear the thread of desperation in his voice.

"Wow, that was seriously blue," she said, shooting him little sideways glances as she continued to stroll down the boardwalk.

"Pardon?"

"Blue is sexy. Or rather, aroused." Her fingers tightened on his, causing a corresponding warmth to spread across his chest at the same time the flow of his blood seemed to halt in its business of keeping him alive, and instead head straight for his groin.

"I'm confused," he admitted. He didn't like the sensation of this perpetual state of uncertainty that claimed him whenever he was around her.

"About the sheriff? Yeah, she has that effect on people—"

No, about whether or not you want me to speak frankly regarding the fact that I wish to make love to you all the while you are thinking about things so erotic, my brain is about to shut down in order to divert all energy to my penis.

She laughed in his head. *Sorry, was I projecting that bit about rubbing you with chocolate cake and licking it off of you?*

"Yes." He thought for a second. "Although I'm sure I'd like the licking, I hesitate in having you spread food across my body. For one, how hygienic is it? Mortals always seem to be getting ill from food, and I would not be happy knowing that you were potentially getting an illness from consuming it off my body. And for another, we'd have to conduct such activities in a location that was not a bed."

Tatiana stopped again, staring at him with a slightly opened mouth that drew his gaze until he felt like he was going to explode if he didn't taste it.

He was just about to do so, leaning in to claim her mouth, when a man who was passing stopped to say, "Got yourself a love poppet, do you, Tat? Have you told him that all your dates end up in disaster? Why don't you send him to my shop where I can make him a protective amulet so he doesn't end up like all the others who were subjected to the Curse of Tat's twa—"

"Eff off, Neil," Tatiana snapped, grasping Finch by the lapels of his jacket, and pulling him forward until their bodies were pressed together, her mouth as hot as an inferno on his. Hunger roared to life within him, joining the inferno of need and want and something soft and warm that he didn't want to look at.

"Who's that?" came another voice, this one a woman's.

"Not sure. Oh, it's that new man, the one who had dinner with Tatty," a second woman answered.

"Really?" the first woman asked. "She had a date that didn't end in dismemberment or a psych ward admission? Wait, is that her?"

"Yup," the second woman answered. "Honestly, the nerve of some people kissing newcomers right here in the middle of the street. The Entity ought to do something about that."

Tatiana sighed into his mind.

"We'd better go. I don't want to stay and be witness to whatever horrible thing is going to happen to him. My cousin Serena still talks about the time she was trying to buy one of Tat's haunted dolls, and a man's unattached leg rolled down the stairs and hit her on the ankle."

The voices moved past them. Finch was about to break off what was truly an epic kiss when Tatiana moved against him, a little wriggle of her hips as if she was trying to get closer to him. His body responded with demands of its own.

"—and I really think you need to take some concrete actions—sheesh, Tat, get a room. What? No, it's just my next door neighbor Tat on the street kissing some man. I don't know. No, I'm not going to ask, for one thing, they're still kissing, and for another, you know I'm the least nosy person around. Now, about your problem with your ex, you absolutely should go for the hex package and blight that bastard with a warty dick—"

The voice moved off, clearly a woman talking into a phone.

Is the boardwalk always this busy at this time of night? he asked.

No. This is unprecedented. I think it's part of how fate is picking on me.

Once again, he was about to stop the kiss, feeling that it was better conducted in the privacy of his room, but just then, Tatiana swirled her tongue around his, and he moaned into her mind.

"Now, that's what I'm talking about."

Finch pulled back from the lure of Tatiana, his mind momentarily overwhelmed with emotions. The fact that he couldn't immediately pigeon-hole his feelings added to the sense of being adrift, out of control, and as helpless as a leaf swirling along the surface of a swollen river.

Clemmie passed them with a grin aimed at Tatiana, and added, "Glad they let you out. Jeremy Finch said they would, but I wasn't so sure. I'll lock up the shop after me, shall I?"

Dark as it was, Finch could see the color on Tatiana's cheeks deepen as she answered, "That's probably for the best."

"Gotcha," she said, spreading her grin to Finch. "Yell if you need any help. Well, not with—you know. I mean, you're in your forties, so by now you probably know what you're doing, Tat. I don't know how old Jeremy Finch is. Er…"

"My age isn't relevant," he told her. "Any more than Tatiana's is."

"Night, Clemmie," Tatiana said with a firm note in her voice, and taking Finch's arm, steered him toward the front door of his shop.

He said nothing until they got inside, making sure to lock the front door. He found Tatiana in the kitchen, staring at the door to the basement, now closed.

"I know this is going to sound weird, but do you mind if we check down there?" she asked.

"Not at all. I was going to do so anyway." He trotted down the stairs; everything looked the same in the basement, although he noted the boxes had been put back into formation. Evidently the deputy's son appreciated a tidy environment, too.

"No bodies. Good. Er…should we go upstairs?" Tatiana sounded hesitant, but considering she was still thinking about licking him, Finch decided she would appreciate him taking charge.

"We should if you don't want me to strip you naked, and make love to you on the boxes," he said pleasantly, fighting with the need that had been building within him ever since her mouth had touched his.

"Oooh." She looked speculatively at the boxes for a few seconds, then gave a little resigned bob of her head. "Tempting as an unusual spot for hooking up is, we probably shouldn't. I mean, there's the whole cursed basement vibe going on, not to mention it's pretty disrespectful, what with Ozy and all."

He wondered if he should point out that he hadn't been at all serious about the offer, but decided that if she had a desire to indulge in sex in out-of-the-way places, he would try to accommodate her. But he drew the line at exhibitionism.

That's fine with me, she said, marching up the stairs. *I'm not into that, either.*

He watched her ass with great pleasure, enjoying the way her hips moved. He'd always had a weakness for a woman's hips, and Tatiana's were particularly splendid, to the point where they made him harder than he remembered being for a long time.

"So, this is your room," she said a short while later, as she stood in the bedroom, and considered first the small table that served as his desk, the wingback chair upholstered in faded, but intricate, embroidery, and the large brass bed.

"It is, although nothing but the laptop, my clothing, and the bedlinens are mine," he said, studying her, confused once again by the emotions he was feeling. This time, however, he realized they were hers. "Tatiana, do you not wish to do this? I assure you that I have never asked a sexual partner to do anything they are not comfortable doing, and if you prefer to take more time to become acquainted, then I will give you that time."

She stopped staring at the bed, and turned her gaze onto him. He felt the effect of those smoky eyes caressing his face, the burn in his soul threatening to consume him. "Would you really?"

"Yes," he said, wanting to add that it might very well kill him, but he refused to put any sort of pressure on her. She was his Beloved—even if he couldn't claim her as such—and although fate conspired to make them attractive to each other, he knew on a primitive level that his reaction to her went deeper than that.

He'd met her the day before, and yet she consumed his thoughts, filled his being with light, and made him feel like he'd been living a shadow of his real self until she'd stumbled across his path, her shining soul and playful spirit enchanting him despite the knowledge that he could never bind himself to her.

About that, he would never change his mind. He would die before he allowed Tatiana to suffer.

"Why do I feel like you're having a conversation with yourself?" Tatiana asked, sitting down on the edge of the bed. "I can feel you thinking things, but they're all dark, like you are hiding them. Also, I do want you to do all the things I was thinking earlier, and since I see you are a bit bulgy in the fly department, I assume you want to, as well, so maybe you could sit next to me and we can proceed."

He sat, grimaced at the pain of his jeans strained across his groin, then stood up and with quick, efficient movements, removed his clothing, folding them and placing them on a yellow art deco dresser that sat in the corner of the room.

"OK, that was good," Tatiana said when he retook his seat next to her. Her eyes were wide, her pupils huge, and she panted a little. "I particularly liked it when you leaned over to put your shoes under the chair. Your butt, Finch."

"What about it?" he asked, unable to keep from looking over his shoulder in a misguided attempt to see his own ass. "If it's hairy, I apologize. My father was born in Hungary, and was fairly hirsute. My mother used to joke about being mated to a bear rather than a man, but that it was nothing a sharp razor and a large bucket of shaving soap couldn't take care of."

Tatiana's gaze snapped up from where it was caressing his chest to his face. "Sounds like your mom had a good sense of humor. Also, your butt isn't hairy. Your chest is, but I like it. It's not 1970s porn star sort of hairy, but enough to make me feel very feminine next to you."

His gaze dropped to her chest. "May I assist you in disrobing?"

She laughed, the sound washing over him with a sense of giddiness that most likely had a lot to do with the fact that no blood whatsoever was reaching his brain since it was all busy encouraging his erection to achieve new levels of hardness. Even his testicles felt tight. "Seriously, when you talk like you're straight out of *Downton Abbey*, it makes me melt inside. Yes, I would very much like help. There's a zipper in the back."

To his delight, she stood and turned around, presenting him with her back, swinging her hair out of the way.

He had the zipper down, and the dress off her before she could do more than utter an, "If you could—"

He placed the dress on the chair, then stood in front of her, reveling in the sight of her bare hips. Her breasts also drew some admiration, as did her woman's mound as highlighted in the pink undergarments that were apparently made almost entirely of lace, but it was the hips that made him feel as if his entire body was alight.

And that triggered the hunger. Since he'd taken receipt of a shipment of blood from his uncle's source earlier in the evening, he hadn't thought he was in need of feeding, but the second Tatiana bared herself to him, the need was back.

No, not just back—it consumed him.

"Wow, you're really—I mean, you look good in jeans, but seeing you standing there—" Her gaze dropped to his penis, her eyes widening a little.

"I apologize for that," he said, unable to tear his eyes from the lush sweep of her hips, the curve of her waist, the perfect roundness of her thighs and breasts and arms. "You take my breath away, Tatiana. How can you even think that you aren't exquisite?"

"I'm forty-three, Finch." Her hands fluttered around her belly. "I used to run, but then things started hurting, so I switched to swimming, but then the pool closed because one day it was filled with lobsters, and no one was able to figure out who'd switched it to a salt water pool, or how to get the lobsters to vacate other than scooping them up and dumping them back in the ocean, but that didn't work because they'd kept reappearing the next day, and then the only other choice was to eat them, and people here don't do that because, well, these were really old lobsters, and it's just wrong to eat something that's lived for eighty or ninety years. Plus, they seem to like the pool, and now the Entity has made it a whole big tourist thing. Why are you staring at my belly? Is it the stretch marks? It is, isn't it? I'm sorry about those, but as I said, I had to stop swimming, and…well…"

"I love your belly. I love your marks. I love everything about you, especially the line of your hips," he said, trying hard to keep from sounding like a man who was desperate to bury himself in her heat.

"Oooh. I like the sound of that. OK, I'm going to peel off the rest."

"May I help?" he asked, only barely keeping from pouncing on her, and that was solely because he wanted her to be comfortable.

Her smile seemed to light up the room as she spread her hands. "Sure."

A moment later his hands were smoothing down the line from her rib cage to her hips, his mind giving a mental moan as her warm flesh filled his mind. *Christos, woman. You are a goddess personified.*

Oooh, it's like your hands are made of fire, she thought, doing a little wiggle that he thought might just end him. He slid the lace undergarment off her, possessing his hands of the delightful roundness of her ass.

If I am made of fire, it's because you turn my blood into an inferno of need, he said.

"You're hungry, too," she said, reaching behind and unhooking her bra, which she tossed in the direction of the chair. "Is it…is it going to hurt like it did before?"

He froze in the act of pulling her against him so that he could breathe in her scent, the need to taste and touch her driving all other thoughts from his mind. He searched her face. "I hurt you?"

"When you bit me outside the city hall. It was over quick, so it wasn't too bad, but if it's going to get worse—"

"I will make sure that you are feeling too much pleasure to even notice the bite," he promised, and with his body tight and hard and other words implying a granite state that he didn't have the energy to summon, he lifted her, his mouth on hers as he set her down in the center of the bed.

"How are you going to do—" She arched up even as he slid one hand up her inner thigh, parting her legs so he could lean down and allow his whiskers to tickle them as he kissed his way up toward her woman's parts. She gasped, her hands clutching the blanket, her thighs quivering as he devoted himself to pushing her arousal to a point where she wouldn't care about a moment of pain.

He let his fingers dance in flesh that he felt would be receptive to such touches. She froze for a second, then her hips bucked as she gasped, her pleasure filling his mind. He kissed a path along her leg, then slid a finger into her as he bit her thigh, bracing himself in case she felt the bite.

"Goddess above and below," she said on another gasp, her inner muscles tightening around him. "This…the way you're drinking…and your fingers…"

Is it too much? he asked, ready to weep with the joy of it all, the sensation of feeding coiled around him, mingling with his body's demand to finish the job.

"Yes… no… Please, do it again…" Her hips, those beautiful, enticing hips, were too much for him, and after swirling his tongue over the bite, he moved upward, gathering her legs as he went, surging inside her, trusting that her excitement made her ready for him.

Oh, so much more than ready. I was ready when I saw your pretty eyes. Bite me, Finch…

I just did, he answered, wondering at the fact that he was able to think even as he plunged, and thrust, and reveled in her heat.

I know. But do it again…

You might feel a moment of discom—

DO IT AGAIN! she all but yelled in his head.

He moved her legs up to his shoulders, and bent down, his breath steaming her shoulder even as her scent wrapped around his head, sinking into his body and soul, binding him to her in a way that he had no idea was possible.

Now, Finch, do it now, she demanded, and he felt her trembling on the edge of a climax.

He couldn't resist. Every last shred of his control, of his intentions to simply engage in lovemaking, but no more, dissolved before her pleasure. He bit her shoulder, the heady, spicy rush of her blood pushing him almost to the point of no bearing. And when she gasped out his name, her body spasming around him, her nails digging into his back, he let himself find his own completion.

"That," Tatiana said several minutes later, breathing almost as heavily as he was, "was beyond impressive. You get several gold stars, an A++ rating, and a testimonial to the effectiveness of your hip action."

Finch laughed as he disengaged himself, rolling off her and onto his back, one part of his mind still reveling in the experience, while the other part, the more analytical side, wondered at the fact that she had tickled his sense of humor. He was a scholar, a man of serious mien, one who did not laugh at something so ridiculous as an A++ rating, and yet there he was, almost giddy with happiness.

When was the last time he'd been truly happy?

"Finch?" Tatiana scooted over, draping one leg over him as she put a hand on his chest. "Is something wrong? Why are you suddenly sad?"

"I was thinking that the last time I was happy was when I was a child, and my parents were alive."

She was silent, and although she hid her thoughts, he could feel her withdraw emotionally. He rolled onto his side, pulling her into his arms, kissing the top of her head. *Until now, that is.*

She melted into him, her body warm and soft and so right, that for a second, he felt a burn of tears behind his eyes. He'd never thought to have a Beloved—he didn't need one, as his friend Ivo had told him so often when they were young men—but now he realized just how wrong that idea was.

He needed Tatiana in his life. He couldn't imagine what sort of a bleak future lay before him if it did not include her saying outrageous things, performing hare-brained schemes, and making plans for his body that were so erotic, he might not survive them. She was his Beloved, and no amount of denial could change that fact.

But that didn't mean he'd offer her up on that altar of tragedy.

His soul wept with the knowledge that in the end, he couldn't have his cake and eat it, too.

TEN

"I think I'll take one of those sour cream apple bars, Billie." I bit my lower lip as I eyed the selections. "And a pain au chocolat, of course."

"Of course," Billie said with a roll of her eyes. She had a tendency to make comments about refined sugars and what they did to the metabolism, but I ignored her. She worked in a bakery, after all. "Is this the boyfriend? Heard you had one who didn't immediately combust, drop off a limb, lose his mind, or run away to become a monk. Also heard the sheriff pulled you in last night because you guys were having sex on the sidewalk."

"What? No!" I shot a look at Finch, who stood next to me texting someone. "We did no such thing."

"Yeah? Well, word on the street is that you were all over a tall, dark, British dude last night." Billie stuffed my choices into a small paper bag and slapped them down with undue force on the counter, giving Finch an overly warm stare to which, fortunately, he was oblivious.

"I'm not British," Finch said, not looking up from his texting. "I simply sound as if I were."

"Jeremy will have a lemon ginger scone," I told Billie, pinning her back with a look that I hope made several points about people who ogled other people's nooky partners. "And a cream cheese brownie."

"You're going to explode if you eat all that sugar," Billie told me, but stuffed the requested items into the bag.

"I said they were for Fi—Jeremy." I waved my hand toward him. "Not me."

"Dude," she said in a drawling tone that made my back itch. "That man has clearly never had a refined carb in his life."

Finch said nothing.

I glared at him.

Why are you annoyed? She's not wrong, he said.

No, but you don't need to stand there looking so gorgeous and sexy and non-carb-eating when some of us have to keep our blood factory going.

Finch shot me a questioning look. *Are you feeling unwell? Did I take too much this morning? You said there was no pain, but perhaps you weren't up to feeding me after last night.*

I'm fine, just hungry, and felt I deserved a bit of sugar after our sexual calisthenics. "He very much does eat, thank you. Oh, and two lattes, please. One decaf, and one...er..." I glanced at Finch.

He cocked an eyebrow at me, then said, "Please make mine without caffeine as well."

I smiled.

You cannot have caffeine?

Nope. I have a thing with my esophagus that means no caffeine.

Billie looked like she wanted to argue with me, but after one last, overly-long look at Finch, bustled over to the coffee machine, and made the lattes.

"Do you mind if I poke through Ozy's stuff?" I asked a half hour later, when we were back at his shop, and I had consumed both coffees and the treats.

"I don't mind, but I assure you that I saw nothing out of the ordinary when I packed the boxes," he answered, eyeing the basement door.

"I know, but I really want to make sure there's nothing that explains why she had such a vendetta against me."

I paused, and then added, "And, of course, why she was killed."

"Or who did the act itself," he said, glancing at his phone when it pinged. "I have a call to take. Will you be all right in the basement by yourself?"

"Of course," I said, wondering why he was suddenly concerned when I broke in to rifle through Ozy's stuff last night, then realized he was being protective.

It warmed me to the tips of my toes, almost as much as the warm, blossoming glow in my chest of something that felt very much like love. I wasn't at all surprised that I was falling in love with him—I'd had an inkling I was heading that way the first time I saw him—but now the emotion had deepened, filling in spaces around my heart that I hadn't known needed filling. It was like all my past love affairs were pale, washed-out imitation of the real thing. This love, the Finch love, was a glorious technicolor version in a world of black and white.

And he wasn't in the least little bit harmed, or showing signs he'd go off the deep end, mentally. Maybe the curse was broken?

"I'll be in my room—come get me if you feel uneasy. I would like to make a few notes after the call, but am happy to forgo that if you need me."

I glanced at the clock above the small sink. "I don't think I will, and in fact, I believe I can help you a bit. There's two hours before we have to open, and I'll have Clemmie come over and we'll pack up Ozy's things in the front room for you. That'll let me be snoopy while also getting her stuff boxed up. Does that sound OK?"

"If you like," he said, obviously distracted.

I wondered who his phone call was with that sucked up so much of his attention, but didn't feel like I could ask him. Everything was still too new, and although I knew he liked me, and we had a major sexy chemistry thing going on, I wasn't sure how comfortable he was with me prying into his personal business.

"Be patient," I told myself as I trotted down the stairs to the basement, pausing to text Clemmie to come over as soon as she could. "You've only known him a couple of days. Right, Ozy, let's see what sorts of things you left behind."

Clemmie showed up about twenty minutes later, when I emerged from the basement covered in dust, the remnants of cobwebs from poking around the non-Ozy boxes, and with a fine appreciation for the tidy job of packing that Finch had done. I washed my hands and greeted Clemmie, who was sitting on the table in the front room. "I take it you are no worse for wear after last night's shenanigans?"

"Me? You know I don't get hangovers," she said with a bright smile, her hair tied up in two balls on the top of her head. "How about you? You look like a cat who not only ate the cream, but milked the cow as well."

"That is an odd simile, although not terribly wrong. I told Finch we'd pack up the rest of Ozy's things, the ones out here. You up for that?"

"Sure, although no one is answering the phone in case someone back east gets their time zones wrong," she said, gathering up the empty boxes I'd stacked on one of the chairs earlier. "How is Mr. Handsome Vampire?"

I flinched as I opened up the drawer to the table where Ozy read crystals. "I was kind of hoping you'd forget that fact about him. I don't suppose you could?"

"Are you kidding?" She gathered a handful of various business cards that I had glanced through and set on the table, tidied them, and placed them in an empty shoebox. "My cousin is dating a vampire. A living, breathing, bloodsucking vampire. Wait—he does breathe, doesn't he? He doesn't look pale and ghostly like the guys in the movies."

"That's because those aren't real vamps. Man, Ozy really did love her office supplies." It took five minutes to scan each of the approximately hundred Post-it notes in the desk, before giving them to Clemmie. There was nothing there other that a few jotted phone numbers of other merchants on Axegate Walk—myself included—and names of clients as well as the amount charged for readings. Evidently she used the notes as a ledger.

The rest of the drawer was empty.

How is it going? Finch asked.

Fine. Ozy's desk is full of stickies. Nothing exciting.

I believe I told you there was nothing of interest.

Uh huh. Are you still taking notes? I wanted to ask him about his phone call, but decided to leave that. It wasn't any of my business unless he wanted to tell me about it.

It would drive me nuts until he saw fit to do so, but I'd just have to survive until that time.

Yes, I'm fleshing out an outline regarding the inefficiency of the sheriff's office, and what she could do to improve both processing time, and interaction with those detained.

I was silent for a few minutes as Clemmie and I took down Ozy's framed posters and wrapped them in a stack of towels I'd brought up from the basement. *That's...helpful,* I said at last.

I hope so. Mortals so often surround themselves with chaos. I like to think I can provide them with an alternative way to live.

There wasn't much I could say to that, so I kept my giggles to myself, and finished packing up Ozy's various bowls of crystals, informative pamphlets, assorted sundries, and finally, stopped in front of the fez-wearing skeleton.

"Do you think Jeremy Finch would let us keep him?" Clemmie asked, her head tipped to the side as she considered the skeleton. "He would be awesome in the window scenarios."

"He's not Finch's to give away," I said, mulling over the idea. "But maybe the sheriff knows who Ozy's heir is. Until then, we'd better pack him up."

I reached for the fez, and something small clattered down the back of the skeleton and slid under his chair.

It was a phone. I sat on my heels after scrabbling under the chair to retrieve it, staring at the object, gnawing my lower lip at the dilemma that presented itself to me.

"Why would someone put a phone in a skeleton's hat?" Clemmie asked, stuffing the hat and skelly into a box.

"It's a hiding place, obviously," I answered, then damning my moral values, turned on the phone and quickly flipped through the screens. There was nothing in the call log, and only one message thread, sent to a number that looked foreign.

The first text was simple enough.

ME
They are here, Morwyl.

Two days later, there were a couple more.

ME
Deacon is helping Angharad. They don't recognize me, but he is seeking sacrifices. They clearly want to bring forth Rhain.

ME
I will alert the Court of Divine Blood that I have located them. I don't know how Angharad managed to free Deacon from the Seventh Hour, but I will find out.

Then the last message was dated three weeks ago, right before Ozy went missing.

ME
Morwyl? I have found the women. I fear Angharad, coupled with the sacrifices, would have enough power to release Rhain should she find the right spell. I'm going to rescue the women tonight, but you may need to help me deal with Angharad since the Court refuses to involve itself.

"What on earth?" I said slowly as I scrolled back to re-read the messages. Clemmie put her chin on my shoulder to read them as well.

"Who's Angharad?" she asked.

"I have no clue, but evidently, she's working with Deacon. Holy shit—he really is intending on summoning an old god!" Fear rolled around in my belly, along with a slight case of panic.

"Is the old god the one named Rhain?" Clemmie staggered forward a step when I hurried toward the door.

"Again, no clue, but I'm sure as hell going to find out—ack!"

I was looking back at Clemmie when I yanked open the front door of Finch's shop, and didn't see Jericho Taf until I almost ran her down.

"If you wouldn't mind not trampling me first thing in the morning," Jerry said, looking down her nose at me. She was very tall, about six foot one, with long butt-length blond hair, and a narrow, ageless face. She also spoke with a faint accent that I had always assumed was English.

"Sorry," I said, backing up a couple of steps so she could enter the shop. I slid Ozy's phone into my pocket, and tried hard to look innocent of all wrongdoings. "Did you want something?"

"Many things, as it happens, but none that you are able to provide me." She spoke with her usual cool disdain. For some reason that always irritated me, she made me feel like I was a child in trouble with the principal. I had the worst urge to scurry to the nearest chair and stare at my shoes, but instead, tried to look poised and confident when she glanced around the room, not even acknowledging Clemmie. "I heard that you had decided to cohabitate with the town's newest bachelor after practically having sex with him on the Walk. Naturally, there's nothing I can do to prevent the poor man suffering from your attentions—other than warning him that he is taking his life in his hands, which I will do at the earliest possibility—but at least finding you here will save me from having to undergo any further action than giving you this."

She shoved a piece of paper at me, and turned to leave.

"What's this...*herewith and henceforth the tenant known as Tatiana Romanoff shall be removed from the lease of #67 Axegate Walk, in the premises known as Three Wyrd Sisters Haunted Curios, effective noon on the eighth of June.* What the hell? You're kicking us out? I knew you didn't like me, Jerry, but seriously? You're kicking us out?"

"It's nothing to do with me," Jericho said, pausing at the door, her hair swinging as she glanced back. She looked like a shampoo model, a golden glow around her from the sunshine streaming in through the door. "It's the Municipal Entity. They have decided they do not wish to rent to someone who is clearly involved with the death of Ozy."

"That's bullshit and you know it," I stormed, shaking the paper at her. There was a lot more legalese on it—and I noticed it was written in a dark reddish-brown ink that made me twitch with its similarity to dried blood—but I didn't bother reading it. "I didn't have anything to do with the death. The sheriff wouldn't have let me go if she thought I was guilty."

"There's guilty...and then there's *guilty*," Jericho said, giving her hair a flip.

"There's also such a thing as state tenant laws!" I marched to the door and flung that last sentence after her despite the tourists that were starting to wander up and down the boardwalk.

She lifted a dismissive hand, and I heard her say, "Pish. The Entity doesn't abide by laws other than their own. You have twenty-four hours."

"She can't do that, can she?" Clemmie asked, worry evident in the pink tinge to her voice.

I didn't answer right away, not knowing what to say. I wanted to ask Finch what he thought, but felt bad that I'd disturbed him so much with my problems, and the fact that he'd had to sweet talk the sheriff into letting me go—I knew she wouldn't have done it without his intervention, despite what he said—solidified my intention to deal with the situation without bothering him. "I kind of suspect she can. Or rather, even if it's not legal, the Entity is going to back her up, and we can't go against them."

"Go against who?"

We both turned around when Finch emerged from the kitchen, his hair delightfully tousled, and an abstracted expression on his adorable face. And his eyes, oh those glorious eyes, they all but smoldered topaz blue heat at me.

"We're being kicked out," Clemmie said before I could think how to phrase the situation. She'd gone from looking mildly scared to annoyed. "By the Entity. Can you believe it? What are we going to do? All the shops are rented, and today is day one of tourist season. Will we be able to find somewhere else?"

"What grounds does your landlord have for evicting you?" Finch asked, moving next to me. I wanted to fling myself on him, but instead, handed him the letter Jerry had given me. He scanned it quickly. "This appears to be legal, although I'd like to compare it with your contract to ensure the clauses they are quoting are valid."

"It doesn't matter," I said, stiffening my resolve to keep from slumping into a ball and weeping. "It was issued by the Entity. It's bound to be down to the letter of the law. Their documents always are. It's over. They've won. Ozy won. She wanted to turn the whole town against me, and she's succeeded. They'll run me out and I'll lose my livelihood, and my friends, and my boon, and…everything."

"I doubt if it's as grim as that," Finch said, putting an arm around me. I leaned into him, taking comfort in his nearness. He was so solid, so warm, that for a moment, I forgot about the hell that my life had become.

Do not despair, he said.

You aren't the one who is about to be homeless.

And neither are you. "The answer, of course, is for you to move your shop here." He gestured toward the front window. "I have no need of a storefront, and since you do, you might as well use it. Your Entity can't evict me since I hold a lease from the owner of the store."

"Would you really let us do that?" I asked as Clemmie gave a little cheer, and immediately set about hauling the boxes we'd packed down to the basement. "And is it horrible of me to admit that I was hoping you'd take pity on us and let us park here for a little bit while I tried to find us some other place to live?"

"It's not horrible in the least," he said, but I felt him thinking things beyond my reach. "You are very welcome to stay as long as you like."

I tipped my head to the side as I considered him. "And if I promised to keep Clemmie out of your hair so you can work on your book during the day? Would that stop you from thinking all those dark thoughts that are rolling around in your brain? I know she seems like a giddy twenty-year-old...well, she is, but she's a nice girl. And she likes you."

"I'm not in the least thinking dark thoughts about you and Clemmie moving in. I'm concerned about something completely unrelated, but it need not have you worried."

Really? Because I'm feeling like you are upset that I'm here.

He pulled me up against him, glancing toward the kitchen, but Clemmie was still in the basement. His hands were on my hips as his lips teased mine. *Sweetheart, I have many thoughts about you being near me, but I assure you they are anything but dark. What do you think of those oils that mortals use to make each other slide around on each other?*

I laughed, and after giving him a swift kiss at the sound of Clemmie clomping up the stairs, backed up and said softly, "I'll definitely have to pick some up."

"We've got a lot to do if we're going to move our shop here," Clemmie said, standing with her hands on her hips while surveying the room. "Honestly, if I didn't fear disappearing like all those others who crossed the Entity, I'd go to the town hall right now and demand that they lay off of Tat."

"People have disappeared?" Finch asked.

"Four women in Ravenfall, and two others from Raven's Bay," Clemmie explained. "Tat knew one of them, a woman who loved her possessed Jane Austen doll series."

"She went to college with me—oh!" I looked at Clemmie. "Six women who disappeared. I wonder if that's what Ozy was talking about?"

"You're right!" Clemmie did an excited jig. "Clues! We have clues!"

"I have no idea what's going on," Finch complained in a mild tone, one that was green tipped with gold.

"We found a phone under the fez," I explained, gesturing toward the box now containing the skeleton. "All that was on it were a few text messages, clearly between Ozy and someone named Morwyl. She mentioned Deacon and missing women, and another woman with a long Irish name, and a plan to get someone else released."

"Gotta be a jailbreak plan," Clemmie said. "And Deacon was going to sacrifice the women somehow. Sex trafficking, do you think? Trading the poor women for help in releasing his jailbird buddy?"

"Possibly," I said slowly. "Although would he need to summon an Old God if he was going to deal in human trafficking?"

"This is all very confusing," Finch said, holding out his hand. "Might I see the texts?"

"Sure—" I was about to hand it to him, but his phone sang a song from a popular musical. He glanced at it, and excused himself with a murmur that he had to take the call.

"He sure gets a lot of mysterious calls," I said, watching him as he disappeared into the kitchen, and I heard him run lightly up the stairs. "That's the second one this morning."

"You think he's two-timing you?" Clemmie asked, picking up the last of the boxes.

"No." I thought for a moment, then shook my head and repeated, "No. He's not that sort of man. But I'd dearly love to know why he keeps getting these calls."

"Ask him," Clemmie advised, then toddled off with the boxes.

"If it was only that easy," I said to myself. *Clemmie and are I going to move the shop stuff over here, so if you want to work, I'll keep her downstairs with me. We'll do our clothing and the rest later, after the shop is closed, if that's OK with you.*

Do you need help? he asked.

No, we're fine. We'll just bring the most popular stuff now, and get the rest later. You do your writing thing.

Very well, he said in a reluctant grey tone. *I have been sorely remiss on working on my book.*

Is…er…I don't want to be nosy, but is everything OK? With whoever called you?

Yes.

He didn't say more, but I could feel an odd mixture of emotions—regret, hesitancy, and oddly, a sense of guilt, but knowing the relationship was still in its early stages, I decided to let him be. He'd tell me when he was comfortable.

And if he wasn't comfortable enough to do so in the very near future, I'd just help him along.

ELEVEN

Clemmie and I put up a sign on the door to our shop saying we were moving to Finch's, and put the landline on forward to my cell phone.

Are you sure you don't need me? I'm happy to help you move, Finch said in mid-move.

No, I told you I wasn't going to let our being roomies interfere with your work. You stay there and write, and we'll be as quiet as possible.

That's thoughtful of you, but I don't mind—

Nope! You write. We'll move. Clemmie is strong as an ox.

We spent a grueling four hours packing up as much of the shop as we could while answering questions from residents, dealing with tourists who were curious about the stock as they saw us ferrying it down the street on a borrowed wheelbarrow, and discussing in rare quiet moments what we should do about Ozy's odd text messages.

"I think we should go straight to Jerry," Clemmie said as she started stocking one of the two metal racks we'd hauled over. I was busy making a sign to hang on Finch's door, alerting tourists to our new digs.

"Jerry? Why her?" I asked.

"Because she's the mayor. And Deacon bought the café from her."

I gave her a long look. "That doesn't mean she knows about him kidnapping six women and intending on sacrificing them to an old god."

"It doesn't mean she *doesn't* know about it," Clemmie said in a confusing sentence that took me a couple of seconds to work through.

"True, but even if she was involved, you know how she is. She'd deny everything while making you feel like an idiot for even suspecting her of wrongdoing." I looked up when I heard the ceiling creak. It sounded like Finch was pacing the length of the bedroom. Probably his literary muse was disturbed by us being below. I'd tried to be as quiet as possible, but it was inevitable that some of the sound of us moving boxes and setting up the haunted items had filtered through to him.

I made a mental note to make it up to him later, in a real and tangible way.

His voice caressed my brain with foresty green warmth. *Why are you smiling at me?*

I was just thinking how I was going to make up to you for the fact that we're disturbing your writing time.

You aren't doing anything of the sort.

I said nothing, sure he was being nice.

What sorts of things are you planning to do? he asked, his curiosity tangible from a floor away.

If I have time to hit up the Touch-a Touch-a Touch Me shop, something with some massage oil.

I look forward to that, he said with a few erotic images of him using it on my hips and belly.

I melted inside at the fact that he thought my problem areas were so enticing. Past romantic partners had never insulted my appearance, but with Finch, I knew he meant everything he said. And thought.

It was both arousing, and heartwarming.

"She might," Clemmie continued. "OK, she probably would deny it, but still, I like the idea of showing her Ozy's texts and asking her if she knows what's up with Deacon."

Clemmie took a step back as she dusted her hands on her legs, eyeing the arrangement of haunted snow globes, demonically possessed antique glass doorknobs (we'd done a roaring business in those ever since a divorce revenge site had listed them as an ideal gift to send to an ex), and rolled up bespelled paper drawings of a gingerbread man that she'd titled Paper Voodoo Dolls.

"I think—drat, now I have a smudge on the word Wyrd—I think I'd rather tackle Deacon, first. He's clearly involved, whereas Jerry isn't. Besides, Deak is weak-minded, so we're more likely to get something out of him."

Clemmie thought for a minute, then made a face and headed for the door. "I guess that makes sense. I'm going to go grab the stuff from the window display so I can set it up here."

I nodded, and finished lettering the big sign as best I could, then with a bit of tape, went to the front door.

Just as I was affixing it, a shadow fell over me. "I'm afraid we're in the process of moving," I said without turning around. "But you're welcome to look at what we have so far—"

I stopped when I finally turned to face the tourists. Two men stood before me, both dressed in hats and long dusters, just like Finch. The blond one eyed the sign behind me, and raised his eyebrows. "We're not in the market for haunted wares, actually. We're here to see Finch Dante."

Instantly, my metaphorical hackles rose. Finch hadn't mentioned anyone visiting him. In fact, I'd gotten the idea that the reason he'd chosen this town is because it was so out-of-the-way. Still…

Finch?

Hmm?

"Who?" I asked, stalling for time, reluctant to share Finch with anyone. The second my brain even admitted that, I forced myself to stop being so selfish. *How many people know you're here?*

He was silent for a moment. *What an odd question. Why do you ask?*

If I said general curiosity, would you believe me?

"Finch Dante," the blond man repeated, glancing up at the number over the door. His voice was a pretty shade of lavender. "We were told it was number 42."

Yes, Finch answered.

I pushed down the guilt that followed his easy answer.

As it happens, he continued, *there is only one person outside of Ravenfall who knows I am here, and I'd like to keep it that way.*

"This shop is occupied by Jeremy Renfrew," I told the men, making a snap decision. If Finch didn't want to be disturbed—which he obviously didn't if only one person knew his whereabouts—then I would make sure he wasn't bothered.

"It says Ozymandra on the window," the dark-haired man said in deep periwinkle, pointing. He had a German accent, while his buddy sounded French. They were both handsome enough that several women strolling down the street sent them more than a few admiring glances.

Oooh. I sense a mystery, I said lightly, hoping he wouldn't press me for an answer as to why I was asking questions.

Hardly that.

"She was here before Jeremy," I said, crossing my arms. For some reason I couldn't pinpoint, I was wary of these men who had come to find Finch, and felt obligated to protect him from them. And yet, I wondered if I shouldn't just tell him that there were people looking for him. A thought occurred that distracted me from that, however. "You don't happen to know Ozy, do you?"

The two men spoke softly in what I assumed was German, then they turned back to me, eyeing me with a thoroughness that had me squaring my shoulders and glaring. "No, we are not acquainted with her."

"Are you with this sparrow guy?" I asked, trying to smooth any deception from my expression.

"Finch, and not personally, no," Blondie admitted.

That solidified my determination to keep Finch from

being bothered by them. Guilt pricked me that I shouldn't make decisions for him, but I really didn't want to disturb him any more than I already had.

I'd mention them to him later, I justified to myself. When he wasn't busy working.

"Sorry I can't help," I said quickly, and flashed them a smile I hoped appeared sincere before returning to the shop to unpack a set of children's books that I marketed as being straight from a dybbuk box.

To my relief, the men left after giving the shop a last curious look.

By closing time, we had almost all of our things moved and arranged, and had made decent sales.

"Ozy's shop definitely has better foot traffic," I told Clemmie as she switched the door sign to closed, and locked the front door. "Did you see that we sold all of the Salt Water Taffy of the Damned?"

"Yeah, that went fast. Think I'll run home and toss my stuff into a bag," she said, gathering up her things before heading for the back door.

I realized I hadn't heard from Finch for several hours, and trotted upstairs to see if we'd driven him to distraction, or if he'd fallen asleep.

It was neither. His room was empty. I hesitated for a moment, but after hearing a voice from the other bedroom, figured he must be making sure it was OK for Clemmie, and hurried to thank him again for taking us in.

"—and I know you know how much the Witness Security Program costs, but damn me, Finch. First a body is found at your place—a fact I'm going to keep from my mother—but now some stranger is chatting you up and you think he knows who you are?" The voice that spoke was male, and had its origins in the phone set on the windowsill next to where Finch stood gazing out of the window.

"Not exactly," he answered. "The man seemed to know… something…about me, however, and it made me wonder if you've ever heard of him."

I hesitated at the door, not wanting to eavesdrop, but being riveted in place by the mention of Witness Security Program. Was that why Finch was here? My blood cooled to glacial level at the idea of him being in danger. Someone wanted to hurt him? Maybe kill him? That's why he had that ridiculous Jeremy name that didn't at all suit him. He was in hiding.

Instantly, the memory of the two men who were asking for him came to mind.

"That's a negative. Is it too much to ask you to keep your head down for the next few months?"

"Of course not, but as I pointed out, the body was hardly—" He turned as he spoke, caught sight of me, and his words stopped dead.

Someone is hunting for you?

He sighed into my head. *How long have you—*

About thirty seconds, but it was enough to hear the words Witness Security Program.

"Was hardly what? Ideal? I wholeheartedly agree with that. I have to go, Finch. Please, for the love of my retirement fund, please don't do anything that's going to bring any more attention."

"I strive to do so," he answered, his eyes wary as he watched me.

"That's all I ask." The call clicked off, and Finch collected his phone, pocketing it before he leaned against the windowsill.

"I suspect you have a few questions," he said pleasantly, his voice fairly spruce in color.

"A fair number, yes," I said, moving into the room and straight into his arms. I kissed along his jaw, tugging his shirttail out of his pants until I could slide my hands under his shirt to caress the lovely flesh of his chest. "But right now, more than anything, even answers to a hundred or so questions, I want to jump your bones."

He chuckled at my statement, his hands wandering up my hips to my breasts. *I have never thought of that phrase as being overly sexy, but suddenly, it is. Are you done downstairs?*

"Yes, and Clemmie is back at my place packing her things. How do you feel about a little afternoon delight?"

His brows pulled together for a moment as I took him by the hand and led him out of the room. "Wasn't that a popular song some years ago?"

"It was, and oddly, was also one of my very straitlaced mother's favorites," I told him, unbuttoning his shirt once we reached his bedroom, and he'd closed the door.

He didn't answer; his mouth was too busy nibbling on a spot on my neck that sent nonstop shivers up and down my spine, his hands as busy as mine as we worked in perfect orchestration to remove clothing, our bodies tumbling, just as synchronized, onto the bed.

"Do you mind if I'm on top?" I asked, kneeling next to him and gently pushing him onto his back.

His eyes were as pale as glacial water…but so steamy I felt like I was bathed with sunlight. "I have no objection to the position, if you would like to try something different."

"It's not that I need variety. Everything with you is new and exciting and so incredibly arousing that just thinking about you earlier made my nipples needy. Not to mention uncomfortable in my bra. You know how men complain about having an erection stuffed into their pants? Well, the same can be said about how uncomfortable aroused nipples are when you have a lace bra pressed against them."

"Allow me to soothe your poor, abused nipples," Finch said politely, filling his hands with my breasts. I had a moment of regret that they weren't the happy, perky boobs of my past, and were instead breasts that definitely belonged to a woman in her forties.

Stop it, he said, pulling me upward to catch the tip of a breast in his mouth, his teeth scraping ever so gently on it. *Your breasts fill me with delight. Your hips make me hard just thinking about them. Your ass fills my mind.*

I laughed into his head as I pulled away to bite the tip of his nose. "It's big enough to do that."

He looked chagrined for a moment before smiling.

"That wasn't my intention, although I do admit I could have phrased it better. How about this—your ass fills my senses..."

This time I laughed out loud, filled with joy at the way he viewed me.

"Christ," he swore, rubbing his face with a hand. "That sounds even worse. Er...your ass looms high in my fantasies—"

I put a hand over his mouth, noting that humor filled his eyes, a fact that tickled me even more than his honeyed words. "Why don't we leave my butt out of it? Your butt, however, is magnificent. I want to mold it like modeling clay. I want to stroke it and touch it and bite those perfect cheeks."

He pulled my hand from his mouth, kissed the palm, and then glared at me. "How dare you compliment my ass when all I can do is stumble over my words like an ignoramus?"

"You used up all your good words writing your book," I said, sliding down to avoid his hands when he reached for my breasts again. "Besides, I can hear all those flattering things you think about some very un-flattering spots on my body, and it melts my insides. No, I think we're going to do this my way. You just lie there and let me, the injured party in this situation, have my womanly way with you. Do you like—"

"Yes," he interrupted.

"You don't know what I was going to say," I protested, spreading his legs so I could kneel between his knees, my hands on the thick muscles of his thighs. As I had noted before, he had dark body hair, but it was a reasonable amount, just enough to make my fingers tingle as I stroked his flesh.

"It doesn't matter. I will like anything you care to do to me. Or with me. Or on me." His eyes were downright hot now, passion shimmering in their beautiful depths.

I gently dragged my nails up his inner thighs, enjoying the way his breath hitched, and his chest heaved. *I shouldn't do this*, I said.

On the contrary, you should do it every opportunity you have, he said, accompanied by a mental moan.

"No, I mean making love. It's getting perilously close to dating if we keep doing this," I said, kissing a path across his belly. "And I'm sorry, but I absolutely refuse to date you, Finch. I don't want you ending up minus a body part or your sanity. Can I bite you?"

I could feel the surprise followed by a hot rush of pleasure in his mind...and then something that he pushed away, like it was painful. "If you like, although I don't know that you'd like my blood—"

"Not hard enough to hurt you," I said quickly, wanting to reassure him that I wouldn't cause him pain at the same time I was quelling the repugnant idea of drinking his blood.

Does it bother you when I feed? he asked, obviously concerned.

"No. You drinking me is..." I bent down to kiss the line of muscle that ran up from his pelvic area around to his flanks. He didn't have an outright six-pack, but he came very close to it. "Sexy. Arousing. Satisfying, somehow. But I do want to bite you."

"Then you may—" He sucked in his breath when I nipped him, not hard enough to do damage, but enough that he felt it.

He froze for about three seconds, then I was flat on my back, and he was over me, spreading my legs, his mouth hot on my breasts, his hands dancing in lower parts, teasing, probing, and in general making me see stars.

"I thought—oh, goddess, right there." My body twitched and shuddered and wound tighter and tighter until I found it difficult to pull air into my lungs. *I thought I got to be on top this time?*

Later. Another time. Right now—

Too much talking and not enough biting, I said, squirming against him, wrapping my legs around his hips and thrusting my own upwards in an attempt to lure him into my so very needy depths.

Are you sure? I just fed—

I slid a hand down between us and positioned him at the same time I bit the part of his neck where it met the shoulder. I must have been a bit more enthusiastic than I realized, because his body stopped moving for a few seconds, shock bouncing around in his brain. He tasted sweet and spicy, and as I ran my tongue over the spot I'd bit in order to ease it, he shuddered, then thrust into me with a strength that simultaneously had me gasping and mentally cheering.

It didn't take long for him to push me into an orgasm, my body tightening in waves around him as he thrust wildly into me, his breath harsh in my ear even as his mind was filled with the most exquisite combination of his pleasure and mine.

And when he rolled us over and I lay on top of him, a boneless, breathless blob of satiated woman, I realized that something wasn't right.

Finch had shared his climax with me, but as soon as he'd regained his wits, he'd gently but persistently closed me out of his mind.

I wanted to demand he tell me why, but a sudden insight hit me—no matter how much I tried to convince myself that sexy times with Finch was just that—enjoyable sex and nothing else—the truth was that I was falling for him. Hard. Harder than I had ever fallen for a man.

And that had triggered the curse. I lay on top of Finch, feeling his heart rate start to slow beneath my ear, his hands warm on my back and behind, his scent and warmth and body filling me with joy…and yet I'd done exactly what I'd sworn not to do.

I'd doomed us. This time, however, the curse didn't affect his body or his sanity—it had ripped from me the chance to have an emotional connection.

I had sworn that all I had with him was a physical relationship, and now I was getting just that. Sex without any emotions that ran deeper than shared pleasure.

"Are you angry with me that I did not let you remain on top?" Finch asked when I rolled off him, wanting to both cry and rail at him. Why wasn't he falling in love with me as I was him? What had I done to deserve this curse? Why couldn't I, just once, be happy and in love?

"No, of course not," I said after the quarter minute it took to get my emotions under control. "And frankly, if you didn't feel the strength of my orgasm, then one of us is doing something very wrong."

He turned onto his side and considered me with eyes that were returning to a deep azure. Idly, I wondered at the fact that his eyes changed shade depending on what he was doing, but I was too busy hiding my emotions from him to spend much time in thought on the subject. "What's wrong, Tat?"

I smiled to myself at the use of my shortened name. Thus far, he'd been careful to use my full name, and it warmed my heart—which was still raging at the way fate was shitting on my life—that he had used it. "Other than the fact that I'm not sure I'm going to be able to use my legs because I'm boneless with satisfaction? Nothing."

He brushed his thumb over my cheek in a gesture that wrung my heart with its sweetness. "That doesn't explain why you're so sad."

I met his gaze, and stopped fighting my inner self. "I'm so not the sort of person to go around clinging to self-pity and moody thoughts."

"No, you are not, and your openness is one of the things I enjoy about your personality."

"Is that so?" I didn't respond to the slow smile he offered. "It seems, however, we both have darker emotions going on."

His eyes widened, and once again, I felt the barriers going down in his mind. "Are you talking about the phone call you overheard? I assure you that there are reasons why I am not allowed to tell you about the situation."

"No, it's not that." I put my hand on his chest. "I felt that moment of panic and regret you had when I bit you, Finch. I thought at first that I hurt you, but it was something else, wasn't it?"

He was silent for a whole minute, then lay on his back, one hand in his hair while he stared at the ceiling.

I didn't speak, giving him the time he obviously needed.

"I told you that there were steps to becoming what Dark Ones referred to as Joined," he said, reluctance wrapped around each of his words.

"Yes, but you never explained what they were." I curled up on my side, wanting to touch him, to comfort him, but I didn't know if that would help or hinder what was obviously some sort of confession.

"The steps themselves don't really matter, just as I thought having a Beloved didn't matter, because I had my soul."

I tried hard not to react to the pain that stabbed my heart with his words.

He turned his head to face me. "I was wrong. It does matter. *You* matter. But therein lies the problem. You see, you're not the only one who has sworn to forego relationships."

I frowned as I studied his face. His voice was as forest green as it could be, so I knew he wasn't hedging around the truth. "You're not cursed like I am," I pointed out.

"No. Yes." He took a deep breath. I ignored what it did to his glorious chest. "I told you that I was born with a soul because my parents were Joined when I was born. My father found my mother in the mid-nineteenth century. Like all of our kind, they fell hard and fast for each other, and spent their time traveling all over the world. My father loved nothing more than having what he referred to as adventures—fighting on the side of right, exploring, serving as ambassadors and trade envoys—while my mother was passionate about social welfare. When I was born, I spent much of my early years with my uncle in the Czech Republic. Later, my mother co-opted me to work for the betterment of mortals."

"Is that why you are a doctor?" I asked, fascinated into this look into Finch's history.

"Yes." He gave a little shrug with one shoulder. "Also, I had a knack for treating mortals, although early on that turned more toward an interest in psychology."

I snuggled up next to him, feeling less darkness in his mind. "Hence writing your book."

"Hence the book," he agreed. He looked at the ceiling again, one hand behind his head, the other around me. "Everything was fine until one day my father encountered an adventure he couldn't survive."

"Oh, no." I withdrew the hand I had placed over his heart, but he took my hand in his, and held it in the same spot. "Did he die?"

"Yes. Dark Ones, as I've said, are hard to kill...but it's not impossible. My father was...well, I'll save you the details since they would upset you. He did not survive incarceration by a tribe in what was then Arabia."

"I'm so sorry." I tried to pour as much comfort as I could into his mind, but didn't know if he could feel it.

"It was a horrible time," he said, his voice now flat and utterly grey. "I was practicing medicine in Germany at the time. My uncle came out to inform me about the tragedies. He was almost as broken as I was, feeling that he was at fault for letting a much-loved younger brother live his life in a heedless manner."

"Tragedies, plural?" I asked, hesitating to interrupt. "Was your mother...er..."

He turned to face me, his eyes midnight blue, and filled with so much pain that tears burned behind mine. "She couldn't live without him. Dark Ones and Beloveds share a life bond, Tat. If one dies, the other suffers incomprehensible agony. My mother couldn't bear his loss, and chose to join my father in the afterlife rather than remain in the mortal plane."

I pushed him back, sitting on his legs as I leaned down, my hands around his face, tears streaking down my face. "I'm sorry, Finch. So very, very sorry. I can't imagine how horrible that was to lose both your parents in such tragic manners."

He brushed tears from my cheeks. "The day my uncle told me what my mother had done, I swore an oath that I would never put another person through such sorrow. I would refuse a Beloved if I found one. I couldn't—can't—risk causing someone I loved to suffer so much that they would take their own life if I was gone."

"You're trying to protect me," I said, insight dawning. I was touched. No one other than my mother had ever protected me. And here was Finch, a man I'd just met, doing just that.

"Yes. Our chemical makeup has guaranteed that we spend our lives together, but I can't do that. I can't have a Beloved. I can't risk that if something happened to me, you'd follow, leaving behind children, family, and friends."

It struck me that he was angry at his mother for leaving him, but I didn't mention it. Later, I told myself, later I would encourage him to get the help he needed to forgive her. "You make it sound like such a horrible outcome is inevitable, Finch. Do you really believe you're so likely to end up like your father?"

"Not like him, no. I wouldn't put myself in the positions he did, but there are other things—" He took a long, shuddering breath. "That call you heard—I witnessed a crime in New York. Since no one else was willing to testify against the men who committed the crime, and I am, my US marshall friend had me sent here so that I would be out of the gang's reach. If they find me here, they would likely try to kill me."

I wanted to protest the idea that someone could kill him since he just got done telling me that wasn't easy to do, but bit back the urge to let my tongue run like it normally would. This wasn't about me, it was his fears, his pain. I needed to be respectful of both.

"We really are a pair," I said after struggling with myself. I slid off him, and sat beside him, my hand still on his heart. "You doing everything you can to help people, and keep from causing hurt to the one person you're meant to be with, and me terrified that just being with me is going to

mean your ultimate doom. In a way, they're the same fears…
just with different spins."

His lovely straight eyebrows pulled together. "I know
you've had bad luck in the past, but clearly, that isn't affect-
ing me. You have no reason to fear that a relationship would
doom me."

"I could say the same thing about you," I said gently,
leaning down to kiss him.

He accepted the kiss, but I could feel a sense of stubborn
denial inside him, and heaved a sigh to myself. There was no
way I could fix the dire straits we were both in.

But that didn't mean we had to stay there.

A faint sound heralded the arrival of Clemmie, no doubt
with the first wave of her possessions. "I suppose we should
get dressed."

"Yes," he said, one hand gently stroking my thigh. He
looked introspective, so I gathered up my things and went to
the bathroom to tidy up and get dressed, my mind busy with
ideas that didn't seem possible.

Unless something changed.

I needed things to change.

TWELVE

Finch waited until Tatiana joined him in his bed that night before making sure his soul-baring hadn't left her with either a distaste for himself and Dark Ones in general, or a firmer belief that she was damned by some sort of a relationship curse.

"Is everything to your cousin's satisfaction?" he asked when Tatiana entered his bedroom, making sure to lock the door behind her.

"Yes, she needed to know which drawer in the bathroom you'd set aside for her stuff. Thank you for that, by the way."

"For clearing a drawer? I didn't, as a matter of fact. I don't have that many things with me that needed storage."

"No, for taking us both in, and making us feel welcome." She sat on the edge of the bed, one foot tucked under her.

Finch, who hadn't been sure if she would feel like any further sexual frolics after their discussion, didn't wish to present her with the sight of his rampant penis and no doubt hopeful pleading look in his eyes, and instead stuffed himself and his willing-to-put-forth-the-effort penis beneath a duvet. "It's my pleasure, I assure you."

She smiled, and thought something flattering about how much she liked his speech pattern, then with a sidelong look, began to disrobe. "Are you, by any chance, naked under there?"

"The phrase naked, willing, and able comes immediately to mind," he answered.

"Music to my ears." It didn't take her long to pluck off her garments, although not nearly long enough, he mused as she hurried under the duvet with him.

That was too fast. I didn't have time to ogle your hips and breasts and thighs, he protested.

And once I've taken up an exercise regime and worked off some of this middle-age spread, then maybe I will be more comfortable with such ogling, but not now.

He turned to her as she primly pulled the duvet up over her bare breasts. "Are you really so uncomfortable with your body?"

She looked momentarily surprised. "Me? No. I mean, yes in that it's not how I'd like it to look like, but I'd also prefer to be taller, have oodles of money, and a pony, and frankly, I don't see any of those things happening anytime soon."

"I think your body is exactly what it should be," he said, fighting the urge to pounce on her and show her how much he appreciated every inch of it, but reminded himself that he was a gentleman, and gentlemen made sure their partner was pounce-ready. "It delights me, as I've mentioned."

Her voice was warm, as was the expression in her eyes. "Oh, I appreciate more than you know the fact that you, a Fitty McFitterson immortal person who isn't ever going to have to deal with love handles and cellulite and varicose veins, think my middle-aged self is desirable. It makes me feel things that I haven't felt in a long time. No," she lifted her hand to stop his protest that she was perfect. "I'm not fishing for compliments. I love the fact my hips hold some sort of magic for you, but I'm not blind to reality."

"I've always wished I was taller, too," he said without thinking.

"Really?" She turned until she was facing him. "But you're like, what, six foot?"

"Barely. All the Dark Ones of my acquaintance are taller." He grimaced at the memories of his youth, when he'd railed against his mother, who had been on the shorter side. That he'd blamed her for something that wasn't in her control shamed him now, but he had long come to terms with that particular regret.

"Are you saying there are no short vampires?" she asked, her expression and mind filled with surprise.

"I'm sure there are, but amongst my friends, I am the shortest."

She pushed him onto his back, lying across his chest and kissing his chin. "You're the perfect height for me, Finch. Any taller and I'd get a crick in my neck. Any shorter, and I'd have to wear flats for the rest of my life."

"Ah, yes, about that..." He was about to address the fact that despite his best intentions, they'd moved one step closer to her claiming the position of Beloved in more than just name, but at that point she began kissing him in earnest, and he then had to allow her into his mind to show her just how much she pleased him, both her body, and mind.

And later, when they both lay exhausted, covered in a light sheen of sweat, and with ragged breaths, he felt his heart breaking at the knowledge that he couldn't stay with her.

"Why not?" she asked, her voice thick with sleep.

He kissed her on the top of her head, and adjusted her slightly against his side. "Because I won't risk the chance that you would have to go through what my mother did."

You're not your father, Finch, she said with a yawn. Sleep pulled at her, making her words come slow. *I don't know why you expect to die, but maybe ask yourself about your friends and other family members. How many of them died tragically?*

He thought about that, his mind busily sorting through the list of Dark Ones who had been Joined, and adding up the ones who hadn't survived to the present day.

A minute flame of hope lit in his soul, and refused to be dampened.

"So, these guys that you saw killing someone." The following morning, after Tatiana had insisted on being on top when he fed—and managed to engage in a lovemaking session that left him as limp as a sodden sheet of paper—he was consulting his phone while she consumed an omelet, a cup of fresh fruit, and yogurt. "Would one have a French accent, and the other sound German?"

"Not that I remember," he said, looking up at her, his heart both simultaneously lightening at the sight of her, and turning to lead at the idea of leaving her.

She made a face. "There were two guys last night who asked for you by name."

"What?" He leaped to his feet without realizing it, the need to protect her from imminent threat overwhelming his common sense—the very same common sense that pointed out there was no current threat. "When? Where? Why didn't you tell me?"

"Yesterday, outside the shop, and I didn't think it was important because I didn't know people were hunting you. You said you weren't expecting anyone, and I…well, I didn't tell you. I'm sorry, Finch. I should have mentioned it. I was trying to protect you, but I realize now that was wrong." She looked guilt-stricken, and pushed aside the remnants of her breakfast. "Oh my god—wait a minute! Men are hunting for you! It's like *Sister Act*!"

"Like what?" he asked, torn between the desire to call Damon and demand that he relocate Tatiana to a safe place while he, himself, dealt with the murderers, and pointing out to her that this was the exact situation he'd feared.

"*Sister Act*. You know, the movie with Whoopie Goldberg. She played a woman who spent time with nuns while she was in hiding from bad guys. This is *Sister Act* all over again. Only, you know, without the actual nuns."

He stared at her for a moment.

"Stop looking at me like I'm insane. And don't try to say you weren't, because I distinctly caught the words 'She's lost her mind' being beamed from your head to mine," she said, looking adorably disgruntled. "Also, stop thinking 'I told you so.' It's not at all nice, and this isn't the same sort of situation as what your parents went through. Although I do appreciate you not blaming me for trying to protect you."

He took a long, deep breath to try to regain control of his emotions, found it didn't help, so took several more in hopes they would do the impossible and calm his panicked need to both stuff her away somewhere safe, and yes, point out that he did, in fact, tell her so.

"Great," she said, getting up to wrap her arms around him. "Now you're hyperventilating. Sit down, Finch, before you pass out. Do you want me to get you a paper bag? Are you having a panic attack? Do you have any meds you want me to fetch?"

He started laughing; he couldn't help himself, the situation was both his worst nightmare, and so ludicrous that he either had to laugh, or break down into tears.

I much prefer the laughter. Are you OK?

"Yes. But I do want to hear about the men who asked for me by name."

She told him about the two men she'd seen the afternoon before, and after asking her to not withhold such information again, no matter how busy he was, he leaned back in the chair with Tatiana sitting across his lap, and thought.

"I just want to remind you that I didn't know you were in hiding," she said in a pitiable tone while mentally he sorted through the information he had read in one of Damon's reports. He didn't recall anyone born outside of the US as being involved.

"No, I don't blame you for that," he said absently, a thought having occurred to him. He scooted Tatiana a little to one side so he could read his phone, and flipped through the messages from his uncle. "Ah. This may well be the answer."

"To what?" she asked. "Getting you out of town? Because much as I don't want you to go, I really don't want you to be here if people are hunting for you."

He showed the message to Tatiana. "I think this explains the men."

"I can't read German," she said, distracting him when she brushed a strand of hair from his forehead.

"It's not German, it's Czech, and I'm sorry, I tend to translate automatically. This is a text from my uncle, and he told me that a couple of his friends were in the area if I needed help. I suspect those are the men you encountered. I believe I will go out and see if I can find them. They may have left town, but assuming they haven't, I'd rather find them before they ask many more people about me."

"You don't know that's who they are," she protested, standing up when he tapped her on the hip. "I'm telling you, those *Sister Act* guys were very clever. The two clowns I saw last night could be trying to look like people your uncle knows just to draw you out. Finch, listen to me."

He stopped when he had taken two steps toward the front door, turning back. She hurried over and wrapped her arms around his waist again, her breath hot on his neck as she hugged him tightly. "I don't for one minute believe you are going to follow your father's path, because you're smart and won't let yourself get into a desperate situation, but you also are filled to the brim with all sorts of heroic feelings that I know you're trying to hide. Why don't you stay here and work on your book, and let Clemmie and me find out if these guys are your uncle's buddies?"

He kissed her soundly, and put her from him with an effort that almost hurt. "I won't be in any danger, Tatiana. I promise you that."

"Gah!" she said, slapping her hands on her thighs as he strode to the front door. "It's like you aren't listening!"

"I am, actually."

"But, in *Sister Act*—"

"This isn't a movie, sweet," he told her, smiling. Before he reached the door, however, a frantic tattoo sounded on the glass.

"Who the—oh, it's Mara." Tatiana rushed past him.

"Who?" he asked, entering the front of the shop with her.

"She's the mayor's assistant. She can be quite cutting when you do her out of a good antique. Hi Mara."

"I heard you were here. The Entity wants to see you," the woman said. She was fairly short, had a shade of blond hair that Finch recalled being referred to as dirty, and wore thick glasses.

"What? They do?" Tatiana weaved a little like she might swoon. Finch was at her side instantly, his gaze narrowed on the woman at the door. "Why? How? What did I do? Oh, goddess, it's the curse, isn't it? Or is it Ozy's body? We didn't kill her! Someone stuffed her here, that's all. They have no reason to summon me."

The woman named Mara had an expression like she's been sucking on a rotten lemon. "The Entity cares not if you wish to be summoned; they have demanded your presence, and you must go before them. They expect to see you at Terce."

"Terce? Terce? What's terce?" Tatiana said, her voice rising with each word.

"Nine in the morning," Finch answered, glancing at his watch at the same time he put an arm around Tatiana to support her. "In slightly less than twenty minutes."

His words drew the woman's attention, and once again, he was subjected to someone he did not know staring at him, and saying softly, "A Dark One. What are *you* doing here?"

"Who are you?" he asked, taking a step forward, but the woman turned and bolted, her voice carrying on the ocean breeze as she raced down the street.

"Terce! Don't be late!"

Finch! Tatiana said, her mind filled with worry and fear. *They want me! Oh, goddesses above and below and everywhere I can't think of at this second because my brain is running around like a squirrel on meth. This is it!*

"It's what?" he asked, closing the door and locking it.

"The end. They're going to do something heinous to me, I just know it."

"I won't let them," he said, wondering if there was something going on with the town that everyone knew what he was. And why had the woman Mara put the emphasis on him being there? Were they expecting a different Dark One? Or was it his kind at all that surprised her? And if so, why? People who could recognize Dark Ones at a glance shouldn't be shocked to see one in person.

Tatiana turned an exasperated expression on him. "You say that just like you can stop them. This is the Municipal Entity, Finch. They have mad powers."

"What sort of powers?" he asked.

Her hands fluttered in the air. "I don't know exactly! But everyone knows they can do things." Her eyes narrowed and her voice dropped to a whisper. "There are rumors of people going to see them and never being seen again. OK, most of them were seen later, but not all, and where there's smoke, there's fire, right?"

"I've never actually found that saying to be true," he said, taking her hand and leading her upstairs.

"What are you doing? Where are we going?" *Finch! You can't want to go to bed right now? We just got up. Are you taking some sort of penis-enhancing pills that I need to know about?*

I always want to make love to you, but that's not what I plan on doing right now. He opened up the small wardrobe and pulled out a suit. "Business-like, I think, would be best. Do you want to change from your leggings to something else?"

"Eek!" she said, and scurried over to the side of the wardrobe he'd given over to her things. "Hell, yes. You don't appear before people who can do unthinkable things to you wearing a pride tee and a pair of leggings with bleach spots on them."

A quarter of an hour later, after having woken up Clemmie, and left her in charge of the shop, Finch accompanied a mildly panicking Tatiana down the street to the building with gargoyles.

"The irony of you lying in wait to see them just a few nights past, and now being terrified of meeting them must provide some sort of amusement to you," he said, her fingers tightening almost painfully on his as they approached the steps leading to the front doors.

"Stop trying to distract me with…with…" She waved a hand, her eyes huge when they started up the eight steps.

"Conversation?" he supplied, both amused and very aware of the surroundings. He shot a suspicious glance up at the gargoyles, but they appeared to be behaving themselves. Nonetheless, he told himself as he pulled open the double doors, he would not allow anyone to frighten Tatiana.

"Yes," she said, hesitating when he crossed the threshold.

She seemed to be frozen in fear until he leaned toward her and said the first thing his brain could summon. "You are beautiful, smart, and brave. And you are mine."

He turned and strolled into the building, sure she wasn't going to let that pass without comment.

He wasn't wrong.

"Excuse me?" A suddenly annoyed Tatiana was at his side, jerking his sleeve until he stopped to look at her. "Did you just claim me, like I'm the last piece of pizza? Dude!"

"Finch, not—"

"DUDE," she said louder, her eyes now lit from within, glittering with ire, annoyance, and what looked very much like humor. She accompanied the word with a slap of her hand to his chest. "I am a person, my own person, and although I much enjoy getting to know your person in a very real and tangible way, that doesn't mean you get to put the Finch Stamp of Ownership on me."

"Greetings." A soft voice accompanied a person who stepped out of a side room, stopping in front of them and making a little bow.

"I don't have any such stamp, and even if I did, I could hardly use it on you. People would be sure to ask you who Finch was." He noticed absently the interior of the building consisted of a large center hall with black and white tiled floor, and walls lined with intricately carved wooden benches. Two doors were evident on both sides of the hall, while at the far end, a podium was set up, with a dozen folding chairs before it.

"Because that's what's important, isn't it?" Tatiana railed.

"You are expected," the person said, and gestured toward the door from which they had emerged. They were clad in an odd mix of what looked to be a Victorian costumer's wet dream, and something out of a Tim Burton movie, with a red full-skirted frock coat topping a gold and brown checked waistcoat, stiff collar shirt, blue cravat, black and white houndstooth breeches, red and white striped stockings, and a pair of bright green plastic shoes.

"What is?" Finch asked, momentarily distracted.

"That people would wonder who this Finch bastard was who stamped me? Gah!" Tatiana snatched her hand away when he tried to take it.

For a moment he wondered if he had really offended her. *Are you angry with me?*

Are you kidding? She took a long, shuddering breath, then turned to face the Victorian person. *I'd get down on my knees with gratitude for you getting me in the building, but I'm afraid the Great Gonzo here would misunderstand.*

The who?

Gonzo. You know, from the Muppets? He…she…they are dressed just like Gonzo in A Christmas Carol.

Ah. I thought more something from a Tim Burton movie.

That, too. OK. I can do this.

You can. He made a bow to the person waiting. "Thank you. I am…"

"We know who you are, Dark One," the person said, their gaze shifting to Tatiana. "As we do all citizens of Ravenfall. This way."

Out of idle curiosity, what color is their voice? he couldn't help but ask as they followed the person to one of the side rooms.

Butterscotch. The same color you had when I first met you and you were amazed by something. I'd never heard it before in anyone.

Interesting. They entered a room that while physically small, struck Finch as being almost cavernous. A long table with a red runner dominated the space, with three chairs beyond it. There was no other furniture in the room.

Two people stood at the table. The unnamed greeter went to join them, and all three turned to face where Finch and Tatiana had stopped.

"Goddess," he heard her whisper, her hand finding his. "It's them. It's really them."

Do not be frightened—

Frightened? She shot him a look that made him want to laugh out loud, releasing his hand to stalk forward, every inch of her delicious body expressing righteous indignation. *Are you shitting me? Look at them, Finch! They're just people.*

Were you expecting something else?

Of course I was! Something Cthulhu-like at the very least. But it's just a woman—wait, is that P!nk? She looks like P!nk— and a man who looks like he just got in from wrangling the back forty's worth of cows, and then Gonzo. Sheesh! "I have to say that I'm a bit surprised you called me before you after all the many times I've tried to see you, and you've refused."

"And hello to you, too," the woman said. She had short blond hair styled in a manner that left her looking somewhat like an annoyed hedgehog, and was clad in a sequined amber jumpsuit that glittered and reflected light with every movement.

Tatiana's lips twitched. "Sorry, that came out more confrontational than I intended. Hello."

"I am Anya Lee, and this is Quinton McGuire." She gestured to the man who stepped forward and pulled a cowboy hat off his head before giving a curt nod toward them. "And you've met Lyric already."

The Victorian person gave a small smile and acknowledging nod, then all three took seats at the table, leaving Finch and Tatiana to stand before them.

"So, about this eviction notice crap—" Tatiana started to say.

Anya lifted her hand. "We are here to discuss the disappearance of Jericho Hall. We understand that you are the last people she visited before she was reported missing."

Tatiana slid a glance toward Finch. He slid it right back to her, not having anything to add to it.

"Missing how?" he asked, then quickly clarified his statement. "That is to say, in what manner is she missing? My Bel—Tatiana said she saw the mayor yesterday when she delivered an eviction notice. Surely, the mayor must have been seen after that?"

"She was not," the man named Quinton said in an easy drawl that indicated he spent some time in the southwestern US. "In fact, she was due to meet with the sheriff at sext, and didn't show up."

He sounds just like Sam Elliott, Tatiana said.

"That is unfortunate," Finch said, wondering why the council felt like the problem was Tatiana's. "But it has nothing to do with either Tatiana or me."

"No?" Anya folded her hands together, her jumpsuit glittering at them. "And yet, the watchers say she was not seen after leaving the shop of Ozymandra."

"Watchers?" Finch asked, a little prickle of annoyance making his voice sharper than he intended.

Yeah, you're heading straight for grey. "Watcher is the name of the town's system of cameras to make sure tourists don't go berserk," Tatiana said aloud.

What—

Mild anger. Fury goes purple. Don't go purple, Finch. They may just be people, but they are still not ones I'd want to meet in a dark alley.

"Regardless of your security cameras, I can assure you that neither Tatiana nor I have knowledge of the whereabouts of the mayor. However, I can tell you that there was a man earlier at the police station who was asking for her. You might consult that department to see if they know of him, and his possible connection."

"A man?" Anya asked. "Describe him."

Finch did so, quickly covering the conversation.

The three council members exchanged glances, then the person named Lyric made a note in a notebook.

"We will, indeed, confer with the sheriff regarding the individual you saw," Anya told them. "However, given the animosity between Tatiana Romanoff and Jericho Taf, not to mention the former's attacks against Ozymandra Tell—and her subsequent disappearance followed by beheading and reappearance in your own basement—the Municipal Entity feels that this, in short, is your problem. You will solve both mysteries, and quickly."

Tatiana stumbled backward a couple of steps. Finch felt like he'd been slammed by a wall of electricity, one that stripped breath from his lungs for a few seconds. His fingers curled around Tatiana's when she moved back beside him and retook his hand.

Did you feel that? she asked.

Yes. He was silent a moment, studying the faces of the three individuals facing them. *One of them, I suspect, is more than they appear.*

How so?

Dark Ones are naturally resistant to compulsions, and yet, I was on the verge of marching out the door to do as ordered. That tells me that one of them is likely a demigod.

"Holy shitsnacks!" Tatiana said aloud, then covered her mouth and looked horrified.

"Your mate is correct," Anya said, standing.

The other two followed suit, the one named Lyric looking decidedly amused, Finch thought.

"About—about—" Tatiana stammered to a stop, and with a bravado that gave Finch new admiration for her character, squared her shoulders and lifted her chin. "Listen, I don't take kindly to people eavesdropping on my thoughts. Only Finch gets to do that, and that's because we have a vampire mark thing going on. So while I'm sorry that Jerry has done a runner—or whatever it is that she's pulling, clearly trying to scapegoat me—and that Ozy died, I will repeat what Finch said: we have nothing to do with either situation."

"It ain't a matter of who's to blame—it's a matter of who can do something about it. Both of you are in it up to your armpits, and you're the only ones who can fix what happened to Ozy and the mayor," McGuire drawled. "Get to fixin'."

It seemed to Finch that the world paused for a second, then gave itself a shake and he found himself walking out of the double doors, Tatiana at his side. They stopped at the bottom of the steps and looked at each other.

"Holy shitsnacks," she repeated, her eyes as big as his felt.

"Yes. That is a significant amount of power one—or all—of them possess." He cast a speculative glance back at the hall, but the double doors slammed shut on their own accord in a manner that Finch felt was pointed. "Very pointed."

Tatiana's eyebrows rose, but she slipped her hand into the crook of his arm when he stuck out his elbow for her. "What are we going to do now?"

He sighed, and started to wonder if the same Fate that was giving Tatiana grief with her romantic partners hadn't turned its sights to him. He certainly felt persecuted at that moment. "We do as we've been commanded."

THIRTEEN

"This is bullshit, utter bullshit, but since Finch has spent the last half hour telling me there's no use fighting with one or possibly three demigods—demigods! What on earth is happening to Ravenfall that we are inundated by demigods, although that really does explain a whole lot about the Entity. I wonder if Mercader knows?—then there's nothing for it. We're just going to have to get our shit together."

I stopped pacing the length of Finch's storefront, and glared at the tourists who stopped at the door, clearly expecting entrance since it was ten minutes past the official opening hours of Axegate Walk.

"OK, but what do you want me to do?" Clemmie asked, getting off the stool we'd placed behind the cash register that Finch had helped us wrestled to his place. It was an antique, and weighed approximately as much as a small horse.

I glanced at Finch. He stood with his hands clasped behind his back, staring at nothing. *Thoughts?* I asked him.

"Hmm? Oh. I will utilize some connections I have back east," he said, shooting me a meaningful glance before raising his eyebrows.

"Sounds good." I wondered what sort of information his witness protection handler could dig out on Jericho and Ozy, and hoped it was enough to get the Entity off our respective backs. "I think I'll go check around town to see if anyone has heard from Jerry. You'll be OK for an hour, yes, Clemmie?"

"Sure," she said, opening the door and greeting the group of four women who were waiting to come in. "Piece of cake. Welcome to Three Wyrd Sisters Haunted Curios. I'm so glad you found our new digs. If there's anything I can help you find, just yell."

I scooted around the ladies and out the door while Finch disappeared upstairs. *You're going to stay in, right? Because of the* Sister Act *people who I can feel are filling the town?*

No. Once I'm done contacting my friend, I will set forth to locate the two men you mentioned.

Dammit, Finch! I slapped my hands on my legs as I almost stomped my way to Mercader's shop, dodging tourists, children, and dogs alike.

I'll be fine, Tatiana.

Just be sure to be overly vigilant when it comes to people who might want to do things to you that would make me projectile vomit over everything within a twenty-foot radius.

He chuckled into my mind, his presence warm and comforting, and touching something in my heart that I didn't want to celebrate. Not yet. Not before I figured out if I could go against the curse. *I know full well that you think you can protect me, and although it warms the cold, hard shell of my heart that you would wish to do so, I assure you that if the two men who seek me are who I think they are, they pose no danger,* he said.

And if they aren't?

I value your hips, and my role in making them wiggle with delight, too much to let anyone harm me, he answered with a mental waggle of his eyebrows.

I didn't know if I could glare straight at his mind, but I gave it my best shot. *See that you do. I have plans for all your bits.*

I didn't respond to the erotic thoughts he sent in response, but tucked them away to enjoy them later. I spent a good fifteen minutes checking in with every shop owner who I could pull away from their clients, but none of them had anything newsworthy to impart about either Jerry or Ozy.

Nor did I see the two men who had been looking for Finch.

"Right," I told myself as I crossed the road to the wooden dock upon which the café sat. I gave it a long, hard look. "Let's see what Deacon has to say."

It was a bit early for the lunch rush, but evidently the nice weather and the official opening of tourist season had brought everyone to town, and they were all hungry, because I had to wait ten minutes before Audra, one of the waitresses, stopped long enough to blow a strand of hair out of her eyes, and say, "I don't know where Deacon is, Tat. But if you see him, tell him we could really use an extra pair of hands. Ricardo is claiming he picked up some sort of medieval pox from an old manuscript, and left Emmanuelle alone to cook everything. Yes, yes, I'm coming."

She dashed off to attend to a crisis, leaving me standing at the entrance to the staff section of the café. I glanced around, but no one was paying attention, so I slid through the swinging door that led to the kitchen and office.

Steam billowed outward, wrapping me in its sticky, moist embrace, the chaos of a short-staffed, busy kitchen sending me reeling backward a step. I gave Emmanuelle the cook and a veritable army of servers, bus persons, and dishwashers a wide berth while sidling my way toward a set of stairs that led downward. I knew from the time Deacon had tried to get me to allow him to draw blood for some weirdo ritual he wanted to perform that his office was on the floor below. I had a feeling he was hiding out there until after the lunch rush was over, and was about to knock on his door when I heard a woman's voice from behind me, faint at first, but growing louder with each second.

There was nothing but a paneled wall behind me.

I listened hard for five seconds, then recognizing the voice, spun around, looking desperately for a place to hide.

Luckily for me, Deacon had a weakness for fancy champagne, and kept a large standing wine fridge at the end of the passage, beyond his door and the door to the staff toilet. With a silent oath, I managed to jam myself between the side of the fridge and the wall, praying he wouldn't notice the slight displacement of the former.

"—and I'm telling you that we can't wait. It's been a year, Cadell. Either you get Rhain out now, tonight, or I will be forced to seek another to do so."

"My name is Deacon," came another familiar voice. I wanted badly to risk peeking out around the wine fridge, but decided it was better to stay put. "I picked Deacon. I *like* Deacon."

"It is not the name I gave you."

"No, but it is the name I gave myself when I came to the mortal world. It suits me. Besides, you have another name. No one calls you Angharad. Therefore, it's only right I should have my own name."

"I am not going to stand here discussing something so trivial when you should be doing as I ask lest I look to others for the help you have failed repeatedly to give me!" the woman snapped.

"And who can possibly do what I cannot?" Deacon asked, a sneer in his voice turning what was normally an ugly shade of brown to muddy grey. "The Entity? They are all bark and no bite. They have no real power against us."

The woman—Jerry—answered, "They are easily distracted, yes, but do not mistake their inability to see through me to mean they are powerless."

"Bah."

Deacon actually said the word bah. I was a bit impressed with that.

"Get the women ready," Jerry continued, a squeak of a door indicating she was going into his office. "It does little to give me confidence that you have only managed to capture six, but it will have to be enough. Conduct the ceremony. Summon Rhain. And don't fuck it up this time."

The slam of the door almost had me leaping up, but instead, I held my breath and listened hard.

Deacon muttered some things to himself in a language I didn't understand, but his footsteps retreated. I took the chance to crawl out from my hidey-hole, and was just in time to see a wooden panel at the bottom stair landing slide into place.

I didn't waste any time. I tiptoed past Deacon's office, half-expecting Jerry to burst out of it and go crazy, but luck, for once, was with me.

So, how's it going? I asked Finch once I escaped the steamy, crowded confines of the café, and emerged into the sunny day, gasping in deep lungsful of tangy air.

Excellent, as it happens. I found the two men.

I stood for a moment, one hand braced against the building, feeling as if I'd run a marathon. My brain wasn't just a squirrel on meth—it was a whole herd of them bouncing off padded walls, but at Finch's words, I straightened up, adrenaline filling me.

They are the two that I mentioned, friends of my uncle. I will introduce them to you as soon as you get back.

OK, but I'm going to go see the Entity first.

Why? I could feel the sense of satisfaction that had filled his mind fading. *Did you find the mayor?*

Oh yes. She's alive and well and living in Deacon's office beneath the café. I decided that I couldn't stand the feeling of itchiness that crawled over me, and started a fast trot to the town hall. *Remember those six women that Clemmie mentioned? Hell, that Ozy mentioned in the text on her burner phone. Well, Deacon has them hidden behind a secret panel in the wall. Also, Deacon isn't his real name.*

Where are you? he asked. I could feel him thinking things, lots of things, but couldn't get a grasp on any of them.

I rounded the corner, the town hall looming up half a block ahead of me. I started to get a stitch in my side, but crossed the street and kept up my pace. I wanted to give the Entity the information I had so I could go help Finch.

I don't need help, and where are you? he asked again.

I didn't tell him that my skin was fairly twitching with a premonition that he was in grave danger. I knew full well how he'd react to that news, and instead, kept my thoughts hidden. *Just coming up on the town hall.*

What is Deacon's name? Finch asked, his voice going sage green.

Cadell. He made a big fuss about picking his own name when he came here, and pointed out that Jerry wasn't her real name, either. Oh good, I'm here. Now if the doors—oh. OK. They've opened on their own. That's not creepy or anything.

I didn't notice for a few seconds the silence that followed my statement to Finch, but as I stood in the black and white tile hall of the building, one hand pressed to my side and gasping for breath (I really, really needed to get back to regular exercise), he spoke in a pale rose tone that was almost pink.

What is her other name?

Angharad, I answered. "Hello again, Lyric. Can I see the Entity, please? I have news of Jerry." *Ozy mentioned it in her text. Angharad...Owen, I think.*

Not Owen, Finch answered after ten seconds as Lyric, with a cocked eyebrow that told me nothing, ushered me into the side room we had visited before. *Owain.*

I was about to ask if he knew her, but a door at the back opened and Anya and the twangy Quinton entered the room.

"Hello again," I said, and made the same sort of bow that Finch made earlier. "Sorry about showing up all sweaty, but I wanted to get here as soon as I could. I found Jerry. She's in Deacon's office, hiding."

Lyric took their seat as the others sat down. All three looked mildly confused.

"You saw her, yourself?" Anya asked.

"No," I admitted, feeling that it wasn't a wise idea to outright lie to a demigod. Assuming Finch was correct and one—or all—of them were such august beings. "I was hidden behind a wine refrigerator. But I heard her. And Deacon addressed her by name. In fact, he made mention of the fact that Jericho wasn't her real name."

"Tell us," Anya said, not looking at the others.

I licked my lips, suddenly nervous, but reminded myself that Finch thought I was strong and brave, and by the goddess, I wasn't going to make him regret giving me those sorts of compliments. I recounted my experience in the café as succinctly as I could.

And then I stood there, fear growing like a fungus in my gut, spreading outward with warm, sticky tendrils when all three of them sat like stones, staring at me.

"You are certain about the names?" Lyric asked me, looking a sickly grey color.

"Yes. Why? Why are you all looking horrified?" *Finch? Who is Angharad Owain?*

Where are you?

With the Entity.

Good. Stay there. I had the sensation of him moving swiftly, his mind carefully guarded but tiny little tendrils of fear and anger sneaked out twice.

"What the hell is going on?" I asked aloud and to Finch. *What are you doing?*

We're going to confront Cadell and his mother.

Jerry? The mayor is his mom?

"You must speak to your Dark One—" Lyric started to say, but Anya interrupted them.

"She has already done so. Let us hope they are in time." She stood, not meeting my gaze, and simply murmured. "I am no seer, but it is clear that what has been set into play must not come about. You have a part in this. You must take up your role, else risk the lives of untold mortals."

I stared in silent confusion, fear, and disbelief as all three of them filed out, leaving me in sole possession of the room.

I'm coming to help, I told Finch, and spun around, pulling out my phone as I did so.

No! I need you to stay safe, Finch said, and for a moment, I felt his fear, so great it swamped him. Fear for me.

What's going on? I screamed at him, slinging the strap of my big striped bag across my torso before bolting out of the door and racing down the street. *Why are you so afraid?*

Sacrifice, was the only word that came through a terrible jumble of emotions. But in the middle of the tangle, one spark glowed bright for a moment. Love. It was love. Finch loved me, and with that knowledge, my mind and heart and being were freed from the fear that I hadn't realized bound me.

Then a scream ripped through me, tearing my soul to shreds with the anguish. I stumbled and fell, pain burning my knees and palms, my eyes swimming as I felt the aftershocks of absolute anguish. *Finch? Was that you?*

The gut-wrenching noise seemed to be on repeat in my head as I sobbed, getting painfully to my feet. Blood streamed down my legs from where I'd skinned my knees in the fall, but the pain of it was nothing compared to what Finch had endured.

Dear goddess above and below—how could he survive such devastation? *Finch, please answer me. Please. I need to know you're OK. Or not OK, but still there.*

I stood for a second, panting, tears streaming down my face, my nose running, and my heart beating so wildly I thought for a second I might pass out. *Finch?* I asked in a word that was thick with torment.

And then I was moving, limping at a gait that would have been more at home in a zombie, scrabbling at my phone until I got a call to go through.

"I have to help Finch," I yelled into the phone when Clemmie picked up. "Deacon's trying to sacrifice him to resurrect some old god named Rhain. If you don't hear from me in a few hours, go to the Entity."

"What?" Her voice was orange with confusion. "What's wrong with Finch? And are you insane saying I should see the Entity? No one sees them—"

"They'll see you. Goddess help us all," I said, then clicked off, and with the café now in sight, forced my aching legs into a run across the road…straight into the oncoming path of a car. I bounced painfully off the hood, falling to the side, scraping both arms and bruising my hip when I rolled a few feet before smashing into a trash bin.

I was on my feet even before the car finished squealing to a stop, and ignored the voices calling out in consternation and concern.

Everything on me hurt. Pain fought the memory of the horror of Finch's blast of emotion, but none of that mattered.

He did. *Finch, hang in there. I'm coming to help.*

Tourists scattered like bowling pins as I half-ran, half-lurched my way down the sidewalk, the horrified expressions of people who grabbed their kids out of my path telling me everything I needed to know about my appearance.

My hand slick with blood, I yanked up the edge of my dress and wiped my running nose and wet face before absently dabbing at the blood on my hands.

Finch? Are you there? Can you hear me but not talk?

Cries of dismay, oaths, and several rude things were scattered in my wake.

I sobbed into his mind. *Please, answer me. Just let me know you're alive and Deacon hasn't done something horrible to you.*

He didn't answer, and worse, I realized that the sense of him that had been with me ever since I'd met him was now gone. It was as if some intangible part of me had been cut off, and now I was left diminished and incomplete.

By the time I yanked open the door to the café, my heart was pounding so hard in my ears, I couldn't hear anything but the tattoo of my own terror.

I'm coming to save you, I told him, unsure now of whether or not he could hear me.

One of the servers looked up when I dashed into the entrance, gasping my name. "Tat, what happened—"

I ignored her, ignored everyone to run painfully to the back areas, making my way through the kitchen and hitting the stairs at a pace that filled my head with pain. But I grasped that pain, and used it to keep from breaking down completely.

Finch needed me, and I had to prove to him that just because his parents' lives had ended tragically, ours did not have to follow the same path.

You're not the only one in love, and dammit, I'm not going to let anyone or anything take that away from us, all right? Just hang on, Finch. Believe in us. Believe in me.

There was no one in Deacon's office. I stumbled in a circle, and headed straight for the wooden panel, snatching up a large fire extinguisher as I did so. I hefted it despite the burn of pain in my hands and arms, and without waiting to see if I could find a switch to open the panel, threw the extinguisher.

The wood exploded in a nova of splinters, leaving a large fire-extinguisher-sized hole in the wall.

"What—" a man's voice behind me said.

I paused long enough to look at back at him, worried for a second that Deacon had come across me, but it was a stranger who was paused at the bottom of the stairs. He had black curly hair, and he squinted at me for a second before saying, "Ah. A Beloved. One a little worse for wear. Would you happen to know where I can find the owner of this establishment?"

"In hell by the time I get done with him," I snarled, and forced my unwilling legs to kick out the bottom half of the panel before careening through the resulting hole.

The passage twisted a couple of times, illuminated only by three naked bulbs that barely lit the space. I limped into a large open room, obviously once used as a cellar, with several closed doors along one side.

But it was the object in the center of the stone floor that caused me to stop, my brain unable to process what my eyes were seeing.

Jerry and Deacon stood on either side of what appeared to be a transporter pad from *Star Trek*. Runes glowed purple on the stone floor, the light of which flowed upward like an inverted waterfall of color. Within it, the air shimmered and wavered, as if it was made up of a million particles each moving independently.

"Get it done!" Jerry was saying when I hunched over for a few seconds, fighting pain and the blackness that threatened to send me into oblivion. Both turned to glare at me.

"What are you doing here?" Deacon asked, one hand outstretched to the transporter light, the other holding a scrap of yellowed paper. "And what the hell happened to you? Oh, now look! You're bleeding all over the floor, and I just got it bleached."

"Where's Finch?" I yelled, fury giving me strength enough to stand up straight, and take a couple of threatening steps toward him.

"Why is this taking so long?" Jerry screeched, coming around the wall of light toward me. "You made the sacrifice. Break the seal and get on with the summoning!"

"Like hell you're going to do anything—" I started to say, jerking away from Jerry when she tried to grab me.

"Ah. You, I assume, are Angharad Owain?" The man who I'd seen on the stairs emerged into the room, glancing around him.

"Who's this?" Deacon asked, his voice grey with annoyance. He made an annoyed tch, and added, "What is going on that everyone feels free to march into my private domain?"

"DO IT!" Jerry screamed at Deacon, who had started to set down the paper, no doubt to address the newcomer.

"Where's Finch?" I yelled again, and made a fist, about ready to deck Jerry if she tried to grab me.

"Where do you think?" Deacon said, glancing toward Jerry before picking up his paper. It looked old, and the writing on it was so faded, I realized it had to be vellum. He nodded toward the transporter light. "He served the greater purpose. Where was I? I'll have to start over again."

A noise sounded beyond the transporter, and a man loomed up, stumbling out of a room. It was one of the men who had asked about Finch.

The curly-haired man pursed his lips, and to my surprise, turned to me. "You must stop them."

"Who are you?" I asked.

"Can't you do anything right?" Jerry spat out, gesturing toward the man, who was rubbing his head. When Deacon started to move toward him, she added, "No! Do the job I asked you to do. It's just one simple job. Even you, the weakest of all my children, should be able to handle a simple summoning."

"You can't do this," the head-rubbing man said, but he didn't get much more out because at that moment, Jerry rushed him, shoving him back into the room. He started fighting, but she kneed him, then did a whirling kick to the jaw, which had him staggering backward.

"I am Leonid of Corinth," the man next to me said in a near whisper. "And I advise you to act quickly. You are almost out of time."

I glanced around the room, looking desperately for a weapon, considering for a moment whether or not I should go back and fetch the fire extinguisher.

"If you do not finish the summoning right now—" Jerry slammed shut the door and slid home a bolt before turning to face Deacon.

"I am trying, but it's difficult when these interruptions keep stopping me," he complained, and consulting the vellum, started intoning what sounded like Latin.

"You must act now, else all will be lost," the man named Leonid told me.

"And I've had enough of you, as well," Jerry said, starting around the transporter beam toward me, her fingers spread like daggers.

For a moment, I felt absolute panic, a fear that froze me to the ground, my brain unable to think. What was I to do? Who was Leonid? Was Finch in the transporter light? Did I have any other choice but to see for myself?

I eyed the transporter light, which was changing color from the purple to a silver tone.

Let's hope this is the right thing to do, because if it's not, I'm about to fuck us both up, I told the silent Finch at the same time I grabbed Leonid and whirled him around straight into Jerry. Without waiting to see what happened I leaped forward, ignoring the pain of my aching body, snatching the vellum from Deacon's hands before flinging myself into the transporter light, praying that I was right.

Jerry's roar of fury echoed in the room as the light filled me, tearing off bits and pieces of me until I became one with it.

FOURTEEN

"Hey."

Finch didn't want to open his eyes. He just wanted to lay there, insensible.

"Mate, you're in the middle of the road."

His body was racked with pain. His brain was stunned to the point he wondered if it would ever work again. And his heart…oh, his heart. What was a sudden realization that he couldn't live his life unless it included Tatiana now became a heart that didn't *have* life.

That bastard Cadell had killed him, sacrificed him to the Seventh Hour.

"I don't want to have to drive over you, because Bertha—she's the laundress around these parts—she charges an arm and a leg to get wheel tracks out of a jerkin. Ask me how I know." The words were accompanied by a robust laugh, and a prod to Finch's lower left leg.

He was dead. It had all come to fruition—the fear that he'd condemn an innocent woman to the hell that his mother had endured for the short time she'd lived after his father's death. He'd warned Tatiana. He'd explained it to her. He'd told her bluntly that he could not accept her as a Beloved because this exact thing would happen, and then he'd have the sin of her death on his soul, too.

Except he didn't seem to have a soul any longer.

"Right. Since you seem determined to not get out of the road, I'll just pull you to the verge, shall I?"

Finch was grabbed roughly under the arms, and hauled across a number of painful cobbles to an even more painful stone curb. "Ow."

"Glad to know you're still alive. Well, not alive, because this is the underworld, but you know what I mean, eh?"

It was Tatiana's fault they were in this situation, he told himself with a self-righteous sniff. If she had listened to him and kept her tempting self, fascinating mind, and truly limitless quirky nature from him, then he'd still be alive, and she wouldn't be, at this moment, no doubt throwing herself off the nearest cliff, or something equally as dramatic.

He spent a few minutes in martyred satisfaction of the hellish nightmare that fate had delivered to them both before the sensible part of his mind evidently woke up and took over running things again.

"Where, exactly, am I?" he asked, sitting up and glancing around.

"Snakespitter Lane," a rotund man with a crown of curly hair around a bald pate answered. He sat in a wooden cart pulled by an ox that looked as if it was dozing off. "You Finch Dante?"

"Yes," Finch said, getting to his feet, absently dusting off his trousers and glancing around. He appeared to be in a replica of medieval London, with narrow lanes, half-timbered houses, and people wearing clothing more suited to a renaissance fair than actual medieval times. Even the man in the cart sported a horn cup strapped to his belt next to what looked like a leather mobile phone case. "How do you know my name?"

"Town crier," the man said, jerking his head in the direction behind him.

Finch noticed an ornate fountain in a small square, around which several women in equally medieval fair garb were collected, chatting and consulting their phones. One sat on the edge of the fountain with a laptop on her knees, tapping away industriously. "You have a town crier?" he asked, trying to resolve the dichotomy of the medieval appearance and modern technology…in the afterlife.

"We do, indeed, and a mighty fine crier she is. Jareth— that's her name—she announces all new arrivals. Welp, best be getting along." He chirruped and tapped the ox's flank with a slender bamboo rod. "Come along, Billy. Let's get you home so you can have din-din, and then we'll watch a few eps of *CSI*, all right?"

Finch glimpsed a crudely made wooden bench at the far corner of the square, and made his way there, his heart sinking with every step. Now that the unhinged part of his mind had been squelched into silence, he realized that his situation truly was one of which nightmares were made. At least, his nightmares were.

Tatiana was alone, with no one to help her, no one to guide her through the pain she was no doubt feeling. He knew she must have felt the moment when Deacon ripped away his soul from him and threw him into the Hour, and his heart wept for what she had suffered. That he was helpless to do anything—he couldn't even contact his uncle to take her in, so that at the very least, she would have some sort of family to help her through the grief—almost smothered him with misery.

A woman about three feet high emerged from a house. Her red hair was piled on her head, and she wore a pink and white striped overall. But it was the bell she carried, ringing it as she marched over to the fountain before pulling her phone out of a pocket, and saying, "Hear ye, hear ye. The population of the Seventh Hour of the Underworld henceforth shall be numbered fourteen hundred and eleven. Welcome Tatiana Romanoff."

Finch was on his feet and in front of the little person before she did more than take a couple of steps, his heart coming to life with an avidity that brought a burn behind his eyes. "Where is she?"

The woman pursed her lips for a moment, then seemed

to understand his question. "Lovers, were you? I'm afraid I can't tell you where anyone manifests once they arrive at the hour. It's particular to each case, you see. But I can tell you—"

"FINCH!" The bellow echoed off the walls of the houses that made up the square. Everyone at the fountain turned to look at a woman posed dramatically at the entrance to the same street he had just trod.

"Thank you," he managed to get out before he was slammed backward several feet when Tatiana flung herself on him, scattering kisses all over his face. He hoisted her up, not caring one whit what anyone thought when she wrapped her glorious legs around his hips, her kisses becoming more urgent with each caress.

You're here! I found you! Oh thank the goddess, I thought you were dead. I wasn't sure if you went into the transporter, but you're here, and I'm here, and now you won't give me excuses about why we can't be madly in love with each other because you could die and you think I wouldn't want to live without you. Which I wouldn't. But we won't go into that because you're not dead, and we're together, and that's all that matters.

He kissed her back, his heart singing despite the situation, ignoring the howling black emptiness inside him where his soul had once resided. "Transporter?" he asked. "Do you mean the portal to the Seventh Hour?"

"The shiny glowy light show, yes," she answered, and kissed him a few more times. *I thought I'd lost you. I thought Deacon had done something horrible to you. I thought he turned you into a puddle of Finch goo that would make me vomit every time I saw you, and that I'd have to live the rest of my life with a Finch puddle. I'd still love you, mind, but I'd barf a whole lot.*

The scent of blood hit him at that moment. Old blood, but it was enough that he managed to get a good look at her. "Are you injured?"

"Not really. I mean, I skinned my knees and hands, and got run over by a car, but nothing is broken. Just a bit bruised. Are you OK?"

"Yes. Is there a—" he started to ask the little woman, but she anticipated his question.

"The Dog Sploot Inn is a block past the fountain, turn left at the ironmonger, and then straight on past the hot yoga shop. Tell Arlene you'd like the newcomer's room." The woman leaned close and said in a near whisper, "It has the vibrating bed, and eight flavors of lube."

"I don't think we need eight," Finch started to protest.

Tatiana slid down until she was standing again, and grabbed his hand, tugging him forward as she said, "Eight sounds perfect to me."

"Sweetheart, I realize you are as enthusiastic to see me as I am to see you, but there are some things we need to talk about before I do all those things you are thinking about. Especially that one. I would need a stack of pillows, and possibly a winch system for that. Really? The wheelbarrow position? I hadn't thought you would enjoy that."

She laughed aloud, her face so full of joy that for a moment, it dimmed some of the emptiness inside him. "OK, that might be a little ambitious—we can save the wheelbarrow for a later time—but you can't tell me you don't want to do all those things."

"I do. I very much do." He waited until they were past a group of children that were riding electric scooters, bouncing along on the cobblestones while whooping with excitement.

It took a few minutes before they were assigned a room—not, Tatiana grumbled in a disgruntled manner, the room with all the sexual aids—and made it up two flights of stairs to find themselves in a pleasant, if minimalistic, room.

"Right, talk first, or do I get to strip you starkers and start at your nipples and work my way down?" Tatiana asked, bouncing on the bed a little to test the mattress.

Finch was torn. Oh, his body knew exactly what it wanted him to do—he'd been shielding Tatiana from all but a few of his erotic desires—but the chill that struck him with her words when she'd arrived, combined with the events of the last hour, left his mind in charge.

"Talk, if you don't mind." He pulled a chair up to sit directly in front of her, wanting to be able to watch her expression, and yet needing to be close. "First of all, what you said a few minutes ago—"

She made a face. "It's because I more or less declared my love for you, isn't it? I'm sorry if that made you uncomfortable, but I've never been one to play mental head games, and I wanted you to know how I feel—"

"No, it's not that." It was his turn to interrupt. He took both of her hands in his, absently stroking his thumbs over the backs of her fingers, sorting in his normally logical mind what he needed to say. To his surprise, what came out was not what he expected. "Normally, I wouldn't have this sort of trouble. My mind has always been orderly. Tidy. Structured, even. I don't have mental battles with myself, Tat. My mind decides things, and then I act on them. But since meeting you, it seems to have morphed into something new. Something discordant."

He thought she'd be mildly indignant, but once again, she made him feel adrift in a sea of emotions. Her laughter rippled like the bubbliest of streams, filling the void within him with a strange effervescent joy that threatened to make him dance and sing and yell from the tallest rooftop about the glory that was his Beloved. "I know, right? I may not have been the most organized of thinkers before I met you, but then you came along and rocked my world, and my brain had to adapt or go under. I imagine it's the same for you. So we adapt."

"Adapt," he said, rolling the word around his mind. "Yes, that's a good summation of the experience of finding you."

"And falling in love," she prompted.

"Of course. As I mentioned before, we are mated in a fundamental, organic level."

Some of her bubbliness faded. Her eyes narrowed, and her hands, which had been lying passive in his, grew stiff. "I'm not talking about the mark thingie that let us mind talk when we first met, Finch. I'm talking about emotions.

Soul-embracing, deep emotions. That's what I feel. I thought that's what you felt, too."

"Ah. And we come to a point that I regret having to discuss."

She withdrew her hands, her back straightening. "Oh, goddess. You don't love me like I love you. I just made a fool of myself, didn't I? Did you even want me to follow you here?"

"No," he said, unable to lie to her.

He thought for a moment she had turned to stone, and with a mental sigh at the fact that he appeared to be doing nothing but saying the wrong thing, he pulled her up, and onto his lap. She didn't want to arrange herself on his legs, but after a few seconds of her squashing one of his testicles, he got her settled comfortably, and wrapped his arms around her, his face buried in her hair.

Normally, I'd feel sorry for the squashed testicle, but not right now, she said.

That's a shame, because it very much likes it when you lavish it with attention. She started to get off him, but he held her tight. *No, don't think thoughts of a gelding knife. I'm not being an ass, I swear. Or rather, I am because I'm not doing this right. Sweetheart, the fact that you would do something as drastic as coming to the Seventh Hour to be with me will remain one of the high points of all my memories.*

"Then why do you have the Finch Serious Face going on? Why are you talking like something is so horrible that we aren't using the one flavor of sexy time lotion I see on the dresser? Why do I have a feeling I've done something wrong?"

"My formerly ordered mind insists I take this step by step, so I'm going to lay those out for you. We'll start with Angharad Owain and her son Cadell."

"OK, but really, that looks like orange flavor, and while not my fave, I'm happy to give it a go. I'm even willing to use it on your balls."

He laughed, so happy for a moment, he was content to simply lean back in the chair, his arms and being full of the woman who had claimed his heart against its will. "This is going to take a bit of a strange turn, but bear with me. Several millennia ago, in the region of southwest Britain, a family of demigods resided. Some of them went on to found the mortal races in that area, and others…well, a few others remained doing whatever it is demigods do. One of them, Angharad Owain, was a member of the Court of Divine Blood."

"What—"

"Heaven. Or rather, it is the organization upon which early mortals based their idea of heaven. In reality, it's a structure of individuals who work for the general benefit of the mortal and immortal worlds."

Tatiana pushed back from where she'd been nuzzling his neck, and met his gaze, her lovely eyes wide. "Are you saying that Jericho Taf, the mayor of Ravenfall, is an angel demigod?"

"Former angel demigod." He made a dismissive gesture. "Minus the angel part. She was a member of the Court, however, so one can assume that at some point in time, she concerned herself with the welfare of others. No one really knows, because much of this history is lost to time, and the only reason I know so much is because my uncle has made a study of it. Where was I?"

"Jerry the mayor used to be an angel, and is a former god."

"Angharad had four sons. They were originally called wealden in the language of the area, but now they are mostly referred to as the four thanes who started the race of Dark Ones."

"Get out of here!" she said, leaping up from his lap, and staring at him with abject disbelief. "Jerry is the mother of vampires? Like in *Game of Thrones*, but with vampires instead of dragons?"

"Not quite. The wealden—thanes—decided amongst themselves that they would save mankind. They wanted to remove evil from the mortal world. Abaddon—the equivalent of hell, although it really isn't at all born of religious dogma—had just been formed by the coming together of ten princes. Demon lords, they are now, and there are only seven of them left, but at the time of forming, there were ten."

Tat sank down slowly onto the bed, her expression one of confusion followed by more disbelief, and finally acceptance. "OK," she said, nodding. "It makes sense that if there are good guys, there have to be bad ones. So the four vamp thanes decided to save the humans."

"They were prepared to fight the demon lord princes themselves to save mankind, but rather than support them, the mortals fell to the lures offered by the princes, and betrayed the thanes one by one. Their sins were bound to them in the form of a curse of blood, stripping them of their souls, and confining them to a part of the Underworld ruled by an old god, one powerful enough to enforce the imprisonment."

"What sins?" she asked, her forehead furrowed.

"That I don't know. Christian—my uncle—guessed that it had something to do with their hubris in thinking that they could save mankind from evil, but the truth is that we don't know. That information was either not recorded, or is also lost to time." He took a deep breath. "This part is where it gets dark. The thanes were bitter that the people they sacrificed themselves to save would turn on them and instead worship the false idolatry offered by the princes, and they swore eternal vengeance against both those who destroyed them—the demon lords—and those who were their tools— the mortals."

"I have to say that I can't really blame them a whole lot," she said, one hand absently playing with the bloodstained tears in the gauzy dress she wore. "I'd be pissed, too, if I tried to do something to save everyone, and they handed me over to the baddies. What I don't understand is how, if these four thanes were so powerful that they could take down ten demon lords, they were stuck in the underworld."

"The demon lords weren't strong enough together to accomplish that." He was silent for a moment, fitting together several pieces of information. "It took assistance from the Court of Divine Blood to bring about their betrayal and containment."

"The heaven place did that? Why?" Tatiana asked, clearly outraged and confused.

He gave a small shrug. "I don't know that, either. All the Court records say is that they were focused at the time in keeping order in the immortal world, and they worked with the princes to bind the thanes to the Seventh Hour."

"But…Jerry was a part of this Court, right?"

"She was until the time came to punish her sons. She refused to participate, and fought to save them. The sovereign—the being who controls the Court—stripped her of her powers, and removed her from the Court."

"Wow." Tat's fingers continued to play with the material of her dress. Finch wanted to get the discussion over so he could turn her mind to more pleasurable activities, but he knew he had to get the worst out of the way, and make it clear to her what had happened to them both. "That's seriously harsh. I feel bad for Jerry."

"Angharad tried for centuries to get the Court to intervene and have her sons released. Particularly her favorite, Rhain. She didn't have any luck. Until now." He was silent for a moment, moving another piece of the puzzle into place. "The weakest of her sons, Cadell, somehow escaped the Hour. I don't know how, but this I do know—they used my soul as part of the sacrifice to summon forth the Old God who guards the Hour."

"Why would they—oh, because without him to stand in front of the door, keeping the thanes in, Jerry could get her other three sons out? But why is that so bad? All they wanted to do was save people from evil, right?"

"And in the millennia following, they swore vengeance against everyone who contributed to their imprisonment," he reminded her. "To be honest, there are few things I'd rather see less than three demigods being set free who are bent on the removal of mortal beings."

Another piece of information moved into place, and he realized that was how Cadell knew what he was. Angharad's assistant Mara must also have been part of the family, since she'd also recognized him for a Dark One. In effect, he was their descendant.

"Yeah, I guess—wait, what? Deacon took your soul?" Tatiana leaped to her feet again, her expression so stark it pierced his heart. He immediately rose and took her into his arms again, the feeling of her there, where she belonged pressed tightly to him, helping to ease the void inside.

"He did. And I will never again think lightly of those Dark Ones who are unredeemed. It is not something I would wish on my enemies."

"Well, he has to give it back," Tatiana all but snarled, pushing herself away in order to storm around the room. "He can't take your soul! We'll have to go back and get it for you. I don't like this blackness I can feel in you, Finch. It's not right. Not right at all."

He sighed aloud. "And we come to the last, and most important point of this discussion. We are in the Seventh Hour."

"The place where the thanes are," she said, nodding, then stopped, her eyes growing huge. "They're here? Are they going to come after us?"

"I don't know why they would, or even where they are. But that is something I intend on finding out as soon as I can. The point, my delectable one, is that the Seventh Hour is part of the Underworld."

"Yes," she said, clearly not understanding.

He slid his arms around her waist, then down to her hips, those hips he loved so much. "The Underworld is inhabited by the dead, sweetheart. When Cadell—Deacon—stripped my soul from me and sent me to this Hour, he also took my life. In effect, I died at that moment."

"I felt it," she said, pressing herself against him. He tried to ignore both the demands of his body and the hunger that rose the second she leaped onto him. "It was horrible. Oh,

Finch, I'm so sorry he did that to you. But…if you're dead, why do you feel so solid? Why do you smell good? Why does your body against mine make me want to do wanton things to your naked self?"

"We are immortals, sweet," he said, giving in to the urge and nibbling the spot behind her ear that made her moan with happiness. She moaned. He lifted her and set her down gently on the middle of the bed. "The Underworld is merely another facet of existence."

"Am I dead, too?" she asked, not looking particularly distressed at the thought. It could be because she was, at that moment, getting out of her clothing as fast as humanly possible, or it could be because he was sending her thoughts of just what he wanted to do to every silken inch of her body.

"You are in the Underworld. You came through Cadell's portal. I'm afraid the likelihood is strong you are."

"Gotcha. Going to deal with that later. Right now, I want you in a way I've never wanted a man, and now I can have you with a clear conscience, because the curse can't do anything to you if you're dead, right?"

He chuckled, something he'd done only once or twice before he met Tatiana, but which now had become a staple in his expressions of amusement, and managed to get his own clothing off in record time, returning to the bed to assist her with her undergarments.

"I don't suppose that I am going to go back to looking like I did when I was about twenty?" she asked, looking askance at her torso. "Please tell me that death will give me perky boobs."

"Your breasts are perfect as they are," he told her, taking the warmth of them into his hands, his mind and body singing a song of happiness despite the situation. He realized that she was right—their deaths had freed them both from the fears that had hung over them. Now he could enjoy having a Beloved without worrying about making her suffer untold pain.

That's one of the few things that's keeping me from freaking out, she told him, her hands stroking down his chest. *That and the fact that I see now that we were meant to spend our lives together. Although...*Pain pierced her for a second, and he knew she was thinking of her cousin.

Let us worry about that later. I must have you now, Tat. My body craves yours. Tell me you want this.

Goddess above, below, and sideways. She pushed him over onto his back, and before he could protest, bent over his erection, her tongue stroking a path up him, causing his body to tighten until he felt like a bowstring about to break. *If I wanted you any more, I'd go up in flames.*

Pulling her over him, his mind overwhelmed with the scent and taste and feel of her as she leaned down, her lips sweet on his as she positioned him before sinking down slowly. "Are you—ah, do not grip me like that, sweet. I won't be able to last if you ripple your muscles again—are you ill? You seem to be hotter than normal."

She laughed, and the tightening of her body around him nearly brought him to orgasm. "You're the only man who could worry about my inner parts' temperature while making love. Bite me?"

With pleasure, my love, he answered, pulling her down and nuzzling her neck, waiting until she had lost her rhythm on him before biting, the pleasure almost too much for him to process.

He gave in to the primal need to possess, bucking wildly even as she gave in to her climax. And when he fell into his own, lost in the moment when their beings joined together, he was content that with Tatiana, he had everything he wanted in life.

The pain of losing his soul didn't return until a short time later.

He lay with her draped over him, her breathing soft and slow as she slept, and swore an oath that he would be happy with the cards he had been dealt. What was a soul when he had the one woman who made everything worthwhile?

His mind started to answer that question, but he stopped it, turning his head into Tatiana's sweet-smelling hair that spread across his shoulder.

She was enough.

FIFTEEN

Two days after arriving in the underworld, I stood at the window of our hotel room, and looked at the street outside. People in the underworld, I'd found, were an odd mixture. Some of them evidently really got into the whole medieval schtick, while others only slightly adopted the theme.

Finch emerged from the bathroom wiping his face. "Do you wish to explore the hour after you eat?" he asked, carefully folding the towel.

I turned to him, and made a face before smiling at him. He had agreed to go two days without shaving because I loved his stubble so much, but swore that by day three, the itching of his whiskers drove him to distraction. "I suppose we should meet with the greeter who came to see us yesterday. I'd like to find out where those thanes are, and who the old god is, and what we can do about leaving Angharad and Deacon in the world doing goddess knows what."

Finch's expression turned dark. "I'm afraid there is little we can do to stop them. When I confronted Deacon, he told me that I was the sacrifice they needed to summon the lord of the hour. By now, he must have completed the summoning."

I stared at him for a few seconds, then went running for my blue and white bag. "Holy mega shitsnacks! I totally forgot about this! I can't believe I did, although just seeing you again—and then we spent two days doing nothing but making love and taking breaks so I could eat—but I *did* forget about it, and Finch! Finch, we're saved!"

"What are you talking about?" he asked, moving over to peer down at the floor when I upended my bag and spilled the contents onto the floor. "Your raven doll? I don't see what that has to do with our situation."

"My raven doll is awesome," I told him, popping her onto a small table next to where I knelt. "Don't disparage Natasha. Where is it? Damn. How do tampons get so grubby just hanging out in a bag? Aha! Here. Look at this." I snatched up the bit of vellum I'd taken from Deacon, and handed it to Finch.

"What is it?" He started reading, his eyebrows rising.

"I hope that means you read Latin," I said, scooping up everything and shoving it all into my bag. I hesitated a second over Natasha, but decided that we'd have to look for somewhere to live that wasn't the inn, so carefully put her into the bag as well, mentally promising that I'd get her out just as soon as I could.

"I do. This appears to be—" He stopped, his pupils flaring. "It's the summoning spell."

"Yup." I got to my feet, strapping the bag across my body. "I took it off Deacon before I jumped into the transporter beam."

He continued to stare at me for the count of eight, then suddenly scooped me up and swung me around. "He didn't complete the summoning! You stopped him!"

I giggled as I kissed his now stubble free chin, and gently bit it. "You didn't think I was going to let him unleash hell on the world? All right, all right, I didn't know that was what he was doing, but still, I didn't want him to do whatever it was that Jerry was demanding. Can we do anything with this?"

"I'm not sure," he said. "Will you allow me to keep it?"

"Sure, I have no use for it."

"Let us meet with the Hour greeter, and perhaps we can see if there is any way we might use the summoning spell to our advantage," he said, one hand on my back as we left the room.

The warmth of his hand immediately had me thinking of going right back to bed, but I told my libido to cool its jets for a bit. The fact that we'd spent the last forty-eight hours making love should have been enough, but the little worry that had grown in the back of my mind came forth as we went downstairs and ordered breakfast for me.

The time in bed had been wonderful. Heart-warming. Inventive and satisfying and so toe-curlingly fabulous, that just thinking about it made me feel hot.

Until afterward, when Finch thought I couldn't feel the emptiness return inside him.

And I wasn't going to stand for that. Deacon had stolen Finch's soul…he had to give it back.

I don't know what I thought the introduction to the afterlife was going to be like, but it was not the dapper man in a salmon-colored suit with teal hair, a face full of piercings, and a small, matching salmon-colored dog of the yappy variety that he held in his arms the entire time he explained to us how the Hour worked.

"There are three houses for you to choose from, although if you wish to build your own, you are authorized to do so once every eighty years, so long as the style matches the current theme." Wyclef, the greeter, gestured toward the ye olde English houses that lined the street.

"Current theme?" Finch asked, looking down at the brochure the Wyclef had given us. "Does it change?"

"Frequently, when the lord is in a bad mood, but he's left this one for the last…oh, what is it, Daisy? Ninety-seven years?"

The little dog curled its lip at me and snarled.

"Yes, ninety-seven years," Wyclef said with a nod. "This concludes the overview of your life here. Are there any questions?"

"Only like a hundred," I said, confused. *Did I miss something? All he talked about was picking a place to live, and that there were a variety of classes we could take.* "For one, how do we pay for anything? Finch gave the inn woman some money for our room, but she didn't seem to be overly worried about payment. Are we renting a house or owning it? Do we have jobs? Where do we get food?"

Wyclef kissed the top of the little dog's head. "None of that really matters here. Money, that is. If you want something, you barter for it. Most of our citizens adopt some sort of a trade that they enjoy, just so they have bartering goods. Others take on tasks in exchange for food and items they desire. I, myself, when I'm not busy with greeting newcomers, work at a bakery making the most delectable of treats for our canine members. Now, if you'll excuse me, I really want to apply myself to a new carrot pumpkin recipe that I'm close to perfecting."

"One moment, if you please," Finch said, with a quick glance at me. "I am, as you are no doubt aware, a Dark One, and this is my Beloved. I understand that some of my...for lack of a better word, ancestors...are being held here. Can you direct us to the houses in which they live?"

"Ancestors—oh, the thanes!" Wyclef tucked Daisy into his pocket. She took the opportunity to growl at me again. "Alas, they are not part of the general population, as they are prisoners. Lord Troy keeps them in a special cloister. It's to the north of the town, and although I'm not certain they are allowed visitors, you can certainly apply with the gaoler."

"Cloister?" I asked. "Isn't that something to do with a convent?"

"The Brothers and Sisters of Perpetual Harmony care for those who were incarcerated in the Hour." Wyclef gave a bright smile. "They have a cracking *a cappella* group."

"The thanes?" I asked, confused beyond all reason.

"The Brothers and Sisters. You might see one of them when they have their walkabout," Wyclef said, his expression brightening. "Lord Troy allows each thane to visit the town for a few hours once a week. Not together, you understand—they are too powerful for that. But singly, and with the Brothers and Sisters accompanying them, they spend time with us. Let's see…today is Tuesday. Yes, it is one of the visitation days. They should be arriving around nonce."

That's noon, right?

Yes. Finch was thinking hard, but I couldn't tell exactly about what. *This is interesting. I believe I will wish to speak with whoever is allowed out today.*

I didn't understand his desire to see one of the guys who intended to destroy everyone if he got free, but to each his own.

It is an opportunity to learn much of the history of Dark Ones. My uncle would never forgive me if I did not take this opportunity to broaden our knowledge of the origins of our kind.

"Does that mean that Tatiana and I are not prisoners?" Finch asked.

Oooh, good question. Maybe we can simply walk out of here.

That's doubtful, but I thought it best to understand the level of our standing here.

"You? Of course you're a prisoner. You were both sent here through an expulsion portal, yes?"

"Yes, but…you said we could get a house and jobs and stuff," I said, waving my hand toward the bustling square. "We're not stuck in a prison with the *a cappella* nuns. Not that I want to be, but I don't understand."

"There are prisoners," Wyclef said, tapping the side of his nose. "And then there are *prisoners.* You are in the former group, and afforded the freedom of the Hour."

"Gotcha," I said, grateful that at least we had that going for us.

He glanced at a pocket watch. "Now, if there are no other questions, I really must trot. Come, Daisy. Papa has some noms for you to try."

"It's interesting that we are not considered as being incarcerated here," Finch said, rubbing his chin as we watched Wyclef hurry off toward the main square. "All things considered, there could be worse forms of existence."

His words were pleasant enough, but I felt the swirling darkness within him.

"Hey, wait a second," I called after Wyclef, and ran after him, leaving a questioning Finch behind.

Tatiana? Is something wrong?

No. Hopefully just the opposite. "Sorry to hold you up," I said, when Wyclef stopped, and glanced back with a frown. "But I had a quick question. Can we leave this place? Like, say, we wanted to go back home to visit people. Can we do that?"

"Leave the Hour?" He blinked a couple of times, and to my surprise, Daisy blinked with him before curling back her lip again. "Why would you want to do this? Lord Troy is most generous, and we want for nothing."

"But if we wanted to leave—just for a quick visit—could we?"

"Not unless you are summoned out," he answered and resumed his quick walk toward a bakery that sat just beyond the edge of the square.

"Damn," I said under my breath just as Finch stopped next to me.

"Unless, of course, you have an expulsion spell, but as Lord Troy doesn't allow those, the point is moot, isn't it?" Wyclef called over his shoulder before entering one of the medieval buildings.

"Expulsion spell!" I said, turning to Finch. "We can use the thing I took from Deacon!"

Finch was shaking his head even before I finished speaking. "I'm afraid that was a banishment spell, not an expulsion."

My spirits, which had risen with the thought of leaving, immediately plummeted. "Well…shit," I swore, wanting to simultaneously stomp my feet in a childish tantrum, and sob with frustration.

Finch watched me for a moment, then gently pulled me up to his chest, kissing my hair. "Sweetheart, I realize you can feel what's happened to me despite me trying to keep it from you, and I appreciate that you think you can get my soul back from Deacon, but I'm afraid that's just not possible. This is our life, now. We are together, and as the greeter said, this isn't an unpleasant place. Do you not think we could find happiness here, together?"

I wrapped my arms around him, and wiggled my hips—which for some reason, Finch seemed to love beyond reason—against him, instantly arousing him.

"I would be happy with you anywhere, but there's no way—crap, sorry." My bag had slid around with all my provocative movements, and was pressed between us. I peeled it off, dropping it to the street before resuming my hold on him. "There's no way I'm going to let you suffer like this. I figure there are two things we can do—we can go beat the crap out of Deacon until he gives you back your soul, or we can do the thing that you said Beloveds do to get souls for their vampires. Do you know what they have to do?"

He shook his head. "I already thought of that. For the most part, we've completed the Joining steps. I suspect, given your description, it's why you weren't harmed when you threw yourself into the Hour. You are, in effect, immortal now. However, the last step is for the Beloved to make a sacrifice, and frankly, I've had enough of those to last me the rest of our lives."

"What sort of a sacrifice?" I asked, panic rising at the thought of something being cut off.

"It is unique to each Beloved, and you can stop thinking about the leg that fell off your past suitor. No one but me is touching your lovely legs."

I accepted the quick kiss he pressed to my lips before he consulted the paper we'd been given. Available houses had been marked on a map of the Hour. "OK, but just so you know, if it's something trivial, like maybe losing a toenail—a pinkie toe toenail—then I would totally do it. So long as it didn't hurt. And wouldn't bleed, or ooze things." I gave a little shudder, and took a step forward when Finch, releasing me, tried to orient the map to the town.

"Shall we go look at the houses available?" he asked.

I stumbled over my bag, swore, and bent to gather up the half dozen things I'd trod on when they spilled out. "Damn! My raven doll! Oh no." I examined Natasha, noting with regret that her black lace mantilla was torn, one of the garnet beads of her necklace had come loose and was dangling by a thread, and the little paper tag with her name had torn off from the tiny safety pin, and now had a smear of mud from my shoe. "It's a good thing I wasn't planning on selling her, because I've severely dropped her sales potential. Could you—thank you."

Finch handed me the minute paper envelope, roughly the size of a large postage stamp. I pulled a silk scarf out of my bag and carefully wrapped Natasha in it, hoping I could repair the damage to her before I studied her envelope to see if I could clean and reattach it.

"I believe the nearest house is on the other side of the square," he said, consulting the map again. "The two others appear to be out in what I assume is countryside. Would you prefer to live in town, or have some privacy—what's wrong?"

I stared at the bit of paper, having brushed off the dirt that I could before I turned it over to read the words stamped on the other side.

Open for spells.

"Spells." I looked up at Finch. "You don't think—"

He looked confused for a second, then his eyebrows rose. "Do I think a doll you bought in the mortal world has the power to get us out of the Underworld? Unfortunately, no. I'm sorry, Tat, but such spells are powerful, and much sought after. They are well-guarded."

"Jerry has a couple of raven dolls," I said slowly, digging through my memories from what seemed to be eons ago, but was actually, I realized with a start, almost a week before. "Mara told me about them at the auction where I found Natasha. She said there were five sisters, five raven dolls, and Jerry was trying to find the others. She didn't know I had two of them already when I found Natasha at the same auction where Mara was nosing around for it."

"I admit that's an odd coincidence," Finch said, watching as I pried open the glued down bit of envelope flap. "However, it's likely to be nothing but that—a coincidence."

"Dammit, this is really glued down…shit. Tore the envelope. Oh well. Here's a tiny bit of paper."

I pulled out a faded yellow paper that had been folded over several times. It appeared to be written on rice paper, or something so fragile it was almost transparent. Finch leaned close to me to read it with me. Around us, people laughed, chatted, and occasionally shouted, while carts rumbled past us, kids shrieked and ran around, followed by dogs, chickens, and a couple of goats. Everything was swept into a background that faded to obscurity when compared with the paper I held between two fingers.

"*Spell to imply the wrongly freed*," I read, squinting and turning the paper to catch the sunlight that filtered in between the tall overhanging houses.

"Imprison the wrongly freed, I think," Finch corrected, and with a *tsk* at himself, slapped his pockets until he pulled out a key chain. He fussed with it for a few seconds until he pulled out a small metal piece that looked like an antique pocket knife, but when he opened it up, it held an oblong bit of glass. He held the magnifying glass over the paper. "Yes, imprison. Is there something on the back? It looks like ink bleeding through the paper."

I turned it over, and we both looked. I blinked at Finch.

He put a finger under my chin, and gently pushed up, closing my open-with-astonishment mouth. "I retract my previous statement," he said.

"Woohoo!" I shrieked, and clutching the paper, threw myself on him and kissed him with as much hope and love and happiness as I could share with him.

Spell to free the wrongly imprisoned read the title on the back side of the paper.

He squeezed my butt, and kissed me back, then abruptly set me from him, and said, "Let us return to our room to examine the paper."

I was careful to slide it back into the mangled envelope, and tucked it away in the folds of the cloth holding Natasha before we hurried back to the inn.

A half hour later, Finch stood up from where he'd been hunched over the paper, handing me the notebook into which he'd transcribed the spidery writing.

"Right, how do we do this?" I said, almost dancing with excitement. "Do I just read it? Should I hold Natasha when I do it? I probably should, shouldn't I? It's her spell, after all." I snatched up the doll, and after giving her a kiss on the black cloth raven beak, tucked her against my arm. My bag was already slung around my body, and I took a quick glance around the room, making sure I hadn't left anything.

Finch said nothing while I bustled about, tidying the bed and replacing the orange lube to the dresser.

His silence finally struck me when I turned back and realized he wasn't even looking at me. He was staring out of the window.

"What's wrong? Oh no—don't tell me the spell isn't complete or something? Are we missing part of it? Some item that is needed to make it work?"

"No." He turned back, and regret and sadness leeching from him. "We can't use the spell."

"Why?" Tears burned in my eyes, immediately making my throat ache. "Why can't we?"

"Take a look at the last sentence." I looked down at the notebook in my hand.

Most of the spell looked simple enough, more like blank verse poetry than anything else, but the last sentence Finch had underlined.

With this sacrifice, grant me that which my heart seeks.

"Sacrifice? What sacrifice? Why are there always sacrifices?" I set down Natasha and the notebook, and stormed over to Finch. "Everyone and everything seems to be obsessed with them! First Deacon, then vampires in general in order to get your soul, and now this spell...dammit, Finch!"

"I know, and I'm sorry. For a moment, I thought this was the answer we sought—" he started to say, reaching for me.

I had a moment of foresight, one that seemed to slow down time so that Finch's hand reaching for me was shifted down to super slo-mo. I had a mental image of us remaining in the Hour, him living with the emptiness inside him, and me forever berating myself for being such a coward that I couldn't do what was needed to fix things.

Fear. It was all about fear. I saw with clarity that I'd spent the bulk of my life acting in response to perceived fear, a fear that hung over my head like a cloud, but which never actually opened into a storm. I stayed in Ravenfall because I was afraid to lose my boon. I suffered Ozy and Jerry's campaign of driving me out, because I was afraid of what they would do if I confronted them. And I was afraid to try to break the curse that blighted my romantic relationships, instead hiding from it, and allowing it to rule my life.

I looked at Finch, at his lovely eyes now the color of the summer sky, at the planes of his face which had become so familiar, at the wonderful body that gave me such pleasure, and which housed his wholly unique mind.

No, I told him. *Not this time. I'm going to be the person you see. I'm going to be brave.*

And before he could react, I snatched up both Natasha and the notebook, quickly reading aloud the four lines of the spell, praying as I did so that the sacrifice didn't cost me the one thing I couldn't live without: Finch.

"Raven ancestor, dark of wing and eye,

Call to you those of heart strong and spirit bright.

Freeing the ones betrayed,

With this sacrifice, grant me that which my heart seeks."

"Tatiana, don't do—" Time snapped back to normal at my words. Finch grabbed my arm just as if he could stop it, but before he could finish his sentence, a percussive blast exploded from nowhere and everywhere, a brilliant golden light dazzling my eyes even as we were thrown backwards, slamming against the wall. For a second, I felt as if I was caught in the middle of a song, one so joyous it made me want to shout in exultation.

And then everything went black, and I knew no more.

SIXTEEN

It was the screaming that filtered through the blackness in my head.

My fingers curled against a cold, hard substance. Cement, I thought. What was I doing on a cement floor?

"You can't blame me for this!" the voice screamed, making my head pound. "It wasn't my fault! Mother—"

"This is the last straw, do you hear me? The last. You are weak, Cadell. You have always been weak, and you always will be. First you kill my sister—which I admit I don't mind, but for what? All you did is end up with a body on your hands."

"It wasn't my fault," the voice repeated, and it occurred to me that it was Deacon speaking. Why was I on a cement floor near Deacon? "And I got rid of the body, so you can't complain about that."

The woman made a little snort of derision. "You stuffed it in the basement of a newcomer. You had to know that would bring in the sheriff."

"He was one of the Children," Deacon answered with a distinct whining edge to his voice. "He deserved any trouble that followed."

"Nonetheless, it was a heedless, foolish act." I recognized the woman's voice, too. Jerry was here. Jerry and Deacon. Together. Something nudged the black mass that was my mind.

Deacon's whine grew. "Why do you always blame me? I did my best. I always do, but it's never good enough for you. You said get someone powerful for the sacrifice to the lord, and I captured Ozy. Besides, I didn't kill her. A demon did it."

Tatiana?

Memory rushed back to me at the soft brush against my mind, and I gasped, my eyes opening as I sat up. Next to me, Finch was stirring. *Goddesses everywhere, it worked! Wait... what did I lose? All my arms and legs appear to be here. Is it an organ? Did the spell eat up something I need to live? Oh no! It's you, isn't it? The spell sacrificed you loving me!*

He laughed even as he groaned softly, sitting up and rubbing his head, squinting a little against the naked bulb hanging over head. *Nothing could make me stop loving you. You are my life, my starshine, my moonlight, the breath in my lungs and the beating of my heart.*

"Can't even handle your own sacrifices," Jerry said, scorn filling her voice. I glanced around, but didn't see either of them. Neither did I see the *Star Trek* transporter, which had been here before. From the sound of it, Deacon and Jerry were just around the corner at the entrance of the basement.

Oh, Finch, I said, my eyes watering a little as I got to my knees and patted him down, making sure all of his limbs were correct and present, too. *That is, hands down, the sweetest thing anyone has ever said to me. I'm going to make you repeat it every day. Are you missing anything internally? Can you see? Hear? Smell?*

"What was I supposed to do?" Deacon's voice rose. "You said sacrifice one of the Children and I did. It's not my fault if that bitch Tatiana ruined it all."

No to all of them. He stood up, and held out a hand, helping me up. *In fact, just the opposite. Somehow, you've managed to return my soul.*

I gasped an open-mouth gasp, then flung myself on him, sending us both toppling over backward. *It's back? Really? Let me feel? Goddess, it is! That whirling black wind inside you is gone. Finch! We did it! We escaped and got your soul back.*

You did both, sweetheart. I had nothing to do with it. Although if you keep squirming on me like that, I will not be able to keep from claiming you as my body, mind, and heart demand.

I gave one last wiggle, then got to my feet, holding out a hand for him. *I see nothing wrong with that idea.*

Nor do I, he said, brushing himself off. *Or rather, I wouldn't, but the conversation going on outside the room is offering much food for thought. Are you hearing it, too?*

Jerry and Deacon? Yeah. They killed Ozy.

So it would seem. His eyes narrowed until they were little chips of blue in a whole lot of handsome face.

Happiness burbled inside of me. He seemed whole, I seemed whole, and he had his soul back. Life was looking pretty damned good. *Shall we go scare the crap out of them?* I asked.

"I'm done with your excuses. I should have left you in the Hour, where you belong. You shouldn't have been summoned in the first place," Jerry snapped.

"Because I'm not Rhain?" Deacon said on a near snarl. "Of course you wanted Rhain, not me. It was always thus. Rhain the golden one. Rhain the highest in your favor. Rhain the everything. Well, it was *I* who responded to the summons, not him."

"Only because you were the weakest. The lord realized that, and didn't bind you as tightly to the Hour as the others," Jerry responded, her voice coming from a distance. That plus the sounds of someone stomping her way up the stairs had Finch and me moving cautiously to the open door. Just behind it, Deacon stood with his back to us, his hands fisted as he watched Jerry ascend.

"I have always only ever served you!" he bellowed. "You can't blame me for circumstances out of my control! This is not my fault."

It was at that moment that I realized what sacrifice I had made to get us out. My fingers tightened around Finch's. *I can't hear colors.*

His eyebrows rose. *In either of them?*

No. My heart felt like it was a contracting into a small ball of unhappiness. *I've lost my boon. That's what the spell took.*

I'm sorry, sweetheart. But perhaps it's not really gone. Let us first attend to this one, and then we will find out what we can.

Sure, I said, but my spirits were sodden blobs of misery until I reminded them that we'd gotten out of the underworld.

"So it was you who killed Ozy?" Finch asked. He had released my hand, and I realized he was poised to move, like a jaguar about to pounce.

Deacon spun around, sputtering at the sight of us. "What—how did you—who brought you out? Where is my spell?"

"Tucked away where it's safe," I told him. *Should we call the sheriff? She'll be super interested in the fact that Deacon admitted to killing Ozy. Wait, did I hear Jerry say he killed her sister? Ozy was Jerry's sister? Does that mean she was...she's a...*

Demigod, Finch said, his mind rife with speculation. *I assume so. And does your sheriff have the ability to control someone of Deacon's power?*

"Then you can just give it back. You've put me in enough trouble," he said, starting toward me with an ugly look on his face.

Finch was instantly there in front of me, slamming his fist into Deacon's face. I expected the latter to stagger back at least a little, but he just shook his head, and narrowed his eyes at Finch.

"You think you have any power against me? You are merely one of the Children. I am a thane. You owe your existence to me! I was so feared it took the Court and Abaddon joining forces to defeat me. You are nothing, and I tire of dealing with you and Tatiana."

I realized then that we had a problem on our hands—he was the son of a demigod. Hell, he was probably one himself, even if Jerry had called him weak. There was no way the local jail would be able to hold him, and certainly Finch couldn't deal with him his own.

There was only one solution. I closed my eyes for a second, and sent up a prayer to the goddess, and pulled out Natasha and the notebook.

"Black of wing and eye, raven queen,
Fly with the imposters,
To the cage made of their sins.
By the light of the silver moon and blackened sun."

Tatiana, why do you insist—Finch started to protest, but he was interrupted when Deacon, with a sound that tore through my mind, lunged toward me.

As spoke the last word, Deacon froze for a second, then turned his gaze on Finch, and said simply, "It's not fair."

He seemed to dissolve into a black smoke that slowly dissipated as Finch and I stood watching it with, at least in my case, a stunned expression.

"All right," I said, looking down at myself. "What did I lose this time? I mean, I don't mind sacrificing something minor to get him stuffed back into the Hour, but I'd really rather it wasn't anything big. I'm still feeling a bit *verklempt* over not being able to hear colors."

"Lose?" Finch shook his head, then pulled me into a fast, hard kiss. "You lost nothing else, you quick-thinking, delicious woman. Did you not notice that the banishment spell did not require a sacrifice? I assume it was considered the lesser of the two magics."

"No—it didn't occur to me—but you're right, there was nothing about a sacrifice. What the hell am I saying? We have to hurry and catch Jerry."

I didn't wait for his reaction, I raced up the stairs, part of me filled with exuberance that we were back in the real world, that we were whole—mostly—and we'd done what seemed like an impossible task, and sent Deacon back to the underworld where he belonged, while the other part was still regretting the loss of my boon.

It's no use, love. I'm sure she's gone by now, he said, but was hot on my heels when I leaped through the still-broken wooden panel, and thundered up the second flight of stairs.

"Have you seen Jerry?" I asked, panting slightly when I skidded to a stop in front of Emma, one of the servers.

"She left a minute ago," Emma answered, eyeing Finch. "Is this the guy you were having sex with on the sidewalk—"

"That's so three days ago," I told her, and ran out the door. *Maybe we can catch her in the parking lot. Or at her office.*

Finch said nothing, but his mind was troubled, although I couldn't get a good grasp on just what it was that bothered him. It concerned Jerry, but he was trying to keep something from me. I made a mental note to have it out with him later.

We searched along the Walk and those people outside Jerry's office, but she was nowhere to be found.

"I'd better call Clemmie," I said after we gave up the hunt. I hit the button for her, adding, "She's probably worried sick about where we disappeared to—Clemmie! Before you lecture me, we're OK."

"Lecture you?" Her voice sounded odd now that it was colorless. Almost tinny. I didn't like it at all. "Why would I lecture you? And why wouldn't you be OK?"

"Because we've been gone for three days."

"Huh? Are you whackadoodle? No, sorry, that wasn't for you. Yes, that is the price, and no, we don't do layaways."

I put my hand over the phone, and asked Finch, who was consulting his own phone, tapping quickly as he obviously sent a text, "Why is Clemmie not concerned that we disappeared?"

He held up his phone, pointing to the date. "Time evidently works differently in the underworld. It's only been half an hour in the mortal plane since Deacon sacrificed me."

"OK, that's just too weird for me to deal with," I said. "Sorry, Clemmie, things have happened that I can't explain now. More later. You OK to handle the store for a bit longer?"

"Sure. But we're going to need to restock. Traffic has been good today," she added in a whisper.

I reassured her I'd attend to it and hung up, looking around and wondering how we were going to find Jerry. "Well, at least we can go clear our names with the Entity."

"Hmm? Oh, yes."

"What is it you're texting? Or am I prying?"

"You're not, but it's not very interesting. The two Dark Ones I'd met here were evidently assaulted by Deacon when he sacrificed me, but they escaped shortly thereafter. They told my uncle I was missing, and I was simply reassuring him that I was not harmed, and that we had news for him. We'll have to do a video call later."

We walked toward the town hall while Finch spoke. I had initially felt a spurt of joy at having returned, but now I rubbed my arms against a sudden appearance of goose bumps, and glanced around trying to pinpoint what it was that had me feeling so…awkward. Unwelcome. Out of place.

It wasn't just the loss of my synesthesia—this was a sense of strangeness that wrapped around me like a thousand silken threads.

We approached the town hall, and for a second, I paused, sure I'd seen one of the gargoyle's head turn toward us, but when I gave it a good, long look, it stared back with a stony gaze. *Remember when I was arrested and you said this building was breathing at you?*

That was my impression, yes, he answered, glancing up at the doors as we mounted the steps. *It was aware of me.*

I believe you. I just caught one of the stone gargoyles glaring at me.

Interesting. We'll have to study them later.

To my surprise, the doors opened just as Finch reached for them. No one stood on the other side.

"I'm not even going to address this," I said, shaking my head at the doors.

"It's probably best."

Without waiting for an invitation, we entered the room on the left, and found the Entity in discussion with two men, one of whom I recognized.

"There, you see?" The larger of the two men pointed at us as we stopped a few feet away. Finch put away his phone while I, feeling somewhat rattled and not in a mood for any crap, held up my mine and took a picture of the men. "They are here. It is as I told you."

"Actually, sir, I was the one who—" Leonid started to say, but the other man interrupted him.

"And I demand that you do something about the situation."

"What, exactly, would you like us to do?" Anya asked, and if I didn't know better, I'd say she was fighting to keep from smiling. "This is your purview, Lord Troy. It has nothing to do with the Entity."

"You're the one who sent these two to my Hour, and look how that turned out."

"One moment," Finch said, holding up a hand. The larger man looked mildly outraged at Finch's interruption. "Am I to take it that you are the god who rules the Seventh Hour?"

"Demigod, and yes." He gave an abrupt nod of acknowledgment. "Troy of Ilios. And you, Dark One, have done irreparable damage. You must be punished for it."

"What damage?" I asked, taking a step forward, but was gently pulled back to Finch's side. "What punishment? We've already been through a hell of a lot. *Literally*."

"I demand action," Troy told Anya, ignoring me. "You must act."

"Action has already been taken," Lyric told him.

"The boon has been removed," Quinton added, nodding toward me. "She has been named nonresident. That is all we are obligated to do."

"Nonresident?" I asked, rubbing my arms again before leaning into Finch. He was so solid, so warm, that just being pressed up beside him provided immense comfort. "What's that? Is it why everything feels off?"

"Your welcome in Ravenfall has been revoked," Lyric explained.

Horror rippled down my back. "But I was born here! That's why I had a boon. You're making me feel like a stranger just because my boon is gone?"

"You have been made nonresident because of your actions," Anya said quietly.

That explains the weird feeling, I told Finch, sadness filling my heart. *I wondered what was wrong. They made me a stranger just because I used the spell.*

Guilt swamped him at my words.

Stop it. I put an arm around him. *I would do it again a hundred times if it meant having you safe and sound.*

That requires much praise and appreciation, neither of which I can give you at this time, but remember it for later, please, when we are alone. I will express myself in a very tangible way for all your help.

You're on, you sexy vampire, you.

"Well, something else has to be done," Troy was demanding, slamming his hands down on the table and glaring at the Entity. "I won't have it said in the Council of Hours that I was at fault when clearly it is the Dark One and his mate who are responsible."

"Responsible for what, exactly?" Finch asked at the same time that Leonid pulled Troy aside with a murmured, "My lord, if I may…"

"It would appear that a spell was enacted in the Seventh Hour," Anya said, her dark gaze on me. I moved my bag so that it hung behind me, just in case she had designs on my raven doll. "One that has the gravest of repercussions…and for which you will be called to account."

"Now, hold on here," I said, wanting to tell her a thing or two. "We've done nothing wrong. Yes, we used a spell to get ourselves out of the Hour, but we were tossed there—well, Finch was, anyway—by Deacon, so he shouldn't have been there in the first place. Not to mention Deacon stole Finch's soul."

"What repercussions?" Finch asked, pulling me close to his side again when I was about to march forward and confront the Entity. *Remember to whom you speak, Tat. They will not suffer foolish words easily.*

They're trying to railroad us!

I think not. Something is badly awry in the world. I can feel it. I'm not sure what it is, but I suspect it has something to do with our escape from the hour.

"It is for Lord Troy to speak of that," Anya answered. "We can only address the wrongs done to Ravenfall."

"Look," I said, still strangely antagonistic. For a second, I marveled over the fact that just a few days ago, I would have died rather than speak to the Entity in such a tone, but now I realized I had nothing to fear from them. I'd gone to hell itself and come back wiser.

The underworld isn't actually hell—

Dude. I'm pumping myself up!

That, my adorable one, is what I'm worried about.

"Look," I repeated, and taking Finch's hand, moved forward a couple of steps since Leonid and Troy were still in whispered conference, the latter waving his hands around dramatically and vehemently denying something Leonid said. "You told us we had to fix the situation with Jerry and Ozy. Well, we've done so. Jerry has been found—not that she was ever lost—and apparently ran off when we tossed Deacon back into the Hour."

"You what?" Troy stopped in mid-protestation to stare at us.

"We were in possession of a spell that returned Cadell to the hour," Finch said, and with that, I could feel speculation starting to form in his mind. "A spell that was oddly specific. It would seem that it was given to Tatiana by purpose rather than chance."

Leonid looked at Troy. "You see? It's just as I told you," he said before they continued their whispered argument.

"And we found out that Deacon killed Ozy," I told Anya et al triumphantly. "So you can scratch that off the list of things you insisted we do."

They looked at each other for a few seconds before all turning confused expressions on us. "Now, why would he be doin' that?" Quinton asked. "That doesn't make one lick of sense."

You want to tell them, or should I? I asked Finch.

You do it. I'm trying to eavesdrop on the old god.

Oooh. Covert action! I like it. I took a couple of steps forward until I was right in front of the table, giving Finch the opportunity to edge a smidgen closer to where Troy and Leonid were talking. "When we popped back from the Hour into which Deacon had sent Finch—after taking his soul—we found Deacon and Jerry arguing. Or rather, she was yelling at him for being incompetent, and one of the things she found lacking was the fact that he killed Ozy—"

"Had a demon kill her," Finch murmured.

"That's right, he had a demon kill her...holy shiitake. Demons are real, too?" I asked, turning to face Finch.

He cocked an eyebrow at me. "You had no problem accepting the idea of demon lords."

"Oh." I made a face and turned back to the Entity. "I guess it makes sense that if there are demon lords, there must be demons, right?"

They all stared back at me like I had a demon dancing on my head.

I cleared my throat. "Anyway, evidently Jerry was demanding that Deacon get someone named Rhain out, and sacrificing Ozy was supposed to do the job." A thought struck me. "I wonder what happened to the six women he was holding? He told Jerry they were for a sacrifice, too."

"The prisoners were freed earlier," Lyric said. "After you spoke to us about Angharad and Cadell, we saw to it that they were freed."

"Oh, good. Anyway, that's what happened to Ozy, although I have no idea why he dumped her in Finch's basement other than sheer spite."

"You will have to ask him that," Anya said, her gaze flickering toward the two men, who were still arguing, now evidently in Greek.

"It's not likely that I'll have the opportunity to do so, but if I do see him again, you bet I will," I told her.

Finch, I was interested to note, was now wholly engaged by Troy and Leonid, and didn't seem to realize I'd moved back to stand next to him, nudging his hand a couple of times until he took the hint and held my hand. *Are you picking anything up?* I asked.

He said something in a language I didn't understand. I had a feeling, however, that he was swearing.

Uh oh. What's wrong? I asked him.

He didn't answer right away, and when he did, I could feel his reluctance to do so. *The spell used to remove us from the Hour...it did more than release us. It released someone else who was falsely confined there.*

I frowned into his mind. *That can't be bad, can it? If someone was falsely confined, it must mean they were good.*

It depends. He turned to face me, his eyes a dark sapphire. "You told me once you loved living here, and could never imagine residing anywhere else. Is that still true?"

I tried to read his mind, but he carefully kept it closed to me. It took me a minute before I could put my feelings into words. "That was true at the time. But now..." I shot a glance at the Entity, who was also now clustered together, obviously in consultation. "But now this isn't home. It's like my tie to the area was severed. So if you're asking if I would go live with you elsewhere, the answer is a heartfelt yes. It'll mean handing over my shop to Clemmie, but I've long suspected she'd make it a huge success. Much more than I could ever do."

"I have made a decision," Troy announced, giving Leonid a shove with his elbow so that he could strut over to us, dripping with self-importance. I didn't miss the eyeroll that Leonid gave when he did so. "Since you are responsible for the release of the thane, your penance will be to take responsibility for the Hour. I so name you as my replacement. Henceforth, you will be known to all as the lord and lady of the Seventh Hour. Leo? I want you to film me as I leave. My followers must have an explanation as to my disappearance for two days. Also, I believe I shall tap the walls with my fingernails as I pass. ASMR, do you see? I wonder if I can incorporate it in climbing…?"

Troy strolled out of the room without a backward glance at us. I, personally, was too stunned to do much more than stare wide-eyed at Leonid as he gave Finch and me a weak smile, then bowed to the Entity before pulling out his phone to film Troy.

"Did he—he just said—we have to go back?" I asked Finch, taking both his hands in mine. Not even the warmth of his fingers around mine could calm the confusion and panic in my brain.

Finch was silent a moment, then with a little squeeze, looked around me to ask the Entity, "Since we committed Cadell to the Hour, it must be another thane who was released. Can you tell me which one?"

Lyric and Quinton left the room without saying anything. Anya stood for a moment behind her chair, studying first my face, then Finch's. "The being released by your spell was Owain."

Finch's shoulders slumped for a few seconds before he squared them, and gave a sharp nod. "Then I will accept the penance placed upon us—upon me—by Lord Troy."

I'm confused. I know that seems to be my default mode lately, but now I'm really, really confused. Epic level sort of befuddled.

The lord of the Hour evidently no longer wants the job, Finch answered.

Does that mean we have to take it? I asked, thinking of the medieval town that made up the bulk of the Hour.

We have freed one who was imprisoned there. I suspect if we did not agree to take over the position of ruler of the Hour, we would face a much less attractive future.

Anya was still for a moment, then she made Finch a bow. I had a feeling she didn't bow to people much. "Lord Troy made a good choice, I think." Her gaze slipped to me, and she gave a wry half-smile. "And much though we will miss your constant stream of complaining emails, we believe that you, also, will prosper in the Seventh Hour."

"Oh, man," I said, my cheeks growing hot. "I didn't real-ize you actually got those. No one ever replied, so I thought they were going to a spam folder. Um. Some of the things I said might have been a wee bit over the line."

"Very much so. It was only because we knew you had a role to play that we chose to ignore them," she said, her lips twitching twice. Then she turned and left, the door closing softly behind her.

"Oh, now that's just bull," I said, slapping my hands on my legs when I turned back to face Finch. "They put me through hell! They put some sort of a curse on my romantic life! They no doubt riled up Ozy and unleashed her on me. And then they evicted me! In no sense of the word did they ignore me."

"Part of me wants to comfort you, and the other part wants to run screaming from the room," he said, looking somewhat dazed about the eyes.

"I'm willing to bet you've never run screaming from any-thing in your life," I said, leaving with him when he held out a hand for me.

"No, but that doesn't mean I don't wish to do so now. We set one of the thanes free, Tat. This is beyond terrifying. I'm surprised they didn't demand we find him and return him."

"I understand that they are not nice people, but Dea-con wasn't that bad. Maybe this Owain will be like him, and someone else will take care of him," I suggested.

"Cadell was the lesser of all the thanes. By all accounts, he was despised by his brothers for his weaknesses. He had power, yes, but it was focused solely on doing his mother's bidding."

"And the guy who got released isn't such a mess?" I asked, my stomach feeling as if it was filled with lead.

"Very much the opposite." He took a long, long breath as we exited the building. He didn't even stop to look up at the gargoyles, although I glanced over my shoulder at them.

One winked at me.

"I told you there were four thanes," he said. "Their names were Owain—the oldest and first to fight Abaddon, then there were Rhys, Rhain, and Cadell. And now Owain is free, and I must explain to my uncle what we've done before we take up our duties. Tat."

"Finch," I said, stopping when he swung me around to face him. I felt such a conflicting wad of emotions, it was hard to separate them.

"Do you mind? Really mind?" he asked, his lovely eyes so filled with worry that I would do just about anything to make them smile at me again.

I touched one of the little laugh lines that emerged from the corner of his eye. "Going to the Hour? Not so long as we're together."

"It won't have to be bad," he said, looking past me. I could feel his mind turning over a number of thoughts, and wanted to laugh. He was making lists, I could tell. Nice, tidy orderly lists for our nice, tidy orderly lives. "As the ruler of the Hour, I believe we will have the power to make changes to its appearance. So if you wanted it to look like something else—"

"Axegate Walk!" I said, happiness filling me again despite everything, despite the loss of my boon, and what was more or less an exile from a home I loved. Had loved…before I met Finch.

Now *he* was home.

"If you like," he said slowly, his eyes lightening to a topaz. "We will present the suggestion to the occupants of the Hour. They might like the idea, although it will naturally lack the tourist element."

"Don't you believe it," Leonid said, strolling up from behind Finch. I jumped, startled by his sudden appearance. "Several of the lords have arranged for cooperative visitations from other Hours. Here is your seal. Troy forgot to give it to you. You have twenty-four hours to wrap up your affairs in the mortal plane before you must assume your duties in the Hour."

"We can have visitors?" I glanced at Finch before asking, "Does that apply to others, as well? People outside the underworld?"

Finch's eyebrows rose as he caught where my question was headed. "I would like to know the answer to that, as well. Are mortals and immortals allowed to visit without giving up their lives?"

"Of course. They always have been. It's just a matter of keeping track of them, and having the correct documentation." Leonid gave us a twisted smile. "Normally, I would offer myself as your steward, since I am employed by the Council of Hours, but Troy insists I facilitate his takeover of Instagram for a while longer. However, I'm certain you will find a suitable steward from your new subjects without any trouble. Good day."

He toddled off, and I looked at the round metal object he'd given to Finch, tracing the symbol on it.

It was a raven.

"OK, that's both weird, and yet, an oddly satisfying end to the whole situation," I said, taking Finch's arm as we strolled through the crowds toward his shop. "At least we know that people can come see us, even if we can't leave. Clemmie will be thrilled. I assume your uncle—"

"He will definitely want to visit, yes," Finch said, looking a bit happier. "You will like him and his Beloved, Allie. And they will be delighted to know that you have found me, and saved me from becoming a solitary Dark One obsessed with categorizing the chaos that mortals embrace."

"Oh, I still want you to write that book. I bet it will be a bestseller. Clemmie can sell signed copies in the shop."

He laughed, and pinched my butt. "Things do seem to have wrapped up nicely, the issue with Owain aside," he agreed. "And the loss of your boon."

"It was worth it," I said, happy despite the setbacks. I marveled a bit at that—I hadn't realized how I had been coasting through life, neither overtly happy or unhappy, just…being. And now…now life was so different. A thought

struck me as I was dwelling on just how wonderful everything had turned out. "Although, dammit, having to take
over in the Hour could be viewed as a manifestation of the
romance curse. Damn the Entity! They got the last laugh
after all!"

His laughter filled the street, my mind, and my heart.

Who needed to hear colors when there was a vampire
who made my soul sing?

EPILOGUE

ME

Hey, guess who got Internet installed in the underworld!

CLEMMIE

Wooties! How are things going there? Did you convince the medieval peeps to go full Ravenfall? Are you and Finch still happy, or has something horrible happened to him (not that I think it would, but I figure it's better to ask)?

ME

Good, yes, and he is one fine specimen of vampirehood. *fans self*

ME

What's going on there? Is the Entity giving you any trouble? Has anyone seen Jerry? And who is taking over the café?

CLEMMIE

Things are copacetic here, although I swear something is going on in Finch's basement. Rolly is back in town, and was going to freak out when I told him that the Entity sent you to the underworld, but then I told him about Finch, and he demanded to see a picture. Also, he sends his best wishes. Oh, and thank you and Finch for buying his shop for me. I swear I'll pay you guys back just as soon as I can! No word on Jerry. Sian is going to run the café. Did you know it's now owned by the Entity? When can I come see you?

ME

Finch is working on getting all the business stuff organized. The man is a whiz with a spreadsheet. Once he has the system reviewed and restarted (the previous guy cancelled visitation when he went off to become an influencer), then we'll let you know, and you can stay with us for a bit. I'm excited about making the underworld version of Axegate Walk. How was Ozy's funeral?

CLEMMIE

Funereal. The whole town was there, and there were lots of snide remarks about her being driven to her death by you, but then the Entity put an announcement in the paper absolving you of any guilt, so now peeps keep their lips zipped.

ME

I'm glad my name is cleared, even if I'm not there to enjoy it. Although, really, it was the least the Entity could do considering they had Ozy picking on me just so that I'd be romantically uninvolved and primed for Finch once he arrived.

CLEMMIE

Really? You think they did all that just so you guys could hook up? I don't want to say that's conceited, but damn, son. That's pretty conceited.

ME

Not really. Evidently they knew I had some role to play, and Ozy told them that it was important I be unencumbered with a romantic relationship, so she put some sort of a curse on me. And picked on me in other ways so I'd be all needy and shit when Finch rolled into town. Mind you, that's speculation because the Entity won't admit anything other than Ozy knew I had a role to play in the town's wellbeing, but eh. It's the only thing that makes sense. Whoops, gotta dash. Finch has just come in with some designs for the new town layout. Axegate Walk: The Next Generation is going to rock!

CLEMMIE

Can't wait to see it.

ME

Right backatcha. Really have to run. Finch just told me that since his uncle has a castle, he feels it's only right that we have one, too, and he thinks it would make a nice tourist addition to the Hour. I can't wait to open up a shop in it! Who could resist haunted crap from the actual underworld? We'll be millionaires!

NOTE TO READERS

My lovely one! I hope you enjoyed reading this book, which I handcrafted from the finest artisanal words just for you.

If you're looking for some fun behind-the-scenes tidbits and exclusive material, hie thee over to my website at katiemacalister.com and sign up for the newsletter.

And finally, if you enjoyed the Finch's story, but haven't read the all the Dark Ones books, here's the list of the complete series, in chronological order:

Made in the USA
Middletown, DE
25 February 2023